"Jean Ewing writes with true Regency wit and charm."
—Jo Beverley on *Scandal's Reward*

"Remember the name of Jean R. Ewing. This major discovery makes a most impressive debut . . . an author on the rise."

—*Romantic Times* on *Scandal's Reward*

★ ★ ★ ★ +

"Destined to become a brilliant star."
—*Affaire de Coeur* on *Virtue's Reward*

"Regency excellence . . . Regency connoisseurs will now have another superstar to cherish!"
—*Romantic Times* Rave Reviews on *Virtue's Reward*

★ ★ ★ ★ ☆

"Jean Ewing is a genius at writing incredible Regency romances. Her plots are perfection . . . impossible to put down."

—*Affaire de Coeur* on *Rogue's Reward*

"This is a book no Regency lover—no historical lover—no romance lover—should miss."
—*Rendezvous* on *Rogue's Reward*

"I was swept along to the end and the rest of my activities could go to the devil. What a master storyteller she is. . . . one of the finest treasures of the genre."
—Mary Balogh on *Rogue's Reward*

WATCH FOR THESE ZEBRA REGENCIES

LADY STEPHANIE   (0-8217-5341-X, $4.50)
by Jeanne Savery
Lady Stephanie Morris has only one true love: the family estate she has
managed ever since her mother died. But then Lord Anthony Rider
arrives on her estate, claiming he has plans for both the land and the
woman. Stephanie soon realizes she's fallen in love with a man whose
sensual caresses will plunge her into a world of peril and intrigue . . .
a man as dangerous as he is irresistible.

BRIGHTON BEAUTY   (0-8217-5340-1, $4.50)
by Marilyn Clay
Chelsea Grant, pretty and poor, naively takes school friend Alayna
Marchmont's place and spends a month in the country. The devastating
man had sailed from Honduras to claim his promised bride, Miss
Marchmont. An affair of the heart may lead to disaster . . . unless a
resourceful Brighton beauty finds a way to stop a masquerade and keep
a lord's love.

LORD DIABLO'S DEMISE   (0-8217-5338-X, $4.50)
by Meg-Lynn Roberts
The sinfully handsome Lord Harry Glendower was a gambler and the
black sheep of his family. About to be forced into a marriage of convenience, the devilish fellow engineered his own demise, never having
dreamed that faking his death would lead him to the heavenly refuge
of spirited heiress Gwyn Morgan, the daughter of a physician.

A PERILOUS ATTRACTION   (0-8217-5339-8, $4.50)
by Dawn Aldridge Poore
Alissa Morgan is stunned when a frantic passenger thrusts her baby into
Alissa's arms and flees, having heard rumors that a notorious highwayman posed a threat to their coach. Handsome stranger Hugh Sebastian
secretly possesses the treasured necklace the highwayman seeks and
volunteers to pose as Alissa's husband to save her reputation. With a
lost baby and missing necklace in their care, the couple embarks on a
journey into peril—and passion.

*Available wherever paperbacks are sold, or order direct from the
Publisher. Send cover price plus 50¢ per copy for mailing and
handling to Penguin USA, P.O. Box 999, c/o Dept. 17109, Bergenfield, NJ 07621. Residents of New York and Tennessee must
include sales tax. DO NOT SEND CASH.*

Valor's Reward

Jean R. Ewing

ZEBRA BOOKS
KENSINGTON PUBLISHING CORP.

Her peerless feature, joined with her birth,
Approves her fit for none but for a king;
Her valiant courage and undaunted spirit,—
More than in women commonly is seen,—

—*King Henry VI—First Part*

Prologue

Northumberland, 1807

The Cheviot Hills to the north lay mottled with shadow as a cavalcade of carriages and outriders swept across the moor and across the little stone bridge over the Whin. A handful of sheep stopped their grazing to look. The horses clattered past the pebble-bedded stream without pausing, and turned in at the peeling stone gates of Whinburn House. As the first coach with its emblazoned crest on the panel drew up before the great sweep of steps, a dashing, dark-haired man in his fifties hurried down to greet it. He seemed to be torn between alarm and hilarity, but he was doing his best to assume an expression of devoted respect.

A very small, very upright old lady climbed stiffly from the chaise, and Sir Shelby Whinburn bowed over the knobby hand of his late wife's aunt, Lady Emilia Shay, come to visit for the first time in thirteen years. He was wearing his plum-colored coat, the one that hid the wine stains, and the collar was twisted as if he had donned it in a hurry. Yet he kissed Lady Emilia's proffered hand with a flourish of graceful gallantry as they exchanged greetings.

"Whinburn is honored, ma'am. Yet we did not expect your ladyship until tomorrow. I trust your journey was everything that was comfortable?"

"On the contrary, it was appalling! I despise travel above all things—and to come so far north! Why, one would think one traveled back in time." Lady Emilia snapped open her parasol as the sun blazed out between the high, drifting clouds.

Sir Shelby waved vaguely in the direction of the lawn. "Pray, allow me to offer your ladyship some refreshment. On such a lovely day, perhaps you might like to take tea outside?"

"No, thank you, nephew." He paled for a moment, but then broke into a smile of undisguised relief as she went on. "I have been cooped up in my carriage these four hours past like a hen being taken to market. What I should like above all things is a stroll about your garden."

The couple began to make a stately progress across the grass, away from the mossy stains on the walls from the broken guttering, away from the dirty, dust-covered windows, and away from everything that Sir Shelby Whinburn wanted to hide inside.

On the other side of the lawn, Jessica was oblivious to this untimely arrival. She had been distracted for a moment by the shriek of a hawk, but now she curled up her legs and reopened her book. The Northumbrian landscape disappeared as Achilles and Hector began to shout their boasts before the walls of Troy.

Sir Shelby had offered one hand to his aunt, but with the other he was making frantic gesticulations behind her back. The faces of two servants appeared at the windows. The gestures were directed at them and were urgent instructions to hurry. Sir Shelby muttered some curses under his breath as Lady Emilia glanced back over her shoulder. Yet with a charming smile and a comment about the view, he distracted her and steered her toward the shrubbery.

"And where, pray, is the child, Jessica?" asked Lady Emilia after the immediate news had been exchanged. "My niece was a great beauty, Sir Shelby, lovely enough to ensnare you without any fortune, though heaven knows you could have used it. Since my income is in trust for my lifetime only, Jessica won't get a penny from either of us. She had better marry well. I sincerely hope she has her mother's looks."

Sir Shelby's brow contracted for a moment. He could see from the corner of his eye that Ben Cameron was desirous of climbing from a downstairs window to join them. Two footmen were trying to persuade him to desist. "Jessica has different coloring," he said absently.

"Where is she? With her governess?"

He swallowed a grin as one of his servants grasped Ben by the back of his high collar and twisted him from the window, then he turned solemnly to his aunt by marriage. Sir Shelby was quite foxed himself. "She's only fifteen years old. I'll not confine her to the house."

Lady Emilia raised an eyebrow. "But Jessica is approaching the age when she should make her come out. She is my only great-niece, and I intend to see to it. Good Lord! What on earth is in that tree?"

"Oh," said Sir Shelby Whinburn. He laughed. "It's Jessica."

And he shouted her name.

The glittering armies of Troy shimmered for a moment, like genies about to dissolve in smoke, then disappeared, taking Hector and Achilles with them. Jessica glanced up, tossing her hateful plaits back over her shoulder. Papa and an old lady were staring up at her. Oh, good Lord! Was this her great-aunt, arrived a day early? And the gentlemen were still in the house!

Jessica slipped from the curved branch that served as one of her favorite retreats, and tried to drop a curtsey.

As her bare foot caught in the torn hem of her dress, the attempt failed so splendidly that she almost fell. She caught at the tree and dropped the book. The aged spine cracked and loose pages scattered over the grass. Jessica knelt and frantically began to gather them up. She had absolutely no idea what to say.

Lady Emilia was the first to recover. "Miss Jessica Whinburn? Where on earth are your shoes, child?"

Giving up any hope of rescuing her copy of the *Iliad,* Jessica stood up and curtseyed again. Several errant pages whirled up around her bare feet and skipped away across the grass in a small breeze. They were in the original Greek. "I don't know, but I'm not a child. I'm fifteen."

Lady Emilia glowered up at Sir Shelby, her voice shaking with indignation. "Whatever are you thinking of, sir? You are laughing! The girl looks like a gypsy—she is as freckled as a hen's egg. I declare I have never been more shocked! This is 1807, not the Middle Ages—to let a girl run around so! Good Lord, she is born to be a lady, not a fishwife!" She turned to Jessica. "Where is your governess?"

Jessica tilted her chin. It was a small gesture, but it betrayed both pride and discomfort. "I don't have a governess."

Sir Shelby tried to look solemn, for Ben Cameron was now waving to them from the top step of the house. The breeze blew his bright hair about his forehead. "I have taught her myself, ma'am. She can ride and shoot better than half the boys in the neighborhood."

"You have taught her to shoot? Good gracious, I might be in need of salts for the first time in sixty summers! Does she have no female companion?"

Sir Shelby shrugged. "There are women on the staff."

"Servants? Nephew, I think you must be mad! Her mother has been dead these twelve years. The child will have to take her place in society. Good Lord, you don't think what you're about!"

Sir Shelby began to look stubborn. "She don't need society. She'll have Whinburn when I'm gone."

"A ramshackle old house in the middle of the wilds, with nothing but sheep for company? It won't wash, sir, and you know it. You think she can grow old here taking care of you? Nonsense! She must marry. She can't spend the rest of her life running wild like a monkey. Without a mother, she needs the influence of a properly reared female. Look at her, sir! She must learn to keep out of the sun and apply lemon water daily."

Not only was Sir Shelby feeling the effects of his wine, but he was uncomfortably aware that he was in the wrong. Whinburn was mortgaged to the hilt. So he lost his temper. "Next you'll tell me that her hair won't do! Well, there's many a border lord proud of such a head, ma'am. Do not think to come to Northumbria and disparage red hair. I've no time for fashion and folderol and women who faint at the sight of a mouse."

Lady Emilia Shay had never fainted in her life. She drew herself up and fixed the handsome features with an angry blue stare. "I am outraged, sir! Send the girl to me in London. She can go to school."

"She'll not leave this house while I'm alive, ma'am."

"Then I shall send a suitable governess here."

"I'll turn the wench off!"

"You shall not! I'll send another."

He leered at her outrageously. "If you do, I'll ruin her!"

Jessica turned scarlet. Spinning away from her father and her great-aunt, she raced into the house. Ben Cameron was waiting at the bottom of the stair. He grinned with easy, open charm and swept her a slightly unsteady bow.

"Well, now, Miss Jessica," he said. "No need to fly into the boughs. It's only an old lady. Find a clean dress and put your hair up, then go and tell your Papa that everyone's gone out the back way, the dice and cards are cleared away, and we'll be happy to offer her ladyship tea in the drawing room. Then I'll give you a kiss for your pains, shall I?"

Jessica pushed past him, and watched from an upstairs window as her great-aunt and her father faced each other ın the garden. Tea was not to be served. With a final, violent gesture Lady Emilia Shay spun about and stalked back to the carriages that had not yet been unharnessed. Jessica knew both despair and anger as the entire cavalcade swept away, out of the gates, and back across the Whin.

Chapter 1

March, 1815

Michael Dechardon Grey, eighth Earl of Deyncourt, was contemplating marriage with very much the same cool, amused indifference that he and Charles de Dagonet had once shared when ambushed by a group of French soldiers in Spain. Of course, that time he had escaped. His narrow lips curved into a smile of faintly sardonic self-derision. With only one manservant riding close at his heels, Michael was traveling rapidly north on his big bay charger, directly into the teeth of a spring storm. It was not the style expected of an earl, and it would very much have surprised his town acquaintance to learn that the exquisite Lord Deyncourt could have so little patience with appearances. No doubt his future bride, whose tastes were going to prove both tiresome and expensive, would disapprove. Nevertheless he had traveled often enough in worse conditions in the Peninsula. Michael narrowed his eyes and turned up his collar. It had begun to snow.

A wavering twinkle of light beckoned through the swirling flakes: the Swan, at last. He was halfway to Tresham.

Michael left his man to see to the baiting of their horses, and strode into the inn parlor. He ordered a brandy, before turning to join his fellow travelers at the fireplace. A dark-haired gentleman at a table in the corner glanced up from his newspaper, then stood and held out his hand. "Good God! That notorious member of the Iron Duke's *jeunesse dorée*, Michael Grey! Or Lord Deyncourt, I should say, shouldn't I? *Enchanté*, my lord!"

Michael laughed. "Devil Dagonet, in person? Dear God, I was just thinking of you, sir, and of a certain Iberian village, best forgotten except for a dazzling display of French swordsmanship."

"Merely *la ruse de guerre*," said Dagonet with some amusement. The swordsmanship had been his, of course, learned as a boy from his émigré French father. "But if I remember, your role in our escape was every bit as wicked. What takes you from town, my lord? I thought you had become an ornament to society and ravisher of hearts?"

Michael sat at the table and crossed long legs at the knee, making the firelight dance in the high sheen of his boots. He was quietly dressed, in charcoal coat and buff breeches, but every understated garment spoke of exquisite taste and perfect quality. Yet his skin was still tanned deeply golden by a foreign sun, making his eyes seem startlingly blue—the same Spanish sun which had touched his dark brown hair with wheat yellow highlights. "Only sophisticated ones, I assure you. You find me on my weary way to Tresham, where my ward languishes in temporary banishment. I have forbidden him the delights of town for a while."

"Your ward?"

Michael grinned. "Peter, the fledgling Lord Steal. His father left a refreshingly old-fashioned will. Peter remains in my care until he comes of age, which is six years away, at five-and-twenty, or when he marries with my permission, if it comes sooner. His affairs are in a sad disorder, you understand. It's a splendid irony that a person like myself is cast in such a gallant role, isn't it?" The waiter brought the brandy and discreetly pocketed Michael's generous tip. "So what the devil are you doing north of London, Dagonet? I thought you had married and come into your estates?"

"Kate stays in Exmoor while I take care of some business for her father. I'm doubly sorry she's not with me, because I'd like you to meet her and I miss her damnably. But thank God I'll be home in three days." Dagonet looked keenly at his friend. " 'Prince, thou art sad; get thee a wife, get thee a wife—' "

"Since I came into my brother's title, I seem to be sought after with that end in view," said Michael dryly. "But I have no wife as yet."

"But rumor says you've had several wives since you returned from Spain."

Michael laughed. "Alas, only a lonely widow, and she has just remarried."

"Yet surely now you are earl you must make a suitable match and provide your name with an heir?" Dagonet's facile voice was deceptively casual.

Michael glanced up at him. "I am aware of my duty, Dagonet."

"In Portugal there was enough sighing and fluttering to quench the candles whenever you entered a room. Having added consequence and wealth to a noble profile, surely *ingénues* are making fools of themselves over your eyelashes?"

"Dear God, I am not interested in innocents."

Charles de Dagonet narrowed his eyes. Quite deliberately, he fired from ambush. "Yes, naive girls are not your style, are they, Lord Deyncourt?"

He had the empty satisfaction of seeing his shot find its mark. "Should they be?" Michael had gone suddenly white about the nostrils. "Since Society is so damned determined to cast me as a leader of fashion, I do what I can to defend the chits from its worst cruelties, but I'm not going to marry one! How could I in honor ask any father to put his innocent daughter into my hands?"

Dagonet recklessly pressed his advantage. "Yet I hear you have been paying marked attention to the Incomparable Melton, a lady of immaculate eligibility, and your betrothal is generally expected any day."

But Michael had recovered his humor and his control, seemingly without effort. He turned his brandy glass in long, supple fingers. "Lady Honoria may be virginal," he said with the faintest mockery, "but she is not innocent."

"So how does the Incomparable survive your absence from town?"

"Very easily. She doesn't lack for admirers. No doubt she will miss the title a great deal more than the man while I am gone."

"You are speaking to a man happily and deeply besotted with his wife. *Chacun à son goût,* of course. But aren't your years fighting Napoleon enough penance for the business with Lady Beaumont? The past is the past. And no one remembers it."

Michael's fingers had tightened slightly on the stem of his glass. "You don't let up, do you? Am I about to pay in blood for confiding in you, or shall I just grovel in humble penance on the floor?"

"I hope not," said Dagonet seriously, "but you cannot spend your entire life living it down."

"Yes, I can," Michael replied, his voice full of insult. "It's such an excellent exercise in self-control, don't you think?"

But it seemed that Dagonet had lost his temper. "There are some things in life that should not be so damned controlled, Deyncourt. I hope to God that the female exists who can rattle that insufferable composure in which you put so much pride."

The earl's smile was cool, and quite deliberately stripped of visible emotion. He stood up. "Dear God! Vainglory is all I have left, Dagonet. 'The sweet, silent hours of marriage joys' are not for me, I'm afraid. The Incomparable Melton has impeccable breeding and would make anyone an admirable countess, and she won't mind in the least if I visit my mistress—when I find a new one." Michael shrugged into his many caped coat. Then he deliberately gave his friend the insolent smile, only thinly veiled with his vivid charm, that had caused the Marquis of Thrawton to demand satisfaction, and then stutter out an apology instead. "If it had been anyone else who had shown the presumption to speak to me as you have just done, Dagonet, I should call him out—in spite of what happened six years ago." Michael carefully pulled on his gloves. His movements were elegant, graceful, and deadly. "And even if he had your skill with a blade, I should kill him."

But then Lord Deyncourt laughed and gave Dagonet a wink, before he strode from the room.

That the night was fit for neither man nor beast was the considered opinion of the earl's manservant, Dover. He knew better, however, than to express himself on the issue. It was still snowing, a thick, wet, spring snow. The road had become a complete mire. Thank God the chaise and four with the Deyncourt arms emblazoned on the door had been left in London. Thank God these deep woodlands were the outskirts of the young Lord Steal's Tresham estates.

Michael was resolutely refusing to think about his meeting with Dagonet. He would arrive at Tresham, convince Peter to follow a sensible future, then return to London and propose to Lady Honoria Melton, with her spun-gold hair and velvet eyes. If he really had the self-control his situation demanded, he would have done so months ago.

His bay snorted, flung up its head, and shied.

There was a large carriage stopped in the road, its wheels sunk in the mud. Michael pulled his mount to a sudden halt, and his servant stopped dead behind him. A team of matched grays stood hanging their heads in their collars, the silver coats darkened with sweat. They were blowing and trembling. The coachman had obviously been applying the whip in an attempt to get the team to move, but now he sat with the reins looped in the guard and his hands above his head. Several other servants stood in the snow and also reached their hands to the clouds. As Michael watched, the remaining occupant of the carriage descended from its cozy interior to stand puffing in the mire. Then he threw up his hands and cried out.

"Outrage! Outrage! I'll see you hanged for this!"

For they were all being held at bay at the point of what looked suspiciously like a very old-fashioned dueling pistol—a weapon held with perfect steadiness in the small hand of the driver of a wicker donkey cart. The donkey stood patiently, idly flicking its long ears, as snow coated its back.

Michael had recognized the coach at once. The rotund lines of the figure now standing in the road and the swollen purpling jowls above the starched collar could belong to only one individual: Lord Clarence. Here was a pretty spectacle! Hanging Judge Clarence being robbed by a woman! For the driver of the cart was undoubtedly female. Wrapped from head to foot in a large, shabby cloak, she stood on the narrow board in front of the seat. Michael signaled his man to stay where he was, while he silently edged his own horse a little closer to the scene. As a precaution he took his loaded weapon out of his pocket and cocked it. At that moment the robber spoke. Her voice was clear and unexpectedly cultured, though with the faint accent of the North Country. Could it be some sprig of the gentry out on a wager? Good God! The girl would hang just the same were the stunt in jest or in earnest! But Michael lowered his weapon.

"The outrage is in your stubbornness, sir," she said coldly. "Now without your weight, perhaps your team may try again? Coachman!" The coachman lowered his hands and again took his whip and reins. At his signal, the grays leant into their collars and slowly began to move forward. Judge Clarence glowered at his assailant. "Now, sir," said the donkey cart driver. "You may walk after your beasts until they reach the top of the hill—then their honest hearts may not be broken having to drag your generous carcass through this mud.''

"But you will first return his lordship's purse, young lady!'' announced Michael. His voice rang with a deadly clarity through the falling snow.

The girl cast a startled glance over her shoulder, causing her pistol to swing toward the earl. At the same moment, as the coach passed him, one of the judge's men grabbed for his blunderbuss. Instantly Michael's hand came up and his finger closed. There was an appalling explosion of sound as powder exploded in his pistol, then in the blunderbuss. As if felled by the roar, the girl crumpled and fell from the cart. The donkey immediately bolted, cart bouncing behind its furry rump, and disappeared into the gloom.

Michael spurred forward and leapt from his bay as the girl turned and glared up at him. The clear gray eyes which looked back into his were dilated a little with shock. Blunderbuss shot had peppered the snow around her. Michael had a sudden wild desire to take her by the arms and shake her. Instead, before she could react, he thrust aside the cloak and pulled her torn dress away from the wound. She was bleeding freely near the shoulder, but she would live.

"For heaven's sake," she said with a clear, fierce bravado. "'Murder most foul!' You tried to kill me?"

Her indignation met nothing but a mask of cool amusement. "But you are only wounded. How very careless of me! It would so wickedly delight my acquaintance to know that I missed my mark."

"Yet you didn't hesitate!" She choked back a gasp as he padded the wound with swift, sure movements. "Is casual murder your habit?"

His nostrils flared just a little. "My past is littered with corpses, though seldom those of women. I aimed for the heart, of course."

"So you think I should count myself fortunate?"

"Very! You survived both my ball and the blunderbuss.

Of course, though the coach guard's shot has a wider scatter, our pistols have more range. If I hadn't shot you, perhaps you would have murdered me." He grinned and pulled the cloak around her. White flakes were steadily coating their heads and shoulders. "With whom are you working? Your friends seem to have left you to your own devices."

"I don't have any friends. Oh, devil take it! Here comes Gargantua!"

The earl looked up to where the judge was struggling toward them through the mire. "By Jove, Deyncourt! Here's the result of your radical ideas, sir: the highway's not safe for honest gentlemen. Yet if you hadn't turned up, this creature would have robbed and murdered me in cold blood. Hanging's too good for such villains!"

Michael rose so that the girl was blocked by his own body from the judge's gaze. An idea had occurred to him and he had no compunction in instantly carrying it out. He was shamelessly pleased that the snow was beginning to fall ever faster, blurring the landscape. "Purely fortuitous, Lord Clarence," he said smoothly. "You are not hurt, I trust? I am relieved to hear that you still have your purse— and your life, of course. For you were about to fall foul of a vicious gang. This is no woman lying here."

Judge Clarence stopped. "What do you say, sir?"

"I have shot down a boy in a woman's cloak—like the infamous Old Mob who robbed coaches dressed as a female. It's the latest ruse of a ferocious band of highwaymen. One waylays a coach in such an innocent guise while the others hide in the woods, ready to spring upon the victims. Fortunately the sound of our gunfire has frightened them off."

"Good God!"

"Did you not hear their hoofbeats?"

"Indeed! Muffled by the snow, of course, but now that you mention it, I did! Yet we have this one in our clutches, at least. I'll see him hanged before the week's out or my name's not Clarence!"

The earl inclined his head. "Very fitting, my lord. Didn't you hang three miscreants together just last month? Yet it's a foul night. Why don't you continue your journey in peace; you must still have some way to go? Whereas I am at the doors of Tresham, my destination. I can take this rogue in hand and happily relieve you of the trouble."

Lord Clarence shook snow from his shoulders. "Be grateful if you would, Deyncourt. Late already for Lady Fletcher's dinner, don't you know. I'll send a man over for the fellow in the morning. Clap him in irons and take him into Bedford."

With that he tipped his hat and turned to slog away up the hill after his coach and servants, cursing as the mud and slush befouled his evening slippers. Michael returned his attention to the wounded robber. She was clutching at the makeshift bandage. Her lashes were damp, perhaps only with snow, for she had made no other protest. As she sat up the hood of the cloak fell from her head, revealing hair that blazed in the dim light like a flame. She immediately grabbed at the hood and jammed it back over her head.

"You shot me. Why on earth are you now protecting me?" she asked.

The deep blue eyes gazed at her steadily. "Perhaps I like an enigma, or maybe I'm the very model of chivalry. On the other hand, how can you be sure I'll protect you? Lord Clarence's man will arrive in the morning with chains, after all. Yet when life presents such a delicious absurdity as a lady in a donkey cart holding up a judge on the King's highway, I'm damned if I'll miss the chance to explore it. Can you ride?"

"I'm not sure." It was obviously a particularly annoying and humiliating admission. "Where do you intend to take me?"

"To a snug pallet of straw in the storage rooms at Tresham Hall—the place whose woods are keeping off the worst of this storm."

"How can I trust you?" She looked at him with open suspicion.

"I am *'a true, a perfect gentle Knight,'* of course."

"Oh," said the girl. "Chaucer? How very erudite! Then why don't you take me to your castle?"

"I can't," he replied gravely. "It's too far. But Tresham will suffice until you're taken to the gallows. You might have thought twice before despoiling the local magistrate."

"I could hardly be expected to know that the object of my venality was a judge, could I?" she said. Then to his immense surprise, she laughed. "Oh, very well. Take me where you like!"

"Then you will have one last dry night before you swing from a tree." He lifted her to her feet. At the movement, however, she paled and stumbled against him. "Devil take it!" said Michael softly. "If you faint, we'll all freeze where we stand. Dover, take the animal!" The servant hurried over and caught the earl's horse by the bridle. "Now, Miss Highwayman, if you will allow me?" In one swift movement, he picked her up in his arms and set her onto his mount. "Thank you, Dover." He nodded to his servant and took his horse's reins. "And if you would find the poor startled ass?"

Dover mounted his own horse and rode off in the direction last taken by the donkey cart. Michael smiled at the girl before vaulting up behind her. It was a smile guaranteed to soften female hearts, but she sat stiffly away from him. "Pray, relax against me, ma'am," he said in her ear. "It would make it easier for both of us. I shall need to put an arm about your waist in order to guide the horse."

"Am I expected to enjoy a close proximity to someone who has just put a ball into my shoulder, sir?"

"Why not? Ladies usually enjoy my company." His breath was warm against her cheek. It promised subtle rewards and seductive intimacy, though the touch of his arm as he gathered the reins was quite impersonal. "Though it's a form of courtship I admit to having shamefully neglected in the past. Would you rather I left you to bleed to death in the snow?"

"I would rather you had not shot me in the first place."

"Nevertheless, I have done so, ma'am," he replied with exaggerated courtesy. "So please rest against me, and I shall be able to take you all the faster to a more commodious location. And while we ride, by all means contemplate all the delightful motives that a gentleman could possibly have for rescuing a damsel in distress."

Chapter 2

A few minutes later they turned in past the lodge of Tresham Hall, and followed the snow-covered driveway into the stable yard. There was a blaze of light from the smoking torches as Lord Steal's ostlers hurried up to take charge of the horse, and the door to the house was flung open to reveal the startled face of a blond young man, dressed in a fantastic blue-and-pink embroidered waistcoat under a bright yellow jacket, who hurtled down the steps toward them.

"Deyncourt! Where's your man? Why didn't you come to the front door? Oh! Whoever is this? Good Lord! Has there been an accident?"

Ignoring the tumble of questions, Michael swung himself easily from his mount and lifted the girl to the cobbles. She straightened her back, but she clung to the horse's stirrup as if she might fall at any moment. The young man in the saffron coat stared at her pale face for a moment before he swept her a deep bow.

"Lord Steal of Tresham, at your service, ma'am. By Jove, you are devilish white! Are you all right?"

She stared at the newcomer. She was several inches

shorter than either of the men, and had to look up into his eager face. "I am very glad to make your acquaintance, Lord Steal. My name is Miss Jessica Whinburn," she said firmly. "There has been the most unaccountable misunderstanding. I have been shot and wounded by this arrogant knave. Now he intends to lodge me in the storeroom. I pray that you will offer me your hospitality and make this lowlife scoundrel apologize at once for his reckless and precipitate behavior."

Peter looked helplessly at Deyncourt. "Oh, dear," he said, his brown eyes as round as teacups. "This is like something from Walter Scott. Miss—Whinburn, is it? Allow me to present my guardian: Michael Dechardon Grey, Lord Deyncourt—eighth earl, you know! Also Viscount Kingston and Lord Marchmont, of course."

"A dreadful mouthful," said Michael gravely. "And without question the titles of an arrogant knave—though rarely reckless."

Jessica still clung to the stirrup, but there was very little color left in her face. "No, your interference was prudence itself," she said with a defiant grin. "Don't say I have enjoyed the honor of being shot down by a peer of the realm. Do you really have a castle?"

"Regrettably I do, Miss Whinburn."

"Then I am among exalted company indeed! Are you also an earl, Lord Steal?"

"Oh, good Lord, no! Only a baron." Then he continued in tones of the greatest respect, only mildly contaminated with youthful indignation: "My lord, you will never lodge her in the storeroom?"

The earl's voice was soft and certain. "I shall do, Steal, as I see fit. Bring me some hot water and towels. Say nothing to anyone, particularly your mother!" He turned back to the girl. "Shall we go in, Miss Whinburn?"

With the elegant courtesy of the ballroom he held out his arm. But as Jessica let go of the stirrup and tried to take a step, she stumbled and almost fell. She bit her lip to choke back a cry. Damnation! Nothing could be worse than to appear helpless before these men.

"Oh, Neptune!" said Peter, his indignation raised to squeaking pitch. "She'll swoon!"

Without another word Michael swung Jessica into his arms and carried her into the house. He strode through the empty washrooms and into a small chamber filled with cupboards and shelves, apparently used to store linen. Jessica noticed immediately that the place had no windows and was provided with a stout lock on the door. Without ceremony, he deposited her onto a narrow cot and began to move the clothing away from her shoulder.

Jessica caught at his hand. "Pray, leave it, my lord! This is surely a task for some female servant."

"Nonsense! There is not a female in the house who has ever seen a gunshot wound and would not faint at the sight of one. Lie still!" He carefully disengaged her fingers and smiled at her. "I am trying to rescue you from Lord Clarence and Bedford Jail. It would make it immensely easier if you would cooperate."

Jessica lay back immediately. Divested of her cloak and with her sensible woolen dress pulled aside, she had no choice but to allow the earl's gentle fingers to explore the wound. A few minutes later Lord Steal appeared, carrying a tub of water and cotton bandages. He watched transfixed as the water in the basin began to turn red. Michael looked up at his ward just in time, for Lord Steal had begun to grow distinctly green about the gills.

Michael's lips twitched, but the tone was deliberately sharp. "If you can be of no more help, sir, than to stand and gape like a mooncalf, pray leave us! You are witness to nothing more than a misadventure of the road."

Peter swayed just a little, but the earl had saved him. He blushed scarlet and rushed from the room.

"Good Lord!" said Jessica. "Do you speak so to everyone?"

He turned back to her in genuine surprise. "Speak so?"

"Like Suleiman the Magnificent." She winced once. "A misadventure? When I am shot down like a pigeon!"

She had closed her eyes, so she couldn't see the expression of faint self-mockery on his face. "Then you should be pleased to know you are only winged, ma'am. Though I had black murder in my heart, it is merely a graze. You have lost some blood, but there is no other harm done."

"Nevertheless I feel remarkably like Pelops, chopped in pieces and served to the gods, as Demeter devoured his shoulder."

"It was a test of divine power to restore Pelops to life," he replied dryly. "I hope my skill as a nurse may match that of the gods of Olympus."

"Good heavens, my lord, you do claim august company! I have no intention of dying, but next time would you be kind enough to shoot the fellow with the blunderbuss instead?"

"May I remind you that he was the innocent party, Miss Whinburn? You were the aggressor. It was his duty to kill you."

Her eyes flew open. "And what excuse do you have, my lord?"

He replied with an exquisite sarcasm. "Only idle pleasure, of course."

Jessica bit back her retort as Dover stepped into the room. He bowed. "I have retrieved the donkey, my lord."

"Well done, sir. I trust the noble ass has taken no harm from his shocking experience?"

"None, my lord."

"And the cart?"

The manservant coughed into his hand. "I regret to say it did not survive quite intact."

"Splinters?" said Michael.

"Unhappily so, my lord, but I took the liberty of collecting the lady's bags." Dover set two leather satchels beside the bed. They were both stained with mud and snow, and one had split along the seam.

Jessica took one look at it. "Oh, dear," she said. "Then

things of a slightly delicate nature must be strewn along the highway. I would seem to have lost my night attire— a minor inconvenience in jail, of course.''

Michael gazed gravely down at Jessica. ''Then apart from your night rail and your cart, on which an ungrateful donkey seems to have expressed the most indecorous spleen, your shoulder is the only casualty of our interesting drama. And it will feel much better in the morning.''

''When you will hand me over to that inflated judge?''

His mouth quirked. ''I thought I had explained that I intend to save you from the consequences of your rash behavior, Miss Whinburn. But then what of my duty to the law? A delightful quandary! I should make a habit of shooting down mysterious ladies.''

He was smiling at her with that ineffable charm—a smile that invited infinite trust and relaxation. Jessica balked immediately. ''Good heavens, do you pride yourself on a reckless disregard for human life? No doubt you have a long and reprehensible history of duels!''

She had struck back more surely than she knew. There was the faintest fading of color beside his nostrils. ''Only one, ma'am.''

She turned away and pulled up the blanket. ''Had you not distracted me, the man wouldn't have managed to wield his blunderbuss—for I am a perfectly adequate shot and could have disarmed him. However, you were in too much haste to demonstrate your own skill. And you told me yourself you have left a trail of corpses behind you. I believe I would rather be put in jail than remain another moment under your care. Good night, my lord.''

Dover gawked openmouthed at Jessica and then at Lord Deyncourt. To his knowledge his master had never been spoken to like that in his life. The earl's expression did not change, however, and without a backward glance, he ushered his man from the room. When they had reached the safety of the corridor, Dover was further amazed when the fearsome and elegant Earl of Deyncourt stopped and gazed blankly out of the window for a moment.

"My lord?" said Dover. "Are you all right?"

Michael looked around and smiled sardonically at his servant. " *"What a piece of work is man! How noble in reason! how infinite in faculties!"* " he quoted lightly. "Do you think I am sold and contracted to the devil, Dover? I shot her down like a dog!"

"As you know very well, my lord, if you had not fired first and knocked the chit over, the blunderbuss would have killed her and the donkey both. There wasn't time for anything else. And, if I might say so, it was a damned good shot!"

"And a devilishly efficient example of strategy; yes, I know. Yet it was done like a bloody automaton, and it was an unconscionable chance to take—I might have maimed her. Damnation to all my nasty and efficient accomplishments!"

Dover boldly laid his hand on his master's sleeve. "Come now, my lord, the lass owes you her life. Don't curse the skill that kept you all alive in the Peninsula—Devil Dagonet and the others do not, I'll warrant!"

But the earl had already regained his composure and his cool smile. "And I'll guarantee that they do, sir—those that live."

As soon as they had gone, Jessica sat up on the narrow bed. She had just come to a painfully obvious conclusion. Whether it had been deliberate or not, the earl's shot had saved her from the deadly scatter of the blunderbuss. And although she had pointed her weapon at him and he'd had every right to shoot, she did not now believe he had intended to kill her. In which case, what truly extraordinary marksmanship! Damnation! Damnation! She owed him her life: a man so obviously used to his effect on women, a type she most despised—all that careless power and charm—his looks alone must fill him with conceit. And to cap it all, he was a peer of the realm, with the infinite confidence given by his station.

Any self-respecting earl ought to travel in a chaise and four with outriders and armed servants, not as simply as a traveling clerk—or as herself, she admitted ruefully. Yet her donkey cart had carried her all the way through Yorkshire and along the byways parallel to the Great North Road without mishap, while she stretched her small supply of coin. Why, why had this had to happen? What would the earl do with her?

She didn't have long to find out. The key turned in the lock and that very gentleman pushed open the door. He was carrying a tray with a wine bottle and glasses, and the appetizing smell of hot soup flooded the room.

"Now, Miss Whinburn, pray eat. Then you will be pleased to tell me who you are and where you are going."

Jessica ignored him and ate the soup. It made her feel a great deal better.

"You might ask after my health, my lord, before badgering me with questions," she said at last.

"You feel considerably improved, but your shoulder pounds like a hammer," he replied without blinking. "Now, why did you hold up Judge Clarence's coach?"

"I had absolutely no designs on his purse, though I doubt not that it's a great deal fatter than mine. As it happens, I was incensed by his treatment of his horses: they couldn't carry that much weight up the hill. They'd have been flogged to death."

"And you thought to intervene with a pistol?"

"Why not?"

"Because Lord Clarence regrettably lacks the sensibility to understand your noble motives. He will be angry and humiliated. I'm afraid he will demand the utmost revenge of the law, which regrettable as it may seem, is hanging."

"But thanks to your fertile imagination and facile ability to lie, my lord, he'll be looking for a boy, won't he? *Maxima debetur puero reverentia?*"

"The greatest reverence may be due to a boy," he replied dryly, "but it was your fairer sex that saved you. I must have absorbed some old-fashioned chivalry with my schooling, after all. Where the devil did you learn Latin?''

"From my late father: Sir Shelby Whinburn, local squire, of Whinburn House in Northumberland. He made sure I was proficient in both Latin and Greek—he liked to lay wagers on it with his friends.''

Michael raised a brow. "A slightly odd education for a lady, surely?''

"Why?'' said Jessica instantly. "Do you think females too idle to study and enjoy the classics?''

"Not at all, I was referring to the wagers.''

There was only the smallest hesitation in her reply. "Nonsense. All gentlemen wager. It was nothing out of the ordinary.''

"No doubt. Like the donkey cart.'' He removed the empty soup bowl and poured two glasses of wine. "Such a very unique choice of conveyance, Miss Whinburn.''

"I am going to London and could afford nothing better. Aren't the streets there paved with gold?''

The earl raised an eyebrow and gave her a glass. Rich depths gleamed in the wine like dark red pebbles in a pool. "Rather with muck and with danger. And when you arrive at the fabled city? I do not imagine you plan to scrub floors. Don't tell me you are going for a governess?''

Jessica inhaled the opulent scent. It was very good wine. "Alas,'' she said with a little laugh. She hadn't expected to ever taste such quality again. "No, I cannot become an underpaid schoolmarm; I have none of the necessary accomplishments. I don't paint in watercolors or know how to make elegant figurines out of butter. Since I lack both decorum and connections, I can't become a lady's companion either. Yet I plan to earn my keep.''

"But what of matrimony, Miss Whinburn? Most young ladies expect to secure their future through an advantageous match.''

"I do not intend to marry,'' she said simply. She put the wineglass on the table beside the bed. "I would rather make an honest living than sell myself into marriage.''

Ah, blessed Fate! So she intended to become a Cyprian? Michael smiled with unashamed delight. He was sadly lacking a mistress for the moment, though not for want of offers, since the beautiful Lady Nest had decided to remarry. Miss Jessica Whinburn wasn't a beauty, but there was something very provocative about her. The smooth white skin had the fine, delicate translucency sometimes found with red hair. Its tantalizing purity was only accentuated by the dusting of freckles over the clean lines of her cheek and nose. How innocent were those clear gray eyes? He was seriously tempted to find out. "You are correct, of course. Matrimony is a mercenary arrangement these days."

"And it's outrageous, don't you think, that females should be allowed so little real employment that they must rely on marriage for their keep. If I were a man, the issue wouldn't arise."

He sat down on the edge of the bed and set his wineglass beside hers. "Then you don't think there are a great many advantages to being female?"

"I wish you could show me one of them," she answered, glancing up at him with that hint of bitterness.

"Good Lord, I can think of several," he said quietly. "This, for instance?"

He ran his thumb gently along her jaw and brushed it over the corner of her mouth. She looked at him steadily as color mounted in her cheeks and the pupils of her eyes seemed to widen into dark pools. Without further hesitation he kissed her, the rich taste of the wine on their lips. It was seductively, entrancingly expert. Jessica felt her nerves turn to water. But as she began to respond, redeeming anger welled up instead and she pulled away.

"How very unoriginal! I think I might with reason expect you to behave like a gentleman."

"But you are not behaving like a lady, Miss Whinburn. Do you think to call on propriety? The demands of respectability didn't seem to be in your mind when you threatened the judge with a pistol. It's a little late for that now, don't you think?''

Her blush made her eyes brilliant. "Because you are a rake?''

He gazed at her thoughtfully for a moment. Her response to his kiss was mystifying, for though it seemed reluctant, she had not been shocked. So she could hardly be the daughter of a respectable country gentleman. "I have a certain reputation and I have indeed enjoyed some discreet but charming friendships in the last six months,'' he said. "You would seem to be alone in the world; may I offer you my protection? Being my mistress would be both comfortable and lucrative, although I should have to insist on giving you dresses. Your present clothing isn't quite to my taste." His fingers still lay possessively under her hair. They moved down to turn the torn collar away from her neck. The touch tantalized her skin and made her blood burn. His hand dropped to the front of her gown, and her buttons began to fall open one by one under his deft fingers. "Wool,'' he said with a faintly mocking disapproval, as he ran his fingertip lightly over the hollow of her collarbone. "So very scratchy."

Jessica took a deep breath and tried to steady her racing pulse. "Don't!'' she said. Her voice sounded desperate in her own ears. Instantly his hand dropped. She gathered all her courage, for that single word had been one of the most difficult she had ever spoken. Rapidly she rebuttoned her dress. "Am I supposed to melt into your arms because you kissed me? It is not my intention to become anyone's mistress. And my thoughts are more taken up with being hanged than being ravished at present."

He stood instantly. Nothing in his manner betrayed how passionately he had wanted to undo all those tiny buttons and then the ties of the linen shift underneath, nor how dismayed he was at his own emotion. His voice was close to raillery. "So you do not want to become a mistress? Or at least, not mine. What a dreadful blow to my pride!''

"Anyone would think you had never been refused before," Jessica shot back.

He gazed at her with open amusement. "I haven't," he said. "But then I don't usually kiss angry young ladies from Northumbrian manors. Perhaps you really are a thief, and this talk of a respectable father is a farrago of nonsense? Can you prove who you are?"

"To your satisfaction? I doubt it!" With hands that still shook a little, she opened the bag which had not been damaged and tipped the contents onto the bed. It was immediately apparent that these were not the possessions of a highwayman or his accomplice. Among the clutter of personal effects, there were several books and a set of silver-backed hairbrushes. Jessica took up one of the brushes.

"This brush was my mother's," she said. "I don't remember her, because she died when I was little, but they were a wedding present from her aunt. It's my only claim to blue blood—rather diluted, but mine just the same. That's my great-aunt's crest on the back, but I am unfortunately the last Whinburn left alive, so I can prove nothing. When Judge Clarence hangs me, it won't matter, I suppose, who I am."

Michael had leaned forward and taken the brush. He turned it in his graceful fingers, so that the back could be clearly seen in the light. A strange, sardonic pleasure crossed his features. "Oh, dear Lord," he said, and to her surprise he began to laugh. "Life cannot surely be so delightfully absurd? Miss Whinburn, I believe we have landed in the most glorious coil—I shall be the one facing the hangman."

"Why? What's the matter?"

His face was still lit with irony. "Only that these are the Shay arms and Lady Emilia Shay is a very great friend of mine—and a great stickler for correct behavior. Now I learn she's your great-aunt. Why on earth didn't you at once make things clear?"

Jessica was looking at him in open astonishment. "My great-aunt is your friend?"

"She and my late Aunt Sophy were inseparable. Why has Lady Emilia never mentioned your existence?"

"She is still alive?"

"Very much so, and every bit as formidable an antagonist as her termagant great-niece. She will not thank me for having shot and imprisoned a long-lost relative. If I turn you over to Judge Clarence in the morning, I very much fear that Lady Emilia will send me to Coventry if not to perdition!"

Jessica's nostrils flared just a little. "Well, thank goodness I don't have to compose a speech for the scaffold after all. But you have done worse than deprive me of liberty, my lord. What will Lady Emilia think of your improper suggestions?"

"And shameless behavior?" He stopped for a moment. "I suppose she would expect it of me," he added at last. Though the tone was light, there was an undercurrent of something very close to pain. "Nevertheless, I most humbly entreat you to forget what has just passed between us, Miss Whinburn. Yet if you have a respectable purpose, I am still in ignorance of it."

Jessica looked down. So that charming, irresistible assault on her senses was simply to be forgotten. There was no reason not to tell him her real plans, but she felt a desperate need to retain some sense of privacy and independence. "I cannot think that's any concern of yours, my lord."

"But how on earth do you come to be traveling alone? And in such a ramshackle fashion?"

"It seemed a convenient way to reach London, for I don't have a feather to fly with. Pray do not pester me for the sordid details, but within six months of my father's death, I was forced to sell up everything at Whinburn to settle his debts—the horses, the paintings, the furniture finally the house. The donkey could survive on the lawn and the rough feed left over in the stable. He wasn't worth enough to go on the block."

"I'm sorry—for the loss of your father, and for the sale of your home," he said quietly.

"No, don't be. I was glad enough to leave. I hadn't reckoned on being shot down, of course."

"To travel as you did was foolish in the extreme. For God's sake, I'm sure I would not have been the only man—" He broke off. "Why did you not write to Lady Emilia? She would have forwarded you the blunt for the journey without question."

"Do you think so? I very much doubt it. I met her only once as a girl. She came to visit at Whinburn, but she and my father quarreled. It was unforgettably splendid and she promised never to darken our doors again. But now that you know I have such respectable connections and was not trying to rob Lord Clarence, I pray you will let me continue my journey."

"I can't. Clarence will have the Watch scour the countryside. You would be arrested again before you had gone ten miles, and your donkey cart is beyond repair. No, the supposed boy who held up the judge's coach will die of his wounds right now, and Miss Jessica Whinburn will become a guest of Peter's mother, Lady Mary, who is an old friend of Lady Emilia. You must stay here at Tresham until the hue and cry is over. If you are accused of highway robbery, neither your great-aunt nor I can protect you."

There was, of course, sense in what he said, but Jessica wanted nothing more than to escape his unsettling presence. Nevertheless, it was obvious, and for more reasons than those of which he was aware, that she would have to agree. "I see that, thanks to your gallant interference, I have no choice," she said. "But if I am still to be your prisoner, my lord, do you think I might have a room with a fire? It is excessively cold in here."

He smiled again. It was a smile that had caused one young lady in London to drop her fan at his feet and faint away. Then he took up the bottle to pour more wine. "Indeed, Miss Whinburn, I am in complete agreement. This place will never do. In fact, I think I had better lodge you in my own bedchamber."

Chapter 3

Jessica looked at his profile, cut clear as a cameo in the candlelight. The clean curve of his upper lip was alone enough to unsettle her. "Surely you don't still propose to secure my future through your protection?"

He turned, glass in hand, his tone teasing. "Alas, no! Though I am dreadfully disappointed, of course. I have always wanted to rescue a damsel in distress and sweep her away to my castle. I am suspected to be an unregenerate libertine, you know. You are missing an opportunity for which many ladies have willingly offered themselves." She could not mistake the glint of laughter in his eye. Nor the fact that when he smiled like that his attraction went suddenly beyond good looks to the promise of some hidden brilliance. "However, there is Lady Emilia to consider. You are great-niece to a lady I hold in the highest respect and affection. I am likely to be deeply enough entrenched in her bad books as it is. If I add seduction to the list of insults I have already piled on your innocent head, she will doubtless hire a champion to call me out. In spite of anything you may imagine about me, Miss Whinburn, you will be quite safe."

"I think I was safer before I met you."

"For I just kissed you and offered you *carte blanche*. I apologize. You see me overcome with contrition, for in spite of my disgraceful behavior and careless assertions, I have no designs on your virtue."

"Then you have a very odd way of demonstrating it!" she insisted.

"My dear Miss Whinburn, I had no idea who you were."

It was the most splendid insult imaginable! If she had not had respectable connections, she would have been fair game? Jessica allowed her anger full rein. "And that should excuse you? Because your charm is empty, your gallantry is only for your own amusement, and your kiss is just a gesture of power! I think, my lord, you are a man without scruple. I will not share a bedchamber with you. How should I trust your word?" She knew then she had gone too far. His expression closed as effectively as if shutters had been pulled.

He stood up and stalked to the end of the room. "If anything, I kissed you as a way to gather information and I will not pretend that it wasn't enjoyable. It was! Considering the circumstances, I made a reasonable assumption that you might welcome it. I'm sorry. But my word is inviolable. Your own actions have placed you in my power. It was your choice to pull a pistol on the local magistrate and risk the gallows! In spite of Lady Emilia, it is too late to turn missish—and because of Lady Emilia, I am bound to safeguard you. You cannot be known to have come here tonight, wounded. Judge Clarence's ire needs time to die away. In the meantime, you must stay hidden. The only place that I can guarantee that you will not be discovered in the house is in my own room. There is another bed in the dressing room that will have to do for me. As of this moment, no one knows of your arrival at Tresham other than myself, Lord Steal, my own man, and two grooms. Lord Steal and Dover are, of course, to be relied on. I shall take care of the grooms."

"What, will you dismiss them out of hand or completely

dispose of them? The grooms are innocent of any wrongdoing in this little caper!"

"The servants are my responsibility, Miss Whinburn. What I do with them does not concern you." She set her chin in a way that promised mutiny, but of course, there was no way that she could intervene. "Tresham contains an army of other servants and they can't be relied upon not to gossip," he continued. "They shall not know that you are here. In a few days, when Lord Clarence returns to town, I will smuggle you out and bring you to the front door where Lady Mary can greet you in style. You may then stay here openly."

Jessica swallowed. It would be distinctly uncomfortable to be forced to stay with this compelling man for several days. Nevertheless, the scaffold was probably a great deal more unpleasant. "Very well, my lord, I capitulate. Hide me where you like."

"A wise lady. Try to get some sleep, and when the servants have gone to bed, I shall come and fetch you. Good night, Miss Whinburn."

Michael stepped silently into the storeroom. The candle had almost burned away. Jessica slept quietly, her red hair tossed about her head. She looked disturbingly open and defenseless, the freckles fading away near the fine curl of her nostril. Although the wound was minor, she must have been in considerable pain. Yet she had hardly complained. How could she have been so foolish as to attempt to travel alone to London in such an extraordinary fashion? And what the devil had she intended to do when she arrived? Yet it was a brave thing to do. He couldn't imagine any other lady of his acquaintance having either so much courage or such resolve.

A half open letter lay under her hand. He reached to move it away, and couldn't help but read a few lines. *We have a steady need for employees skilled in the classics, and for translations from the Latin and Greek. If you would kindly apply in person at our offices in Hunting Lane* . . . Good God! Michael shook the page open. It was from Bromley and Finch, the well-known London publishers. The superscription at the top of the page told him exactly what he expected. They thought she was a man: the letter was addressed to J. Whinburn Esq. Such a firm of staid old businessmen would never hire a young lady, however talented in the ancient languages. What would have happened to her after they had refused her? She'd have been lucky to find a protector instead of a brothel. Thoughtfully he set the paper aside and moved her gently by her good shoulder. The gray eyes opened.

"It is time to remove you to more comfortable quarters, Miss Whinburn. Everyone is safely abed."

Jessica sat up. She felt a little faint and dizzy, but he should not know it.

"I am to follow meekly to the lion's den? I'm afraid I cannot, Lord Deyncourt. You see, in addition to being shot, I have also damaged my ankle. I believe it caught and twisted as I fell from the donkey cart."

He knelt and took her stockinged foot in his hand, carefully feeling the bones. "Not broken, I think. Yet you cannot walk on it. Why on earth didn't you mention this before?"

Because if I had you would have touched me as you have just done, she thought. But what she said was: "Because it is, damnably, the thing that makes it impossible for me to leave."

"Then you must stay longer at Tresham."

"And then what?"

"I will send you to your aunt."

"I do not wish to go to my aunt!"

Michael stood. "Nevertheless you will do so. It is out of the question for you to arrive in town alone. I can assure you that Lady Emilia Shay will greet you with open arms and have you married off within two months."

"I cannot—" she began in something close to panic,

but then she stopped and looked down. "I do not see, my lord, that you have the right to order my future."

She was expecting another argument, but instead he said quietly: "Then I appeal to your chivalry, Miss Whinburn. Do you wish to see me hanged with you as an accessory who deceived Lord Clarence and tried to rob him of his rightful revenge?"

Without allowing her to answer, he swung her into his arms. In silence she was carried through endless hallways and up several flights of stairs. Great marble columns soared away into the vastness of arched ceilings. Paintings of bewigged Steal ancestors crowded the walls in their gilt frames and gazed at each other across paneled alcoves. The staircase under his feet swept in a gracious curve of polished granite to innumerable other rooms and halls. Tresham was obviously a home of great age and matching magnificence, but Jessica barely noticed the grandeur, her senses were filled with the disturbing presence of the Earl of Deyncourt. She had been forced to put her arms about his neck and lay her head against his shoulder. It was a sensation that brought as much pain as pleasure. A massive oak door opened, and with a blank face Dover bowed them into his master's bedroom. The manservant left them together without a word. Michael set her in a high-backed chair beside a roaring fire. In front of the hearth stood a bronze hip bath filled with steaming hot water, and a stack of fluffy white towels hung on a mahogany rack beside it.

"Now, Miss Whinburn," he said. "You will remove your regrettably bloodstained dress so that I may burn it, and perhaps you would like a bath. Here is my cane to lean on. You can manage with your sore ankle?"

He pulled a screen around the tub, and with a courtly bow, left her. The hot water was the most inviting thing Jessica had seen in several days. Half an hour later, she was done. She had attempted to keep the bandage dry, but without success. In dismay she noticed blood beginning to seep once more through the cloth. She dried herself by the fire, and looked around for something to put on.

There was only one available choice: a gentleman's silk nightshirt and dressing gown, draped over the screen. They smelt delightfully of fresh air and spring sunshine. She shrugged into the nightshirt and wrapped the dressing gown around her body. Taking the cane, she limped into the room. Deyncourt sat casually in an easy chair, his long legs crossed at the knee, perusing a newspaper. At her movement he looked up.

"You are about to bleed all over my dressing gown?" He rose and strode over to her. Setting the screen aside, he gestured her into the chair by the fire. "Like Pelops, perhaps you need a new shoulder of ivory?"

Jessica dropped the nightshirt from her shoulder, and allowed him to unwrap and replace the bandage. She was painfully aware that she was naked except for a thin garment of silk, in a gentleman's bedchamber, with her disgraceful carrot hair, still damp, curling in reckless abandon about her head. With a man who had already stolen a most seductive kiss—a man who had offered to make her his mistress. He knelt and, with a strip of linen that she suspected had once been a cravat, bound up her sprained ankle. Pray that he didn't offer her any more empty gallantry! Jessica Whinburn had no interest in charming rakes; in fact she had no interest in men at all. Though not because she didn't find him attractive. His carved lips were only inches away. It was only too tempting to lean forward and touch them with her own. What would it be like to kiss him again? No doubt many ladies had already found out; no doubt, for a while at least, she wouldn't have to worry about making a living.

But he set down her foot as if it burned him. "Now, it is extremely late and I have to cope with Judge Clarence in the morning. Until then." He bowed and strode across to the dressing room door.

It closed behind him with a distinct thud. With the help of the cane, Jessica limped to the fresh sweet-smelling bed and curled up beneath the covers. He had made no bones about his prowess with the female sex. What would he think of her, had he known her reaction to his casual flirtation? Of course, now that he knew Lady Emilia was her great-aunt, he wouldn't try to find out; he would assume a concern for convention and propriety. And Jessica Whinburn knew nothing of either! Yet she dismissed the memory of those fascinating lips, and instantly fell into an exhausted sleep. The thick walls and heavy oak door prevented her from hearing the footsteps of the earl as he paced backwards and forwards in the small dressing room.

Eventually he stopped and eyed the empty bed, then he tugged off his jacket and cravat, and ran his hand through his hair. The movement drew his attention to his reflection in the mirror on the wall. With distaste Michael looked at the familiar features for a moment—the straight nose and dark brows, the sun-touched hair falling over his forehead. The words he had said to his manservant seemed to echo in his ears: *Do you think I am sold and contracted to the devil, Dover?* Very deliberately he pulled off the rest of his clothing and flung himself onto the narrow cot. The sleep of Michael Dechardon Grey, eighth Earl of Deyncourt, was a great deal more troubled that night than that of his unexpected guest.

Jessica sat up in the bed and looked around the chamber. A beam of sunlight crept in between the curtains. Someone had been in while she slept, built up the fire, and swept and tidied the room. Her meager possessions had been placed on a table, and her dresses had been sponged and pressed and hung from the front of the large wardrobe. It must all have been done by Dover. Thoughtfully, she shrugged into the dressing gown, then winced at the movement. A memory of long, gentle fingers binding her hurts came flooding back. She could not stay here with Deyncourt, and she would not be sent to Lady Emilia Shay and offered on the Marriage Mart. She climbed out of bed and limped to the window. A thaw had set in. The snow was gone and the landscape dripped water.

The door opened and Dover appeared carrying a tray. There was the smell of hot rolls, with butter and eggs, mingled with that of a large jug of steaming hot chocolate. The manservant set the meal on a small table.

"Where is his lordship this morning, Dover?" asked Jessica as she buttered a crusty roll.

"Lord Deyncourt is about to greet Lord Clarence in the drawing room, madam."

Jessica gave one glance at Dover's impassive face. "Then for all our sakes, I hope he has his wits about him," she said.

There was the slightest lift of the manservant's eyebrows as he bowed and began to leave the room. "But of course, madam. I have never known his lordship lacking in wits."

"Oh, heaven save us! We shall all be murdered in our beds!" The frantic voice of Lady Mary Steal echoed into the hallway.

"Hush, Mama," said Peter, and with a flourish of invention he went on: "We are quite safe. The fellow slipped away, even though he was horridly wounded—Lord Deyncourt shot him, you know."

Thus as Michael appeared in the doorway, he found disaster awaiting him in the drawing room, for Lord Clarence was already there with Lady Mary Steal and her son, and hysteria ran loose in Tresham.

Lady Mary turned to Michael and threw up her hands. "Deyncourt! Lord Clarence tells me you brought a desperate villain back to Tresham last night! A highwayman! How could you?" Then with a small scream she collapsed onto the drawing room sofa. The gentlemen looked at her with varied expressions of dismay and several voices spoke at once.

"But the man has escaped," insisted Peter.

"Escaped, you say, sir?" Lord Clarence had turned purple. "He won't get far, wounded!"

"Escaped!" Lady Mary screamed again. "Oh, then he

may be hiding about the premises! The house and grounds must be searched. I insist upon it! I insist! Everywhere must be turned out. You have your men with you, Lord Clarence?''

''I have more than men, my lady,'' replied the judge with triumph. ''I have dogs!''

Within minutes the Watch was scouring the house and grounds, accompanied by several of the local yeomanry who had tagged along to enjoy the sight of a felon being dragged away to his hanging. With such a wonderful excuse offered for a holiday from their labors, the household staff joined in the search, and the stable boys ran whooping and laughing after Lord Clarence's pack of hounds as they cast about for a scent in the muddy yard.

Lord Clarence attached himself instantly to Michael and plied him with suspicious questions. Where had the fellow been held? How could he possibly have escaped? Could he run far when he was so badly wounded? It was impossible to get away, impossible to get a message to Dover or to Jessica. Michael steadily reinforced in the judge's mind that they were looking for a boy. There was nothing else he could do. It took only half an hour for the hue and cry to reach the second floor and begin turning out the bedrooms.

''You will not need to search any further, Lord Clarence,'' Michael said with a calm that was far from his emotions as they reached one particular door in the guest wing. ''This is my own room.''

''No, no, Deyncourt!'' It was Lady Mary, hurrying up behind them. ''Lord Clarence must look everywhere. They say the dogs have found nothing outside.''

''The dogs cannot possibly find a scent with half the county trampling about in the mud, Lady Mary,'' said Michael. It was said with an air of regret, but secretly he thanked God for it. Yet any scent from the room where Jessica had first been held would lead them right here. ''We should probably assume that the fellow had accomplices who helped him get away.''

"But supposing the villain is hiding in the house? I have let them bring a brace of hounds inside, Deyncourt. The rogue must be captured. Oh, what a disaster this is!"

As she spoke a man in a leather cap and gaiters ran down the hallway, two hounds coupled together coursing in front of him. The excited dogs were barely under control.

"For God's sake, I hardly need my bedchamber trampled over by hounds!" snapped Michael. "In fact, I forbid it. They are only following my own scent, which they picked up in the storeroom where I left the miscreant."

"But the man may have come into the house through a window," wailed Lady Mary. "And we have looked everywhere else. Pray, go in and search, Lord Clarence. I shall never sleep sound again if you do not!"

In spite of his rank and a frown that made most of the servants hang back, Michael was only a guest in the house. Lord Clarence grasped the door handle and thrust open the door, and Lady Mary, Peter, and the judge tumbled into the room with the hounds, their handler, and a cluster of servants. Michael suppressed a sudden desire to knock them all to the ground as he tried to invent a plausible reason why Miss Jessica Whinburn should be found in his bed.

Chapter 4

She was not there. There was no sign that she had ever been there. The room lay innocent of anything feminine, and the bed was empty. Michael watched the men and dogs rampage about for a few minutes, then they all tumbled back into the hallway. Meanwhile he picked up a sheet of paper which lay on the table. The hounds had snuffled ecstatically around the table legs, and one of the searchers had glanced at the paper, then set it down again. It was written in Greek with a scattering of Latin quotations. Beside it lay a copy of the *Odyssey,* and a little pile of other books.

"Now, Lady Mary," Michael said calmly, folding the paper and putting it into his jacket pocket. *Hounds, for God's sake! There were hounds after her.* "Are you satisfied? No doubt the fellow died in a ditch and his friends have buried him. Even if he lives, he will not survive long if he is hiding outside. He is wounded, and it has begun to pour."

There had been a steady drumming of rain for several minutes. No one but Michael had noticed it, but now Lord Clarence looked out of the window.

"This sits very ill, Deyncourt," he said scowling. "But there's no sign of the villain at Tresham. I'll scour the countryside, and put a guard on every road and at every toll gate. He won't last long in a cold rain like this."

It was another two hours, however, before Lord Clarence left. First they must all drink a toast to the law, and the men who had been searching the grounds must be given hot drinks and their orders. The hounds must be rounded up and temporarily put in the stable. The housemaids must be sent back to work and the cooks to the kitchens. With a calm smile Michael sat in the drawing room and was charming and witty, while the rain beat at the windows and turned the countryside into a sea of mud. Dear God, where the hell was she? *Even if he lives, he will not survive long if he is hiding outside.*

At last the judge left, and Lady Mary retired to her room with the headache, insisting that Peter come and read to her. Michael was left alone. He quickly unfolded the note. It began with a quotation from Publilius Syrus: *Beneficium accipere libertatem est vendere.* The rest, in perfect Greek except for the lines from Phaedrus at the end—*Non semper ea sunt quae videntur*—was short and to the point. She thanked him for his kindness. Her ankle and shoulder felt much better. She had taken some money from his dresser, but she would pay it back. The books were security for the loan; he could keep the donkey and her pistol as interest. She had left.

Instantly he collared Dover, but the manservant could tell him nothing. Miss Whinburn had eaten her breakfast and Dover had left her in the bedroom. So Michael began to make his own very meticulous, very thorough search of Tresham.

Jessica lay on the roof of the orangery and shivered. She had no idea how she'd found the strength to get up there. She had known she must leave Tresham since the moment she awoke. As soon as Dover had gone, she had packed

up her bag and cleaned up the room. Her books were too
heavy to carry. She would leave them as security, with her
grandfather's dueling piece which Lord Deyncourt had
never returned to her. With her bound ankle she could
walk quite well if she didn't hurry, and the pain in her
shoulder she would just have to endure. It had taken a
long debate with herself to justify taking the earl's money,
but she would pay it back once she began working, and
now her donkey cart was destroyed she would have to buy
a seat on the stage. Jessica had gone down the back stairs,
meeting no one. It seemed that all the servants had disappeared elsewhere. She slipped into the garden and was
limping away from the house, when she heard the hounds.

She ran. Gasping with pain, she managed to get to the
orangery and, hefting her bag behind her, climb up a
neighboring elm. Then she dropped both the bag and
herself onto the flat roof, and prayed. The baying came
closer. Jessica peeked over the parapet that edged the roof,
and saw the hue and cry racing toward her hiding place,
the hounds in full tongue, when the clouds fractured and
it began to rain. Within seconds the downpour was so
blinding that the hounds began to mill about helplessly
and their handlers called them off. Soon everyone had
gone, and Jessica was left to the mercy of the elements.

Now she wasn't sure that it mightn't be better to be
discovered and hanged, after all. For she was very cold and
shaking uncontrollably, and she knew that she didn't have
the strength left to get down from the roof. She could no
longer dream of walking to a staging inn. Her ankle was
pounding with an insistent throbbing and she could feel
her foot swelling below the bandage. Miss Jessica Whinburn
was going to die up here and never be found until birds
built nests in her skeleton and raised their fledglings in
woven beds of red hair. Would Michael Dechardon Grey,
Lord of Deyncourt and all those other places, wonder why
she never paid back his money and redeemed her books?
Jessica put her arms about her bag and laughed weakly to

herself as the downpour battered at her. Better that than allow the betraying tears to come.

"It's all right," said a quiet voice. "They have gone."

Jessica opened her eyes and looked up. It was getting dark. Lord Deyncourt stood over her and the rain had stopped. "Why, I am quite the thing, thank you, my lord," she said with a desperate bravery. "How did you find Judge Clarence?"

Michael dropped on his heels beside her. The blue eyes seemed perfectly serious, his features as grave as a priest's. "On the verge of apoplexy, as it happens."

"Not really! Will you tell me what he said?"

Unthinkingly he brushed the wet hair from her forehead and smoothed his hand over her cheek. "He is convinced that had I not so fortuitously turned up, he would have been murdered as well as robbed. What he most particularly cannot forgive, however, is the deliberate attempt to humiliate him in front of his own servants and the total loss of a pair of expensive evening slippers."

Jessica tried to stop shaking. "Yet he could have sat there all night and had his coachman flog his team, but that would be less humiliating than walking a hundred yards through the mud?"

"Certainly, if one is wearing shoes dyed at great cost to exactly match one's stockings. Especially when one plans to cut a dash in front of Lady Fletcher, for whom one is developing a *tendre.*"

He put an arm around her shoulders and helped her to sit up. Jessica tried to make her voice light. "Did Lady Fletcher recoil from his muddy feet, or is she a sensible woman who could offer Gargantua a pair of warm slippers?"

"Undoubtedly she recoiled. In fact, she fainted at the sight and had to be revived with salts."

Jessica wanted very seriously not to lean into his warmth

and strength, but she couldn't stop herself. "You have sent Lord Clarence away satisfied, I hope?"

"Of course. He believes the villain escaped. I would rather have strangled the lad myself, so that he could have died here, but unfortunately I could not produce a body." He paused and gave her a wicked grin. "The grooms were both of a heavier build."

"When you promised to silence them, I was so convinced that you intended murder!"

"Alas," replied the earl. "You have found out that, unlike you, I lack sufficient mettle for a life of crime. Yes, the grooms are quite safe—I sent them with the donkey to Castle Deyncourt. And now if I do not get you back to my bed, I believe I shall have your death on my hands instead. Come, I will help you back to the house, where you may now remain as hidden and secure as a dormouse."

"Your bed? Then you still want to make me your mistress?"

"No, my dear innocent, I thought I might make you my countess."

Instantly, in spite of her sodden state, Jessica colored. "Oh, no, Lord Deyncourt," she said. "None of that! I might accept, then mend my fortunes by bringing a suit for breach of contract. How lucky you are that I don't intend to marry!"

He lifted her face and kissed her briefly. His lips were as chilled as her own. "Well, it was worth a try," he said lightly. "But you're thinking of Publilius Syrus, aren't you? *'To accept a favor is to sell one's freedom'*?"

No, thought Jessica to herself. *I was thinking of Phaedrus: Things aren't always as they appear.*

Jessica awoke with a raving thirst. Trying to sit up in bed made her head spin. Weakly, she pushed back the covers. How had it become so hot in her room? The fire had burned away to ash, and cast only a faint glow over the chamber. She called out. Instantly the door to the room opened and someone came in with a candle; a tall man in some kind of long robe, the flame casting the planes of his face into sharp relief. He sat beside her on the bed and laid a cool hand on her blazing forehead.

"Please, I'm so very thirsty."

"Hush, Miss Whinburn. You are quite safe. You were caught out in the cold and the rain all day. You have a little fever, that's all."

A few moments later strong, capable fingers were helping her guide a glass of cold water to her mouth. She clung to the strength that she could feel there. When he disentangled her fingers from his own, she felt bereft. Hot tears scalded down her cheeks, and a cool, damp cloth sponged them away.

"Ben has been killed?" It came out as a muddle of sounds; only her distress was clear.

"Hush, now, Jessica. Don't try to talk. Listen instead, and I will entertain you with absurdities, shall I?"

Strong arms gathered her in and held her securely. The man in the soft robe lay back on the bed, still holding her, and pulled the covers over them both as he began to murmur odd rhymes and snatches of nonsense. She burrowed into his chest listening to the soothing tones of his voice, while the fever shook her and his hand stroked her hair away from her forehead. Before long the tremors ceased, and she fell into a deep, exhausted sleep.

Michael lay still for a while and continued to hold her. What a bitter irony this was! The accomplished seducer playing the innocent nursemaid! Yet should it ever become known, she would be hopelessly compromised. He was suddenly furious with himself. *Naive girls are not your style, are they, Lord Deyncourt?* Why on earth hadn't he already offered for Lady Melton? He intended to make a suitable match that would leave him unencumbered; Honoria was perfect for the role and everyone expected it.

As soon as he was sure that Jessica was in a sound sleep, Michael extricated himself and slipped from the bed. He stood for a moment, looking down at her. The riot of red hair was spread across the pillow, and the freckles stood out strongly against her pale skin. With careful, impersonal, compassionate hands, he changed her bandages, combed her hair, and bathed her long limbs. However intimate it might be, however improper, however disturbing, she needed nursing. Yet Miss Jessica Whinburn was not his concern, other than saving her from Judge Clarence and delivering her safely to London. He would not become entangled!

Jessica opened her eyes upon a room dimly lit by one candle. The earl was sitting at the fireplace, staring into the fire. He was fully, even impeccably, dressed, as if his crisp white collar and correctly folded cravat could act as armor against emotion. As she moved, he stood and walked over to the bed.

"How long have I been ill?" said Jessica. On a table beside the bed lay a basin and some towels.

"A few days."

She closed her eyes for a moment. "And you nursed me?"

"I fought in Spain for years. I have seen fever before."

"Soldiers," said Jessica.

He seemed remote, untouched by her distress. "Some of them died, but I was called upon to help my sergeant's wife upon one occasion. Fortunately, both baby and mother survived."

"An odd task for you, surely?" *A few days! Dear God!* "And you take on these decisions naturally, don't you? Did you give no thought to how I would feel about it?"

"Don't refine upon it," he replied. "It was nothing personal. Dover offered his expert assistance. Before he became a widower he raised six girls."

His tone was cool and reassuring, but Jessica felt the humiliation burn to her soul. "Did I rave and mumble?" she asked.

"Nothing intelligible."

"Then thank God for that." She sat up and looked at him. Was he always like this? So damned cool and in control? She wished with a fierce passion that she had never met him, had never tried to save Lord Clarence's horses. She would have been in London by now. "How many persons' lives are at your disposal, my lord?"

He looked surprised. "Too many," he said.

"Yes, of course. There must be all the tenants of your vast estates who are at your mercy."

"I suppose they are."

"But then growing up as the heir to an earldom, you have always taken it for granted."

"I did not grow up as the heir. The title came to me on my brother's death, just six months ago."

"I'm sorry!" Jessica watched him as he walked back to the fire and added more coal. There was a hushed, intimate quiet in the room, broken only by the steady tick of a clock. The rest of Tresham lay in deep sleep.

Michael stirred the fire with the poker. "He was twelve years my senior—an unbridgeable gulf for boys. Nevertheless, his death was sudden and unwelcome, and was followed very quickly by his wife's. The tenants adored them, but unfortunately they had no children. Thus all those poor souls have fallen under my despotic sway."

"Your tenants don't like you?"

"They resent me. But it's none of your business, is it?"

"No, I suppose I should be more concerned with the fate of the nation. You have a seat in the House of Peers, do you not?"

"Indeed. And I serve my country where I may, Miss Whinburn. But affairs of state are not among the usual interests of young ladies."

"Because our understanding is too weak and our sensibility too delicate, of course. It is only men who have independence in their lives, isn't it?"

"Is it? I had a great deal more freedom of action before I became earl, I assure you."

"Fiddlesticks! Now you are earl, you may do as you like!"

Michael looked at her and laughed. "It may interest you to know, Miss Whinburn, that I am very far from being able to do as I like. Before I left London, for instance, I had a very uncomfortable conversation with the Prime Minister, and not only because he is concerned with riots over the price of corn and whether or not my radical politics might countenance revolution."

"And do they?"

"If the poor are starving, they will make their discomfort known whether it is convenient for the government or not. Remedial action would hardly come amiss. Nevertheless, Lord Liverpool has plans for me. I am considered sound when it comes to foreign policy. My brother was invaluable to Britain's diplomatic efforts in the past; now the government hopes it can rely on me. Since more is always achieved under the auspices of a fine meal and a charming entertainment than was ever formally secured around the diplomatic table, Lord Liverpool believes it would be easier if I had a wife to act as hostess. He even has a particular lady in mind."

Jessica frankly met his eyes as Deyncourt smiled lazily at her. "And how did you reply?"

He laughed. "You may imagine what you will, Miss Whinburn. But I will no doubt marry the lady."

In fact he had swallowed his anger and said: "There are a great many things I would do for my country, but I'm not sure that immediate marriage to the Incomparable Melton is among them."

Lord Liverpool had frowned. "Lord Deyncourt! It is common knowledge that you and the lady have an understanding. Are you saying you won't help us?"

Michael had risen to his feet and held out his hand. It was the first he had heard that he and Lady Honoria were considered as good as engaged. "I didn't say that, my lord. But I will assure you of one thing: Lady Honoria may make a charming hostess, but she has no interest in either the travails of the poor or the fate of the Congress of Vienna."

Jessica watched him as he looked back at her. Why on earth he had told her that he was planning marriage—was he warning her, or reminding himself? "It's a touching tale, is it not?" he said. "Perhaps I am only trying to engage your tender sympathy for my own nefarious purposes. You can't know, can you?" She felt angry color stain her cheeks. She had been fascinated for a moment by this glimpse into his life—so he was a diplomat! But now he was saying that it was all part of some disdainful manipulation. Yet she would not look away, even when he gave her his most devastating smile. "However, you are correct in one thing: I have more freedom of action than you. Judge Clarence has called off the Watch. It is time that we put an end to this irregular arrangement, and I brought you to the front door like a typical guest."

"I would rather that you took me to a coaching inn where I can catch the stage, my lord."

He seemed distracted, almost angry. "For God's sake, Miss Whinburn. I can't risk your fleeing again. You will remain here until I deem it safe to leave, and will then meekly travel to your aunt's and stay with her for at least two months. I want your word on it."

"Why? Why do you insist on this?"

"Because nothing else will suffice," he said firmly. "You have become my responsibility, and I won't discharge it by allowing you to try to make your own way in the world. You can have no idea of the dangers that await you in London."

"I had no idea of the dangers that I'd meet on the road," she said sarcastically.

"Exactly. Don't think to gainsay me in this, Miss Whinburn."

"This is outrageous! What earthly concern is it of yours?"

Because if she arrived alone in London, he knew perfectly well

what would happen to her. Of course, that was not something
he could put into words. "I owe it to your great-aunt," he
said instead. "Lady Emilia will take you in and dote upon
you."

"But as I told you, she and my father quarreled most
dreadfully!"

"Did he also have red hair?"

Jessica flared up immediately. "What on earth does that
have to say to the matter? Why must everyone always assume
that the color of one's hair determines one's tempera-
ment? My father had dark hair and was always up in the
boughs. Yet in spite of looking like a tree full of oranges,
I do not have a temper!"

"Obviously not," Deyncourt replied dryly. "Nor do I
imagine that you are a typical young lady. Your behavior
so far wouldn't quite meet the demands of the dowagers.
Never mind, Lady Emilia will teach you how to go on."

He could have no idea! How could she cope with the
ton? "It is unconscionable that you should do this!"

"Two months, or Lord Clarence may send his men with
the chains."

It made no difference that she knew the threat was
empty. And perhaps, because of the blunderbuss, and the
orangery, and the personal, intimate tasks he had done
for her for the last several days, she owed it to him. With
foreboding and reluctance, and filled with anger at her
own helplessness, Jessica said: "One month, no more."

"Then thank God for that. You won't regret it. Nothing
is more amusing than life among the *beau monde.* You will
be diverted, Miss Whinburn, and entertained. We shall
repair to London as soon as I finish my business with the
Steals."

"Do you run their lives completely?"

He smiled very much as he had done while assuring her
that black murder had been in his heart. "Of course. Lady
Mary is hen-witted when it comes to money, and my ward
is an impulsive boy. Tresham is encumbered with debt,

but with proper management it can be brought about. In the meantime, it needs an infusion of capital.''

"Which you will provide?''

"Which a certain Miss Caroline Brandon will provide.''

"Why, is she a relative?''

He grinned. "She soon will be. She will marry Lord Steal.''

"Oh, so they are betrothed.''

He rose. "Not yet, Miss Whinburn. But they will be. Peter just doesn't know it.''

Jessica had almost begun to believe she'd misjudged him, though she had been outgunned and outwitted, and had capitulated to his plans for herself with hardly any fight at all. Was Lord Steal as willing a victim?

"Good heavens, Lord Deyncourt!'' she said, lying back on the pillows. "Is everyone's life to be arranged to suit your convenience?''

"No, Miss Whinburn,'' he replied softly. "Not everyone's. Only yours.''

Chapter 5

Jessica dressed the next morning in her gray sarcenet and limped to the fire to await breakfast. It was not Dover, however, who came in with the tray, but Peter, Lord Steal. His bright blue coat lit up the room.

"Are you feeling more the thing, Miss Whinburn?" he whispered, his eyes full of concern. "I can't stay. Deyncourt would flay me alive if he was to know I'd stolen in here like this, but I had to see how you did."

"Then I am much better for your visit," said Jessica. "Do you go in such fear of your guardian that you must creep about and whisper in your own house?"

"Oh, Deyncourt's a dreadful stickler! At least as far as my behavior goes. It's a pretty rum go having him control all my affairs, I can tell you. He thinks I'm going to turn out like Father, who was a famous gambler!"

"So was mine," said Jessica gravely. "So I empathize."

"Do you?" Steal's brown eyes were locked on her face. "You're most kind to say so. But at least you don't have Deyncourt to answer to. I have to get back to town, but I don't even know if he'll let me go up for the season."

"Why on earth not? It would be monstrous to force you

to rusticate in the country if you didn't care to. Anyway, how can he stop you?"

"Good Lord, any number of ways! He could cut off my allowance for a start."

"He wouldn't dare! It would make him appear badly before his friends if he did so."

"You don't know him, Miss Whinburn. He don't care a fig for anyone's opinion. Besides, I would rather stand in a cage full of Bengal tigers than face him down."

"I won't believe it, Lord Steal!"

"That's because you're a sweet-natured female. He has a devilish temper, you know! But he don't rant and rave. A fellow could cope with that, I think. It's more a kind of killing frost. I can't stand it anyhow."

Jessica didn't want to criticize the poor fellow for his lack of backbone, and had she not capitulated to the earl's plans herself? So she merely said: "Well, I shan't tell him you came to inquire after me, so you're quite safe."

"Thanks, Miss Whinburn. What a monstrous thing to happen to a tender lady—to be attacked on the highway! You were fainting from the horror of it when you arrived. And I suppose it's very shocking for your sensibilities for you to have a gentleman in your room like this. I'm terribly sorry!"

His face scarlet, Peter bowed himself out. Jessica stared thoughtfully at the fire for a moment. There was something that young Lord Steal was afraid of; a glaze of anxiety overlay everything in his manner. Was he really so terrified of his guardian? And the earl intended to force this match with a Miss Caroline Brandon. It was outrageous! Jessica was not sure if she was glad or sorry when Lord Deyncourt did not come back to his room. Once again that evening she donned his nightshirt and slipped into his bed.

Someone was giving her an insistent shaking. The earl was sitting casually on the edge of the bed.

"It is morning," he said simply. "Pray, dress yourself.

Dover has brought breakfast. We are to go gallivanting about the lanes. Regrettably I shall first have to carry you into the garden.''

Jessica pulled on the dressing gown and hobbled behind the screen to dress. She brushed through her hateful hair and bundled it into a knot, knowing that it would follow its usual wayward habits and end up looking like a bird's nest. Then with the aid of the cane she stepped into the room. Deyncourt poured her a cup of hot chocolate, and she sipped at it while he buried himself in his newspaper. She watched his hands as he folded the paper—hands full of strength and grace. They didn't seem to be the hands of a bully.

He carried her outside and within a few minutes set her down in a small stone building. It was a folly: a small replica of a Greek temple, built with great pride by the previous Lord Steal.

"There's no fire in here, I'm afraid. But Dover has provided some hot bricks. As soon as I can respectably leave the house with a curricle, I shall come and fetch you and we shall duly drive about until we can be expected to have returned from Bedford."

"You always have everything planned, don't you, Lord Deyncourt?" said Jessica as she sat down on the stone seat. "I gave you my word. I shall be waiting here, as douce as a lamb."

"I imagine you will, since you cannot walk. In the meantime, here is your luggage."

"This box?" asked Jessica in surprise. There was a very respectable trunk sitting on the floor.

"You can hardly arrive at Tresham carrying your battered leather bags with their diminished contents, can you? You're supposed to have been traveling like a lady. And since it would raise eyebrows among the maids if I were to continue to lend you a nightshirt, I have taken the liberty of rectifying the situation a little.''

She looked up at him, but he laughed and left her. Jessica opened the box. Her dresses and other belongings had been carefully packed inside. But at the bottom lay something which slithered sensuously through her fingers. Jessica held it up in the dim dawn light. It was a nightdress. The garment was perfectly modest, cut high to the neck, with long sleeves and a hem that would sweep the floor, but the fabric was the finest she had ever felt. The seductive silk rustled a little as she laid it back in the box. The gift undoubtedly meant nothing to Deyncourt. Yet with a sudden rush of shame, Jessica blushed scarlet.

They met no one as they bowled along together through the damp lanes. Sodden sheep looked up disconsolately as they passed. Jessica could feel little beads of water beginning to form on her hair and cheeks and the end of her nose. She brushed them off.

"Why does Lord Steal hold you in such fear, my lord?" she asked suddenly.

"Good God! For what reason do you suppose that he does?"

"Because you appear so confident that you can order him to marry where you like! Is it your reaction to Lord Liverpool's request, to bully your ward into matrimony also?"

He seemed merely amused. "I cannot see that it is any business of yours, Miss Whinburn, whether I chose to act the tyrant to my ward or not."

"Then you don't deny that you would force him into a marriage where he had not the slightest inclination?"

"Force is a strong word."

"Why can't Lord Steal wed where he likes?"

"Because of his father's will he cannot marry without my consent. Of course, when it was written it was my late brother, not I, whom the late Lord Steal had in mind. Yet the guardianship fell to me along with everything else. It's a charming arrangement, don't you think?"

"Yet I should like to see what you could do about it, if he did not agree to marry where you direct! Suppose he should fall in love with someone other than this Miss Brandon?"

"Do you think if Peter fancied himself in love, I should change my mind?"

"Obviously you would not. You would make him marry for a fortune even if his affections were elsewhere engaged. You show no scruples at all."

"Don't tell me you're a romantic, Miss Whinburn! When you yourself plan never to marry?"

There was only the slightest hesitation in her reply. "Because I am so situated! I have no dowry, for a start."

"Tell me the real reason."

"Very well," she said. "I intend to write. It would be impossible to achieve my goals with a husband and children hanging at my skirts. Will that do?"

"If it is the truth," he said.

Jessica turned her head away so that he couldn't see her face. The truth! She had not lied to him, but such a partial truth was hardly honest.

Lady Mary's smile was charming, if a little absentminded, as she exclaimed over her guest's sore ankle. "I have always said that the steps on those carriages are too treacherous for words! You poor creature! To suffer such an accident!"

Two footmen had carried Jessica into the drawing room, and set her beside Peter's mother. Lord Steal lounged on the small sofa opposite them. His mother wouldn't have guessed that they had met before, yet Peter's look was very solicitous. The footman brought in the tea tray and set it between Jessica and Lady Mary. Jessica waited some time while Lady Mary fiddled with her handkerchief and looked vaguely anxious.

Casually Michael rose and came over to them. "I really fail to see," he said with gentle charm, "why it is always the lady guest who has the honor of pouring tea. May we gentlemen not have a turn?''

Jessica watched him deftly handle the pot and the dishes. Oh, good Lord! Lady Mary had been waiting for her to fill the cups! She hadn't known because they'd never served tea to guests at Whinburn. But Michael covered the moment with idle conversation, and tea was taken without further incident, until at last he rose and gestured to his ward to accompany him.

"If you will excuse us," he said, bowing smoothly to Lady Mary. "There is some estate business that needs our attention. Good day, Miss Whinburn."

The gentlemen left the room.

"Does Lord Deyncourt order all your affairs, my lady?'' asked Jessica when they had gone.

"Oh, indeed, Miss Whinburn. He is everything that is kind. I don't know what we would have done without him after my dear husband died. And now he has become Peter's guardian, Lord Deyncourt is of untold assistance to us at Tresham. Of course he has his own ideas. All the latest notions! Crop rotations and newfangled machinery! And the earl insists that the tenants' children attend school. Not at all the thing in my day!''

"School?" said Jessica, surprised.

"Oh, indeed, my dear. He's done the same thing at Castle Deyncourt. He's quite a radical, you know. I'm very afraid that the children will get ideas above their station, and it is a great vexation to the parents to lose the extra hands on the land. Yet we have a dame school now in every village.''

Jessica felt a sudden rush of confusion. Why should a careless rake care about rustics' children? "Do his radical ideas reflect badly upon him, then?'' she asked.

"Oh, no, surely not! The earl is generally considered above reproach. He would never do anything to offend even the most delicate sensibility.''

Jessica almost choked. If Lady Mary had any inkling that her guest had already spent a considerable length of time in that perfect lord's bedchamber in this very house, she would probably have an attack of the vapors on the spot! Deftly, Jessica shifted the conversation to a safer subject.

Lord Steal turned to his guardian as they rode out to inspect the home farm. "That was splendidly done, Deyncourt! Miss Whinburn is like the heroine of a romance! Mama suspects nothing."

The earl smiled at his young ward. "And neither will she if you keep your head. I could not help but discern that you never once took your eyes off our new guest."

Peter blushed furiously. "Well, her hair color ain't top of the trees, but she's so very delicate and has the tenderest sensibility!"

The earl raised an eyebrow at this extraordinary description. "Miss Whinburn is the penniless daughter of an obscure country squire, who has not the slightest idea how to behave in polite society and had enough temerity to travel alone to London. She's headstrong and obstinate. She also—" He stopped. What was she? A mystery, surely? Yet with an innocent, valiant heart! "She also has freckles and a temper. Perhaps you should look more carefully to your own situation."

Peter looked down. "I know. Thanks to Papa's recklessness, I must marry an heiress. Yet even people in our position in society are beginning to marry for love."

Michael's voice was only a little goading as he quoted gently: "*'Go to; it is a plague / That Cupid will impose for my neglect—'*"

Lord Steal had no patience with Shakespeare. "Anyway, how am I to meet anyone cooped up down here in the country?"

"If you had minded your manners in town, sir, you might still be there."

"All the fellows game and drink!"

"Yet they don't usually turned up foxed at Almack's and ask the Dowager Countess of Hawksley to dance!"

Peter began to look a little petulant. "How could you understand? It was a wager! Yet I don't suppose you ever stepped out of line, did you?"

The earl's horse jibbed a little as if his rider had unexpectedly tightened the rein. "Do you think not?" Michael said quietly. "I know a great deal more about folly than you imagine. Yet this discussion concerns your future, dear Steal, not my past."

Peter couldn't imagine what Lord Deyncourt was talking about. Everyone in town was intimidated by the earl's unflappable style—though of course he had an enviable reputation with women. "I should think even you might concede that a certain amount of compatibility would be desirable in a lifetime mate," he mumbled at last.

To his surprise, his remarkable guardian laughed. "Peter, our unusual guest is penniless and she's a veritable hoyden."

"Never!" said Lord Steal, his round brown eyes very serious. "She's all alone—she needs someone to protect her! And she's as soft, pliable, and complete a lady as . . . as Miss Caroline Brandon!"

"I'm glad to hear that Miss Brandon has attracted your attention."

Peter looked astonished. "Who, Caroline? She's as plain as a mouse! If you hadn't led her out at the Kales' ball, she'd have been marked down as a wallflower. Of course, your lead was enough to make all the fellows ask her."

"Including yourself, as I remember. I trust you are aware that Caroline Brandon is in possession of fifty thousand pounds? Perhaps you might be interested to learn that I would not object if you were to make Miss Brandon an offer. Marry her, and we need not have any more of these uncomfortable conversations."

"If I were to offer for her, might I return to town, Deyncourt?"

"Certainly! In fact, I should expect you to cut a dash!"

"Very well then. I'll have her."

"Will you?" The earl's voice expressed genuine surprise.

"Good God! Then you have just made a very wise decision, sir."

The earl touched his horse with his heel and the bay bounded forward. *It is a splendid, but temporary, thing to be nineteen,* he said to himself as they galloped away. *But why the devil has he agreed to marry Miss Brandon? And who is it that he's so afraid of?*

The house party was proposed immediately after dinner that evening. It seemed to be Lady Mary's idea, but Jessica was sure that Deyncourt was behind it.

"Let us have Lady Honoria Melton visit us," Peter's mother said absently. "Her cousin Cranby will be happy to bring her, no doubt, and perhaps Miss Caroline Brandon may complete the party."

Jessica saw an expression of pure panic cross Peter's face at this pronouncement. It could only be at the mention of Miss Brandon's name, surely?

"And after the visit," said Michael, idly watching his ward, "it will be time to revisit London. With your permission, Lady Mary, I shall go and make the arrangements." Michael bowed and left them.

"Who is Lady Honoria Melton?" asked Jessica.

"Sir Gordon Cranby's cousin, you know," said Lady Mary. "She's the loveliest thing."

"She was the toast of the season," added Peter, his face suddenly white. "She's known as The Incomparable. She's a raving beauty and Deyncourt plans to marry her!" And leaping from his chair, he charged from the room.

Chapter 6

April seemed determined to make up for all the storms of March. By the time the guests were due to arrive, Tresham smiled over woods and gardens bright with spring flowers. The earl and Peter had disappeared for two weeks to inspect the farms at Castle Deyncourt. Jessica was left at Tresham. She burned with impatience, yet the prospect of eventually being delivered to her great-aunt in London filled her with dread. In the meantime, she could not walk on her ankle at all; she certainly could not travel. Since Lady Mary seemed essentially oblivious to her presence, Jessica spent a great deal of time alone in the library. She amused herself by translating Greek epics and putting them into simple stories. Her injured ankle excused her every time she was late for dinner or unwittingly revealed her appalling ignorance of etiquette, since Tresham was run with an exact and efficient correctness that Jessica had never experienced before. For there was a great deal about Whinburn House that she had not told Deyncourt.

Yet at last the gentlemen returned and they were all gathered in the drawing room, waiting for the company to arrive. The earl came up and leaned over her.

"I hope you are managing, Miss Whinburn?" he said politely. "And that your shoulder is entirely mended? It would hardly do for me to visit you in your bedroom now that you are an official guest of Lady Mary."

"I am perfectly cognizant of that, my lord," she replied. "I am quite competent to handle my problems by myself. There is no further need for you to concern yourself with my situation. Besides, I would have thought you had your hands full with everybody else's."

He merely raised an eyebrow. "Indeed? What makes you think that I enjoy such a role?"

"Because you obviously do it all the time!"

He leaned close enough to make her pulse race uncomfortably as he whispered: "But I do it only for my own malicious pleasure, ma'am, and the wanton amusement afforded by playing God."

There was a sudden bustle in the hall, and the footman opened the door to announce the visitors. Lady Honoria Melton entered the room, smiling, confident, and exquisite. Jessica was instantly entranced. Everything about the Incomparable was perfect: from her golden ringlets to the pale buff kid boots that peeked beneath her elegant skirts. Her features were lovely, pure, and calm, like a medieval Madonna. How did anyone get their hair so smooth? And her skin! The Incomparable Melton had a complexion like white cream. Jessica realized instantly that Lady Honoria would make a perfect Countess of Deyncourt.

"My dear Lady Mary!" Honoria said in a clear, low voice as she came forward and held out her white hand. "It has been positively this age since I have seen you! How delightful of you to invite us down to Tresham. Town life is filling everyone with the most horrid ennui. Our journey was quite Gothic, of course! Yet I believe the sun will shine tomorrow. Ah, Deyncourt! How do you do?" Michael bowed over her hand. Lady Honoria smiled, a smile of clear beauty and muted invitation. "You know my cousin, Sir Gordon Cranby, of course? And Miss Caroline Brandon?"

Jessica forced her attention to the other guests. As she was introduced, Sir Gordon Cranby peered at her rudely through his quizzing glass. His face had the smooth, polished look of old ivory, and the heavily-lidded eyes were set deep. He pronounced himself charmed. Miss Caroline Brandon, on the other hand, gave Jessica a sweet soft smile. She was tiny and thin—surely not more than seventeen?— and her pale brown hair was pulled back too severely into an elegant knot, set with ribbons. Her dark green dress made her skin look sallow and swallowed her delicacy in its elaborate ruffles and folds. *Poor Miss Brandon!* thought Jessica, suddenly wanting to protect this young girl who seemed as shy as a deer. *So she is to be the latest victim of Deyncourt's arrogant manipulations!*

The entire company was soon settled and Lady Honoria was given the honor of presiding over the teapot. "What do you say we all ride out tomorrow?" said the Incomparable with charming grace. "Lord Steal's stables can mount everybody."

"But Miss Whinburn has a bruised ankle," objected Peter.

"No, pray go without me," said Jessica immediately.

"Oh, Miss Whinburn may keep me company," said Lady Mary, and soon the guests launched into a debate as to the most desirable destination. Sir Gordon Cranby seemed to take particular delight in soliciting Lord Steal's opinion.

"This is, after all, your domain, my lord," he said, gazing idly at Peter through his quizzing glass. "You are master of Tresham, the loveliest house in this part of England! Have you no suggestion?"

But Peter sat silent, fists clenched, staring at his feet.

They all met the next morning in the breakfast parlor. It had been determined that the riders would trace the old Roman road to the ruined abbey at Holy Cross. Honoria had declared herself unutterably thrilled at the prospect.

"A ruined abbey! It is simply too grotesque for words! Shall we encounter the ghosts of monks babbling horridly in the misty cloister, do you think?"

"Or bats?" smiled Cranby.

"Better and better," said Honoria gaily. "I hope you gentlemen will be ready for fainting ladies."

"I shall do my best to offer my arm should you pass out from horror," said Michael dryly.

"Oh, will you, my lord?" she replied archly. "Tell me, Miss Whinburn, is that the fashion for morning gowns in the north?"

The question caught Jessica entirely off guard. "Why, no!" she replied innocently, glancing down at her shabby muslin. "We North Country females follow London fashion as best we might. It is just that I am too much of an eccentric to keep up."

Lady Honoria arched her delicate brows. "And you have no personal maid, I understand. I insist that you borrow Cicely while you are here. I have two maids and shan't miss Cicely at all. You will be amazed at how she can improve the most impossible hair. Not that I meant to imply, of course . . ." She trailed off in charming confusion.

"I couldn't possibly accept. I dress my own hair, and would not trust any lady's maid not to collapse in horror if confronted with the task of trying to tame it."

"But I insist, Miss Whinburn. You would not deprive me of the pleasure of being able to make such a simple gesture of welcome, when you are otherwise so left out of activities? I consider it settled and shall send Cicely to you first thing. I refuse to hear another word! Lord Deyncourt can tell you: I always get my way, don't I, my lord?"

The party returned from their outing to find Jessica restlessly perusing a book, while Lady Mary snored gently in the opposite chair. The riders had not encountered any wailing spirits, but a sudden flurry of bats had indeed given the ladies some excuse to scream and clutch at the arms of their escorts. Peter seemed disappointed, in fact, that Caroline had not been more upset by the animals' flight.

"It was most shocking," cried the Incomparable Melton, once they were all changed and gathered in the drawing room. "Those horrid bats! Indeed, Lord Steal, you are correct. Miss Brandon displayed far more fortitude than I."

"Well, I have spent most of my life in the country, Lady Honoria," said Caroline gently. "I should be ashamed if a few simple creatures should cause me much disquiet."

"No doubt Miss Whinburn would share your sensible attitude," commented Michael idly.

"Oh, no!" cried Peter. "I imagine Miss Whinburn would have fainted clear away!"

Jessica looked up in astonishment. Dear Lord, did the fact that she had a sore ankle make her seem such a frail damsel? If it was not for her promise to Deyncourt to stay meekly at Tresham until her ankle healed and he could take her to London, she would take considerable pleasure in disabusing Lord Steal. But she had no chance to reply to his extraordinary misconceptions, since dinner was announced at that moment. Her chair was carried into the dining room by two burly footmen, and she was seated next to Sir Gordon Cranby.

"You missed quite the outing, ma'am," said that gentleman, once the soup had been served. "My cousin was in need of considerable support from Lord Deyncourt when the bats made their appearance." His heavy-lidded eyes looked down the table to where the earl and the Incomparable Melton were deep in conversation. "They make a graceful couple, don't you agree?"

"Undoubtedly, sir. Apart from the bats, were you impressed by the abbey?"

"Alas, I spent an hour lost in lonely contemplation, while the earl fanned my cousin's agitated brow, and Miss Brandon and Lord Steal wandered the ruins together. I have the unfortunate facility for discomforting poor Lord Steal; he envies my style, don't you know, so he avoids me.

Such a tiresome thing! I was tempted to frame a sonnet to 'Solitude in Ravaged Grandeur,' but Deyncourt and the Incomparable came back to disturb my meditations.''

Jessica was relieved when the ladies left the gentlemen to their port. Lady Mary suggested that they play piquet, and Jessica was paired with Caroline, while Honoria sat at another table with Peter's mother. After discarding the necessary number, Jessica shuffled the cards for the first deal. Caroline burst into giggles. "Oh, pray, do not handle the cards like that, Miss Whinburn! You will have Lady Mary in a faint!''

"Whatever do you mean?" Jessica smiled at her partner. Since the return from Holy Cross, Caroline seemed to be changed. "Like what?" She had put the pack back on the table at the other girl's words.

"As if you were about to perform a magic trick!"

Jessica laughed. "Like this?" She made a waterfall of the pack, then fanned it rapidly and with a quick flip of the wrist, slid the entire deck through her fingers into an elegant reshuffle.

"Yes!" cried Caroline. "However did you learn to do that?"

"From my late father. Is it not done?"

"Not for a lady! Peter's mama will think you have frequented gaming hells.''

"Well, my father had done so often enough, and he liked to be stylish when he entertained gentlemen at Whinburn. How am I supposed to do it?"

"Like this." Caroline took the pack and quietly reordered them. "Did your father play deep?"

"Very," said Jessica. "But he just taught me his skill for our own amusement.''

Caroline made no judgment on this glimpse of a most extraordinary upbringing. Instead she dealt the cards. "See? You must not look too proficient."

"So competence in a lady is cause for the vapors?"

"Indeed it is, Miss Whinburn." It was Deyncourt. He stood casually at her elbow. The gentlemen had finished their port and rejoined the ladies. "Miss Brandon is right. Should you display it in polite society, your expert handling of the deck would be enough to preclude your being granted a voucher for Almack's at the very least."

She looked up at him. His expression seemed to hold nothing but polite disinterest. While Caroline was to be offered to Peter as the sacrificial lamb! Miss Brandon was a little shy, but beneath the mouselike exterior she had a simple and sensible attitude to life, and Jessica genuinely liked her. Anger flooded through her. "But that's absurd! In order to keep females dependent they may not do anything well, not even shuffle a deck? And society will allow us no occupation of real consequence. We may play games of chance based on a rapid calculation of the probabilities of the cards, but should not worry our pretty heads about accounts, for the figures would be too hard. The human relationships of the family are our domain, but we could understand nothing of international relations. We are so delicate we can be expected to faint at the sight of a bat, yet we must face the rigors of childbirth—" Jessica stopped herself in mid-sentence. "Oh, fiddlesticks, I've done it now, haven't I?"

Caroline had blushed scarlet and seemed ready to slide beneath the table, yet she couldn't help but grin. "That's a lot worse than shuffling cards, Miss Whinburn. The lady patronesses would have the vapors instantly!"

"I am sorry! It's just my wicked tongue when I get angry. I didn't mean to be indelicate."

Michael smiled. "What you have missed, Miss Whinburn, in your cogent analysis of our social foibles, is that ladies rely for their safety on their ability to elicit protective instincts in men, and must behave appropriately or face the consequences."

She looked at him with fury. "Because otherwise the gentlemen would use their superior strength to enforce their will? That is exactly what happens now! However, I don't want to throw everybody into the boughs everywhere I go, so I am indebted to Miss Brandon for her advice, and I shall try to guard my wayward tongue and handle the cards like an incompetent in the future." If only she had not made him that promise!

"Not like an incompetent, Miss Whinburn, just like a lady. And now I beg that you will allow me to take Miss Brandon away. Lord Steal would like to try your game, and Cranby would prefer playing with his cousin."

He walked away with Caroline on his arm, and Peter sat at the table with Jessica. Lord Steal seemed distracted and anxious. Jessica glanced across the room at the earl, and was not surprised to see that his blue gaze was idly watching the Incomparable Melton, where she sat with her cousin Sir Gordon Cranby at another card table. A calculating smile seemed to haunt the corner of Deyncourt's firm mouth. *It truly is as if he were some eastern potentate,* thought Jessica, *controlling the lives of all of us. Even mine!*

"So the earl would rather partner the plain little Miss Brandon than the Incomparable Melton?" asked Cranby idly as he dealt the cards to his cousin. "Doesn't it worry you to watch Deyncourt pay attention to another female?"

Lady Honoria looked up at him and gave a charming laugh. "To Miss Brandon? Are you serious? All the innocent young chits are safe from Deyncourt. She is one of his lame chickens, taken under an avuncular wing. Really, Cranby, right now he is watching me! For God's sake, gallantry is as natural to him as breathing. He can't help it. Anyway, I trust possession of Castle Deyncourt will prove sufficient compensation if I am neglected."

"Yes, Castle Deyncourt is very fine, of course." Then Cranby smiled. "Though Tresham is more to my own taste."

"Don't be too sure of your plans, Cranby. I see that Lord Steal is making sheep's eyes at the penniless Miss Whinburn."

Cranby glanced at Jessica and Peter. "Have no fear of that, my dear. Deyncourt would never allow it. She has no fortune and I believe our puissant earl doesn't even like her. For although as you have so cogently pointed out, he cannot prevent himself from enthralling the ladies—even the homely Miss Brandon—Miss Jessica Whinburn would seem to be the exception. Haven't you noticed? Our hero does not flirt with her."

Yet as Caroline Brandon faced Michael over the cards, she was merely concerned that he would allow her to win. She was not enthralled by the handsome earl, and she was very nearly immune to his charm. Caroline was perfectly aware that Deyncourt was very dashing, of course, even if he was at least ten years too old, but she was quite desperately in love with someone else. "I must thank you, my lord," she said shyly. "I have been made very happy."

Michael smiled at her with none of the dangerous wit the *ton* had come to expect. "So Peter has proposed? And you have accepted him. Why thank me?"

She looked up at him. "Don't deny it was your doing. After I was so foolish as to tell you my feelings!"

"That you have loved him since you were ten years old? Alas, I could never resist bravely restrained tears in a young lady. Very well, I won't insult your intelligence by pretending otherwise. I have done as you asked, dear Miss Brandon—I hope it was wise?"

"Oh, yes! Now we are engaged Lord Steal must notice me, which he never would otherwise, and thus I have a chance. He thinks of me simply as the sister of his old friend, and of course I'm so very plain. It must seem excessively foolish to you that I am so sure I want Peter, when he doesn't want me."

"I trust he will want you when he discovers how very delightful you are, Miss Brandon."

She blushed. "Oh, stuff! I know I am a veritable antidote. If you had not been so kind as to dance with me at the Kales', I should have been a wallflower for ever."

"Never."

"Yes, it's true, and you shan't gainsay it. You may pretend it was an idle whim, but I know better. You're just a compassionate person, aren't you? You would help anyone in need."

"Hush, Miss Brandon. If anyone overheard this, it would ruin my reputation!"

"You're still kind to help someone so ordinary."

The earl smiled. "But I don't think you ordinary, Miss Brandon, which is why I have taken your part with my feckless ward. I think that when he realizes the treasure to whom he is betrothed, you'll be the making of him."

Which was the very moment when Jessica learned that Deyncourt had succeeded in his diabolical scheme, and that Lord Steal had become engaged to Caroline Brandon. Between dealing the ace and laying over it the ten of hearts, Peter announced that he and Miss Brandon had come to an understanding at Holy Cross Abbey. Jessica could do nothing but offer her felicitations, and watch Lord Steal's miserable young face as he glanced across the room at Cranby and Honoria, then at the earl and his betrothed. They played out the rest of their game in silence.

After the card tables were finally put away, Michael came up to her and smiled. "Has Lord Steal told you? I seem to have succeeded in my wicked machinations already, Miss Whinburn."

"Don't be too sure, Lord Deyncourt," Jessica replied quickly. "Anyone could tell that Lord Steal's affections are not truly pledged."

"And you intend to do something about it?"

"I would if I were able! It is unconscionable for you to so manipulate them."

He smiled sardonically at her. "Do not try to set yourself against me, Miss Whinburn. My plans for my ward are not your concern. If you interfere, please be assured that I will exact immediate revenge."

"There is not a thing you can do to control my behavior."

"I can turn you over to Judge Clarence."

"You would not!"

He grinned with that exasperating charm. "Try me, madam. Now, perhaps you may keep Lady Mary company while I play fast and loose with the lives of the rest of the company?"

Chapter 7

The next morning Jessica was obliged to accept the services of Honoria's maid. It was a mixed blessing. Cicely Pratchett was a sharp-faced woman with prying eyes, and Jessica disliked her, but she could not deny that she was a clever lady's maid. She could indeed do wonders with the most impossible hair. Within a few days, Jessica was amazed to find that her carrot crop began to behave itself. Cicely mixed a rinse that tamed the bright color into a deeper, softer shade and brought out rich mahogany highlights.

"I'm stunned," said Jessica one morning as she watched this transformation once again. "Could you do the same for Miss Brandon?"

Cicely sniffed. "A rinse wouldn't answer *there*, ma'am. Miss Brandon should cut her hair and put it in curls. She's too fine-boned for the style she has now, and her maid ought to know it."

"And those clothes," said a cool voice from the doorway. "Miss Brandon is drowned in ruffles. I declare her mother has the taste of a gypsy." Lady Honoria Melton smiled charmingly at Jessica as she came into the room. "Miss

Brandon should dress in the simplest lines and plainest fabrics, then she would look delicate and appealing, and Deyncourt wouldn't have to work so hard.'' She began to leaf idly through some fashion magazines which the chambermaid left in all the ladies' rooms. "Like this, or this merino walking dress. Don't you agree, Miss Whinburn?'' She gave the magazine to Jessica. "Nothing is more important in society than looks, other than reputation, of course—especially to someone like Deyncourt who must keep up his position. Appearances can always be mended, but a lady's reputation, once damaged, is irreparably lost. Yet the gentlemen may sow their wild oats without it making them in the least ineligible to marry well. Sometimes I think it's unfair, don't you?''

"I don't know,'' replied Jessica. "I would hope that character counted for something.''

The Incomparable laughed aloud. "Character! Lord Deyncourt doesn't care a fig for character. He just wants an unsullied bride. I expect him to offer for me, but I don't expect him to admire my character!''

Jessica felt totally at a loss. "Yet I think you are very kind, Lady Honoria, to lend a complete stranger such a skilled lady's maid,'' she said.

"Think nothing of it,'' replied the Incomparable in her lovely, low voice. Then she gave Jessica a dazzling smile. "When my future husband has decided that you are another of his lame ducks, what else could I do?''

The Incomparable Melton accompanied Jessica down to breakfast, where they found the company in an uproar. Everyone was talking at once, while Peter plied Michael with questions.

"What is it?'' asked Jessica. "Has something happened?''

Michael gave her a quick glance. "Indeed, Miss Whinburn. You may know that when Bonaparte escaped Elba in March, royalist resistance collapsed in France and he entered Paris unopposed. Wellington has been gathering our men in Belgium for the last month. Yet Napoleon has been deplorably unable to take the hint. He plans a

great military spectacle to effectively thumb his nose at
all the great powers; war is inevitable. We face movement
and machinations all across Europe." He turned back to
Peter. "Ambassadors are up in the boughs. I must return
to London, dear Steal. The Corsican Monster gave no
thought to our domestic convenience, I'm afraid."

Immediately after the meal, Michael shook hands with
each of them and made his farewells. Jessica looked straight
into his eyes as he took her hand. He met her gaze and
gave her a slight wink, which she found infuriating, then
he bowed over her fingers with the perfect, impersonal
courtesy of the trained diplomat.

"Goodbye, Miss Whinburn. I trust when we meet again
in London, you will be entirely recovered from your indis-
position?"

"It is a matter of complete indifference to me, my lord."

"What, that you recover?" He looked at her in genuine
surprise.

"No, whether we meet again. For I find your use of Miss
Brandon unconscionable."

But he merely smiled at her, before he strode away to
mount his horse for the journey to London. The house
party was to break up the next day. Cranby would escort
Lady Honoria and Miss Brandon back to London in his
carriage. Jessica was to remain in Lady Mary's care for a
few more days until her ankle was entirely mended, then
Peter would bring the ladies to town. Honoria insisted that
Cicely, the maid, stay with Jessica until they should meet
again in London, and it seemed churlish to refuse.

As soon as his most urgent business was done, Michael
had gone straight to Lady Emilia Shay. Her parlor was
ablaze with cut flowers brought up daily from the country.

"This story you tell me of my great-niece is most singular,
Deyncourt! To travel alone in a donkey cart! She was a
very odd and outspoken girl, if I remember. Tell me, is
she pretty?"

Michael smiled. "She is unusual."

"You mean she grew up to be plain? I won't believe it. Even as a child she had good bones."

"Which she still does. No, I mean that she has extraordinary eyes, a clear profile, and a neat figure, and many of your acquaintance might well consider her attractive. But then she also has freckles, and, in her own words, a head of hair like a tree full of oranges. Yet she would seem to have a curious attitude for a young lady. I don't believe she takes any thought to her appearance."

"Well, we'll see about that! Unusual! Yes, I remember the hair. She shall start a rage and make a grand match."

"That does not seem to be her intention," said Michael quietly.

"She must! What else can she do when there's no inheritance? I don't have enough to provide for her. That fool of a father—to leave her desperate and in want! My poor niece married him for love and he was a charming, handsome man, but feckless. After his wife died, he raised Jessica without any propriety. I declare I have never been more shocked! Sir Shelby let the girl run around without chaperon or guidance. He raised her like a boy—taught her Latin and Greek and how to bring down a bird with a gun. It was beyond anything."

"You offered your advice?" asked Michael.

The old lady laughed a little bitterly. "I offered to send a governess."

He gazed absently at his fingers. "Since Miss Whinburn behaves with a certain imprudence and does not seem to understand society's finer rules, I am to assume the offer was rejected?"

Lady Emilia leaned back and Michael looked up. He was amazed to see tears shining in the old lady's eyes. "It was."

There was the briefest pause before the earl replied. "What was Whinburn House like?"

"Oh, a ramshackle old place out on the moors, the

Cheviots brooding to the north. There was nothing there but sheep."

Which was not what Michael meant at all. What of that expert fall of cards sliding through Jessica's hands? He feared that a great deal more had taken place at Whinburn than was related to the care of sheep. "So you quarreled," he said.

"We never corresponded or saw each other again. Yet Jessica is all that is left to me of family."

"Then you will give her a home, Lady Emilia?"

"Of course! Indeed, I am most anxious to have her join me in London."

"So am I," said the earl with a wry smile. "I am afraid that if she stays much longer at Tresham, my ward will make a cake of himself over her."

"Fustian! You told me yourself that Steal has offered for Miss Brandon. He has too much honor, surely?"

"He is also very young."

"And how did you manage to bring the engagement about so rapidly?"

"To be honest, I have no idea. It was no sooner suggested than done. It's absurd to think that my ward holds me in that much awe! And he is definitely becoming enamored of Miss Whinburn."

Lady Emilia sniffed. "If you think that my niece is so lost to decency as to encourage Peter, it is surely not beyond your powers to distract her attention. Besides, if I am to launch her in society, I should appreciate your help."

Michael gave the old lady an amused glance. "She doesn't wish to be launched in society. She wishes to do Greek translations and earn her own keep."

"Balderdash! We'll see her wed, Deyncourt. I rely on you to help me find her a match."

With an odd lurch of the heart, the earl remembered Jessica's brave defiance at Tresham. Yet he could not allow himself to become involved with her! Thank God it seemed that he had kissed her with impunity. And then he shuddered at the arrogance of the thought. "Unfortunately she has taken me in a strong dislike."

"Fiddlesticks! You are the most accomplished rake in London! Surely you could exert a little innocent charm?"

Michael leaned back in his chair. "Oh, no, Lady Emilia," he said. "Miss Jessica Whinburn is your protégée, not mine."

Yet it was some time before Jessica was able to travel, for in her impatience to be well, she twisted her ankle on the stair. Lord Steal pressed her hand with solemn meaning, but disappeared instantly to London. Jessica was once again left alone with Lady Mary. "I declare, we are so fortunate in Lord Deyncourt!" said Peter's mother. "I thank heaven every day that such a *nonpareil* has charge of Peter! The earl does everything to perfection!" And every day the sentiment was repeated with small variations. Then one day the dry sticks of hawthorn along the lanes began to swell with buds. Abruptly the hedge was alive with white blossom, like an unseasonal snowfall of petals, and Peter returned to escort his mother and her guest to London. At last Jessica's ankle was healed.

The morning before Jessica and Lord Steal were to journey to London, Peter insisted that she allow him to show her the blossom in the orchard. Taking her hand in the crook of his mulberry sleeve he led her into the lane, and they walked together between the banks of hawthorn bloom. A gust of wind sprayed them suddenly with petals. As Jessica stopped to brush them off, Peter grasped her by the hand.

"I wish you weren't so dashed pretty, Miss Whinburn," he said awkwardly. "With the petals on your shoulders, you look like a bride!" Jessica gazed at him in amazement. This was too much! Before she could respond, he had rushed on. "Well, hang it all, can't you see? I'm in love with you! If I hadn't made such a dashed botch of everything, I'd have asked you to marry me."

"Whatever are you saying, Lord Steal?" Jessica felt torn between embarrassment and laughter. "We have barely seen each other these last weeks, and you are betrothed!"

"Only because Deyncourt would never have allowed me to offer for you! Actually it's not all his fault. He can be a jolly decent fellow really—stood me the blunt to cut a dash in town last season, though I know he don't care for my taste in clothes or friends. Well, that don't signify. It's just that he's afraid I'll go the same way as Father. It didn't seem to matter until I met you." He dropped suddenly to one knee and threw out an arm in a dramatic gesture. Jessica hastily swallowed the laughter that threatened to disrupt. She could not be so cruel as to let her amusement show, but really Lord Steal did look quite ridiculous.

"Lord Steal, this is outrageous!" she said as sternly as she was able. "You have no business saying such things to me when you have an understanding with Miss Brandon, and though I hold you in the esteem with which I might hold a brother, I have no desire to marry you. Please get up, you are spoiling your trousers."

He scrambled awkwardly to his feet, and gave a rueful look at his blue Cossack pantaloons, which now sported a mud patch on one knee. "Not even if Miss Brandon cried off?"

"Especially if Miss Brandon were to cry off."

He gazed at her with an unmitigated infatuation. "Well, you have to say that. It's only ladylike."

"Fustian! I have never in my life cared for being ladylike and I shan't start now!"

"You're only bamming me, aren't you? You would never do anything to truly cause comment out of the ordinary."

"How can you say so? Lord Steal, you have entirely mistaken my character!"

"Well, dash it all." His face was the picture of self-indulgent misery. "Forget it then. Shouldn't have said anything really."

They traveled back up the lane toward the imposing edifice of Tresham Hall in a distinctly uncomfortable silence.

Early the next morning, Jessica sat beside Cicely in the Tresham chaise. Lady Mary had decided not to come to town after all. The countryside was too pretty to leave, and London so tiresome! Peter could escort Jessica, and with Cicely as chaperone it was quite proper. Jessica could not suppress a surge of excitement. The capital! She quickly thrust aside a fleeting concern about the upcoming meeting with her great-aunt.

Peter came out of the house and climbed up on the box where he had decided to sit with the coachman; two footmen stood up behind. Jessica was finally to travel in style. Taking a last farewell of Lady Mary, with much waving of lace handkerchiefs and blowing of kisses, they bowled out of the drive and set off for London. It should have been an uneventful journey. There had been a low-lying mist producing a distinct chill in the air as they left, but it was confidently expected to burn off. Instead, as they trotted along the country lanes on a shortcut that Peter was sure of, the mist thickened to fog until every landmark disappeared in the murk. The horses dropped to a walk and then to a crawl. Several times they stopped altogether, as Peter and the coachman debated their route. Jessica was not surprised when several hours later, a very damp and disheveled Lord Steal joined the females in the carriage, and announced that they were lost.

"I'm afraid we're not going to reach London today," said Peter with the most woebegone expression.

"Then let us find a suitable inn as soon as we reach the next place and put up for the night."

"This is just the kind of ramshackle tangle in which a

gentleman should never land a lady," wailed Peter. "You must think me a perfect nincompoop."

"Why? Because we have been caught in bad weather?"

"Deyncourt would never have let it happen!"

Jessica laughed aloud. "Of course not. The earl can order the rain, sun, and snow to his liking! Pray do not distress yourself, my lord. It's of no consequence at all if we arrive today or tomorrow."

She was not sure if that was entirely the case, however, when they pulled into the yard of the Blue Boar. It was not quite the standard of place to which Cicely, at least, was accustomed. To make matters worse, a band of soldiers was encamped there for the night. Nevertheless, the landlord was able to provide them with his best rooms, and they ate a filling, if not elegant, meal in a private parlor. Jessica eventually sank gratefully into a chair in the bedroom that was provided. She was surprised to find herself quite exhausted. Her weeks as an invalid must have robbed her of much of her usual energy. Cicely had been given a room on the floor above, and after laying out her temporary mistress's few things, she bobbed a curtsy and disappeared. Peter had pressed Jessica's hand as he said good night, and disconsolately gone off to his room just down the hall.

Peter was thoroughly miserable. He had done his darnedest to overcome his feelings, but to no avail. To be suffering from unrequited love was bad enough, though very romantic, but when a fellow was engaged to someone other than the object of his affections, it was the end of anything! And then to land in such a place as the Blue Boar when his only desire had been to impress the lady. The worst of it was, of course, that she had no fortune, and he was rather enamored of his expensive London lifestyle. Still, it was a situation that rather gratified his fancy, and he felt suitably sorry for himself as he pulled the brandy bottle from his case.

Jessica was startled a few moments later by a knock at her door. She opened it to find the chambermaid. "I'm sorry, miss, to disturb you so late, but there was no time earlier for me to make up the fire, and landlord'll have my hide if it's not done ready for morning.''

"Of course, go ahead." Jessica stepped aside to allow the girl into the room, and decided to walk down the hallway and look out into the yard to see if the fog had begun to lift. As she did so an officer came running up the stairs and they nearly collided. His hands caught her by the arms to steady her.

"My sincerest apologies, ma'am. I trust you are not hurt?" he began.

At that moment, the door to Lord Steal's room was flung open and they both looked around into the barrel of a pistol held in the uncertain grip of that young gentleman. He was obviously foxed. Waving the pistol in a grand gesture, he staggered toward them.

"Unhand the lady, sir, or answer for the consequences!" The last word tangled itself up into a flurry of sibilants.

The officer looked from one to the other. He was fully prepared to have the young lady faint in his arms at such a shocking situation, yet she seemed quite composed. "Is this gentleman of your acquaintance, ma'am?" he queried softly.

"Oh, yes, he's my cousin," Jessica lied quickly. "You had better go! I do apologize for his behavior, but I'll be quite all right." With a surprised look at the young lady and one more glance at the wavering pistol, the officer bowed and quickly left them. Jessica had no intention of having ladylike vapors. Instead, she hurried over to her would-be rescuer. "Lord Steal, you are quite overset! I am gallantly rescued! Please, come to your room." She took him by the arm and steered him back through his open doorway. As they entered, he mumbled something about protecting her from all comers. Then he turned the key in the door behind them, before thrusting it into his jacket pocket.

"Mush keep you safe!" he insisted.

"Lord Steal, please give me the key!"

"Better have a drink first." Peter dropped into an arm-chair beside the fire. "Ought to have a drink after such a shocking experience!" It was his last conscious thought before his head dropped to his chest and he emitted a thunderous snore. Beside him lay the evidence that he had finished the best part of a bottle of brandy. Jessica tried to reach into his pocket and extract the key, but his entire weight was upon it and she couldn't move him. She picked up the pistol and found it wasn't even loaded. She shook the recumbent form firmly by the shoulders.

"Lord Steal, wake up!"

Her efforts were greeted with another shattering snore. From the looks of him, he wouldn't wake until morning. She glanced around the room. The bed lay empty and inviting. Well, why not? If there was no escape from Peter's room until he awoke or stopped sitting on the key, she might at least make herself comfortable. Without further ado she lay down on the feather mattress and pulled the quilt over her shoulders. She would get up in a little while and see whether her hapless captor had shifted his position. Instantly she fell into a dreamless sleep.

Jessica awoke with a start. Someone was cursing. "What in the blazes! Oh my head!" Weak early morning sunlight streamed into the chamber and across Peter's yellow hair. He sat up in the chair and clutched at his head with his hands, groaning loudly.

"Have you the headache, my lord?" Jessica inquired mischievously.

Peter turned carefully. "Good God! What are you doing here? Devil take it! I remember. I must have been three sheets to the wind!"

"Indeed you were. You threatened a perfectly innocent officer with your pistol, then proceeded to lock me into this room with you while you snored like a steam engine and sat very thoroughly on the key.''

"Oh, Lord! This is an unmitigated disaster!''

"I can't see why. You didn't actually kill anyone. The gun wasn't loaded.''

"Don't you see? You have spent the night in my room. I shall have to marry you after all! Oh, God. There'll be the devil to pay when Deyncourt finds out about this! We'll be complete paupers, I'm afraid.'' The prospect of actually having to make a match with the penniless object of his infatuation was suddenly a great deal less attractive than it had been as a fantasy.

"Oh, fustian! Who's to know? If nobody knows, then how can my reputation be affected? Now, if you will just let me have the key, I shall creep away and no one will be any the wiser.''

Peter reached into his pocket and handed it to her. "Are you sure?'' He groaned and clutched at his head again. "I have the most beastly headache.''

"And well deserved.''

"My heart will break!''

"No, it won't. You will discover that I am nothing like you imagine me and that Miss Brandon will suit you admirably. Now, put your head in a basin of cold water and you will feel a great deal better.''

He rose gingerly to his feet and followed her to the door. As she stepped into the corridor, he suddenly pulled her to him and clumsily kissed her. "I won't tell anyone and I shall do my damnedest to treat you like a friend, but a fellow was never in a worse predicament!'' Pushing her away, he flung himself back into his room.

As Jessica slipped down the corridor she was entirely unaware of the sharp eyes of Cicely Pratchett, watching from the shadows at the end of the hall. An hour later, accompanied by the maid, Jessica climbed into the chaise to resume her journey to London. A white-faced Lord Steal sat glumly opposite them. Cicely's knowing little smirk fell on blind eyes. She had gone into Jessica's chamber just to make sure. The knowledge made her positively smug and might be worth quite a bit in the right quarters. Not only had she witnessed Miss Whinburn and Lord Steal kissing in the corridor, but the young lady's bed had gone unslept in last night.

Chapter 8

The sights and sounds of London broke over them with a crash. Hawkers and traders of all descriptions were crying their wares to the passersby—milk, muffins, strawberries, ribbons. The crush of carriages and carts was overwhelming. Dirty children scuttled away from the moving wheels, then crowded around at each stop, hoping to earn a farthing for holding the horses or sweeping a walkway. Everywhere was noise and bustle, cries and laughter, dirt and splendor. The sunlight was orange in the haze of smoke from all the morning cooking fires. Somewhere church bells were ringing, and the clatter of pattens and rumble of iron-shod wheels formed a deafening background to the raucous gabble of human voices. Jessica hung her head from the carriage window and drank it all in like wine. She imagined for a moment how she might have felt had she arrived in these streets alone in her donkey cart, and reluctantly recognized that she was glad she was safely riding in a carriage.

Then the bustle was left behind as they turned into the modern, fashionable part of town, laid out in gracious squares and crescents. It was still early, there was almost a hush in the elegant streets. The fresh white stone of the buildings had not stood long enough to gather a grimy coating of soot, and the houses sparkled at each other across the charming formal gardens in the center of each square. Lady Emilia's imposing residence stood in a quiet crescent not far from Hyde Park. Wrought iron railings separated the classic façade from the pavement. How would her great-aunt greet her? As the chaise pulled up in front of the portico, a bewigged servant flung open the door. Peter escorted Jessica up the steps. The butler relieved her of her dowdy cloak and, as his eyes swept over her windblown hair, he gave a disapproving little sniff.

"Lady Emilia is in the drawing room, madam; if you would care to step this way?"

Jessica followed him up the stairs to where a tiny old lady sat rigidly beside the hearth, like an extra poker.

"Come in, come in, my child. Don't stand dawdling like a schoolgirl. Let me take a look at you. Good heavens, I see I shall have my work cut out! Some tea, Jenkins." Lady Emilia turned to Peter. "I thought Lady Mary was to accompany you? I suppose she is just being hen-witted as usual. Never mind. What's the matter with you? You look positively haggard. Are you quite the thing? I must offer you my felicitations on your engagement to Miss Brandon and my thanks for bringing me my great-niece. Stand aside so that I can see her." She gestured to Jessica to sit beside her and subjected her to a searching scrutiny. "You have quite the look of your mother about you, my dear. Although you don't have her coloring."

"No, my lady, it is quite my own," said Jessica promptly.

Lady Emilia laughed. "Carry it off with style, that's always my motto. I declare, Steal, she'll be a *nonpareil* if I outfit her in some decent clothes."

"If you'll forgive me, Lady Emilia, I must go and see Deyncourt right away."

"So that your guardian can set you up to cut a figure about town, no doubt."

Peter rose to go and mumbled his goodbyes.

"Now!" said Lady Emilia once she was alone with Jessica. "We're family, my dear. Your mother was my favorite niece. You must call me Aunt Emilia, none of this my lady stuff, and I shall call you Jessica. I am very sorry about your father, my dear; he was a stubborn man, and we didn't get along, I shan't pretend that we did. He had positively ramshackle ideas about everything and was a careless scoundrel to leave Whinburn so encumbered, but it's a hard thing to be left alone in the world. However, we'll soon put all that to rights. You can make your home here with me for as long as I live."

Jessica watched her aunt's animated way of talking— the old lady's head tipped to one side like a bird's—as memories flooded back of that one visit all those years before. "You are most kind, Aunt Emilia," she said sincerely.

"Nonsense. You are my own flesh and blood. Now, I intend to show you to your chamber myself. Come along."

Jessica followed her up the stairs and along a carpeted hall. Her bedchamber was at the front of the house, overlooking the quiet gardens in the crescent beneath. The tall windows were swathed in ivory satin curtains. It was a truly lovely room. As they entered, Cicely had just finished unpacking Jessica's few dresses and was hanging them in the copious wardrobe.

"My dear child! Is that all your luggage? And so out of style! We shall get you a new wardrobe immediately. And is this your maid from Whinburn House?"

"No, Aunt, this is Cicely Pratchett. Lady Honoria Melton was kind enough to lend me her services at Tresham. She will be anxious to return to Lady Honoria now, I'm sure."

Lady Emilia turned to the maid. "But you will stay on until I can find my niece a suitable replacement? Lady Honoria could have no objection." Cicely bobbed a correct curtsy and nodded. Her face was the mask of the perfect servant. "Well, freshen up, Jessica, and join me for luncheon, and you can explain all this. You and I are to become the best of friends. I can feel it in my old bones."

And with a sudden, surprising kiss to her cheek, Lady Emilia bustled from the room.

By the next morning Jessica had discovered how much pleasure her visit was bringing the old lady. To spurn Lady Emilia's generosity out of pride would be cruel, and there would be time enough yet to pursue her own living once the month she had promised Deyncourt was up. Besides, that glimpse of the overwhelming size of London had slightly shaken her confidence. Later, as they sat together in the withdrawing room, Aunt Emilia pored over fashion plates and fabric swatches and tossed those she liked to her great-niece. "I shall see that you look a credit to me. What do you think of this? In a sprigged muslin with russet ribbons—and this riding habit, in gray to match your eyes. White piping, I think, and a hat with a white plume. You would seem to need absolutely everything. The mantua-maker will be here this afternoon to take your measurements."

"To be honest, Aunt, I hardly know what I like. I have never given much thought to fashion."

Her great-aunt squinted at her over the top of a pair of pince-nez. "So I understand, young lady, nor to correct behavior. You would just as soon run wild like an urchin or travel the highways like a tinker. Nevertheless, I intend you to dazzle the beaux and make a good match. But you will have to learn the rules of propriety or you will get nowhere."

"But I do not wish to marry," said Jessica.

Lady Emilia gave her a shrewd glance. "Because you have a head full of wild notions placed there by your father? Stuff!"

"No, no, I cannot marry, truly, Aunt!"

"Good heavens, child! No one will force you! But there's no harm in having a little fun in society! And if you think you will make *faux pas,* all the more reason to cut a dash.''

Jessica was prevented from making a reply by the footman, who entered the room and announced a visitor. "The Earl of Deyncourt, my lady."

"Show him up. Show him up. I don't stand on ceremony with Michael Grey. He shall give us his opinion. I know of no one with such impeccable taste."

Thus Jessica was destined to next see Deyncourt in a room strewn with frippery, pattern plates, and a patchwork of muslin, satin, and silk. It was intensely humiliating. Particularly when that gentleman's keen blue eyes seemed to take in her situation at a glance and revel in her discomfort. She bridled immediately.

"I am having a wardrobe made up for her, Deyncourt," announced the old lady. "We shall be in your debt if you will give us your opinion."

"That is, I do not wish to impose upon your valuable time, my lord, with my private affairs," announced Jessica. "No doubt you have important business in town?"

"Not at all, Miss Whinburn. It is my pleasure if I may be of service. Besides, if Lady Emilia beckons, humbler mortals must obey."

The old lady laughed and Jessica's objections were overridden. She burned with chagrin as her aunt discussed hats and fabrics under the apparently careless scrutiny of Deyncourt. Jessica became aware immediately that the wardrobe that would result would almost entirely reflect his judgment, even though Lady Emilia was left with the impression that each choice was her own idea. How could he be so shameless?

Michael stayed to take tea and greatly amused the old lady with an account of the latest events to scandalize the city. A new exhibit of art was doing much to raise eyebrows.

"You are unusually quiet, Miss Whinburn," he said to her suddenly. "Do you have no opinion?"

"Indeed, I know nothing of art, my lord," she replied stiffly.

"Then I must attempt to remedy such a deplorable state of affairs. Might I prevail upon you to accompany me to the gallery later this week?"

The rejection that sprang to her lips was cut off as Lady Emilia interrupted and accepted for her. It was instantly settled that he should collect her one morning and take her to the exhibit. The minute he left, Jessica turned to her great-aunt. "Aunt Emilia, I must beg of you not to accept invitations for me. I am three-and-twenty: no longer a child! It is very distasteful to me to be forced to go out with this gentleman."

"Stuff and nonsense! No one else of my acquaintance has so much consequence. He is a charming and cultivated man, as well as a bit of a rogue, but I would trust you with him as I trust myself."

Trust him! He had begun their acquaintance by offering to make her his mistress. It was insufferable! Nevertheless, a week later, dressed in a devastating new outfit of dark blue jaconet with matching bonnet, Jessica accompanied Michael through the fashionable streets.

"It is very kind of you to escort me, my lord," she began. "I hope, however, that in future you will not allow my great-aunt to persuade you to do anything contrary to your own wishes."

His eyebrow lifted a little. "If you think that I do anything against my own inclination, you do not know me very well, Miss Whinburn, in spite of our enforced intimacy at Tresham."

"An intimacy that was not of my choosing!" she shot back.

"No, and then you were sadly excluded from activities. The trip to Holy Cross was most edifying, for example. You had horses at Whinburn, I believe you said. Perhaps we could ride together some time?"

"I don't have a mount."

"You will, never fear. Lady Emilia has asked me to pick out an animal for you."

"She has not! If she is to provide me with a horse, I would rather select it for myself."

"No doubt. But ladies do not attend Tattersalls, and you have no acquaintance from whom to make a private purchase. However, if you prefer it I will leave you to ride a hired hack when you make your entrée in Hyde Park."

"Why must ladies' choices be restricted to either the trivial or unfair? I probably know more about horseflesh than half the gentlemen in London!"

"Do you indeed?"

"Papa often traded horses—" She stopped. "Even when I select my wardrobe, others' opinions must be consulted."

"Are you unhappy with the result? You look beautiful."

She laughed. "Your professional opinion as a rake? I really don't care about my appearance, except that it pleases my aunt to dress me. But you might concede that you would have felt humiliated had you been served so."

"I?" He appeared stunned for a moment. *"Touché,* Miss Whinburn. I shall never advise you on your wardrobe again. But I pray that you will allow me to select you a horse. You shall have complete veto power."

She was forced to agree. They walked on together toward the exhibition of paintings, and straight into Peter with Miss Brandon on his arm.

"I'm so glad to see you again," said Caroline warmly, as the two gentlemen dropped behind and followed the ladies up the street. "It will be such fun to have a friend in London." Glancing back at the men, Jessica was horrified to find that Peter was gazing at her like a puppy with the megrims, and that Deyncourt was lazily watching them both. Her brow contracted in thought, Jessica was hardly aware of Caroline's friendly chatter.

* * *

Michael returned to his town house with a similar expression. He was not surprised that his ward was head over heels in love with Lady Emilia's great-niece. She might be unconventional, but there was definitely something very appealing about her. But how dared she encourage him! Steal had come straight to Deyncourt House on his arrival in London, ostensibly to report to his guardian about estate business, and Michael had noticed immediately the stricken look on his young features.

"I trust Miss Whinburn is safely delivered to her great-aunt, Steal?" he had asked casually. "Are you of the same opinion of her good qualities? You were becoming rather enamored, if I remember rightly."

Peter blushed scarlet. "Well, if you must know, I'm dashed well in love with her! If you didn't have control of my affairs, I'd marry her and to heck with Tresham!"

"Do you believe Miss Whinburn returns your affections?"

"Of course she does. But she has the most delicate sensibility, and is too much the lady to express her feelings where is it not proper."

"I see you have it bad," said Michael. He looked out of the window, idly stroking the feathering of the quill on his desk with one hand. She had threatened to interfere in the engagement. Was this her chosen method? Could Jessica Whinburn really be so perfidious? He dismissed his vague feeling of pain at the thought. "You would no doubt live blissfully in a cottage and subsist on potatoes and green peas. How fortunate that I am your guardian and you may not marry without my permission. Though you may not believe it, I do not wish to see you unhappy. I shall not allow you to cry off from Caroline Brandon; only marriage to an heiress can correct your situation. Unless you really wish to give up your sumptuous wardrobe and the undoubted pleasures of town life?"

"It's monstrous!" shouted Peter.

The earl looked back at him. "Yes, it is rather, isn't it?

However, I ask you to uphold the honor of your name and not do anything foolish. Miss Brandon is to know nothing of this. I will not see her hurt by your thoughtlessness. Do I make myself clear?''

Peter's face was splendidly miserable. "I knew you would never understand," he muttered.

"On the contrary, I understand perfectly," said the earl.

Michael could not ignore it. Peter was his responsibility, and he must make sure that his ward lost interest in Jessica Whinburn. *You are the most accomplished rake in London! Surely you could exert a little innocent charm?* Michael smiled a little grimly. He had been trying so hard to disengage himself! But he didn't hesitate to present himself at Lady Emilia's and thus he had found his old friend setting up her great-niece with a wardrobe.

When they finally arrived at the gallery, Jessica seemed to lose herself as she gazed at the paintings. Michael realized with some irony that she was barely aware of him. With no self-consciousness at all, she gave her rapt and unfashionably sincere praise or criticism on each piece. He found himself joining in.

"You realize," he said after a moment, "that the expression of such genuine emotion is frowned upon in society?"

Jessica turned to him. "Oh, yes. Rakes don't have any real emotions, do they? Thank you for correcting me. I'm sorry if I indicated any enthusiasm."

It touched him as surely as if she had reached out her hand. No wonder she had Steal wrapped around her little finger! Yet if she was to be a success among the *beau monde,* she would have a great deal to learn to avoid raising eyebrows. And Lady Emilia expected that the controlled, sophisticated Lord Deyncourt could harmlessly be Jessica's teacher? Dear God, must he prove himself, again and again, forever—when he was secretly terrified that he could not trust himself? Yet because of Miss Caroline Brandon, he could not bow out. Michael did not notice, as he deliberated his course of action, that at no time had he given any thought at all to the Incomparable Melton.

Lady Honoria was not pleased that Lord Deyncourt seemed to be suddenly enamored of the red-haired chit. Why should his indifference at Tresham have suddenly turned to escorting her about? Two weeks later Honoria unburdened herself on her cousin, as he lounged opposite her in her pink drawing room.

"What does Deyncourt see in Miss Whinburn, Cranby? They are seen everywhere together."

"Nothing but a vague annoyance, I should imagine, that takes his mind off what should be his real pursuits."

"Which are?"

"His plans against me."

The Incomparable was beautiful even when she frowned. "Why on earth should he have plans against you? You do say the most absurd things!"

"If he knew where Lord Steal stood with me right now, I assure you he would have plans."

"Yes, but he does not. As I trust he does not know how you stand with me! It could ruin every chance I have of becoming a countess."

"Deyncourt doesn't even know there's anything to look for."

"Good. Because I'm a lot more concerned about this Jessica Whinburn, and you would be better off finalizing your scheme against Lord Steal."

Sir Gordon raised his quizzing glass and stared at her until she blushed. "Am I to have nothing to amuse me until I am master of Tresham?"

"I hope to be more amused when Cicely Pratchett comes back and reports to me."

"Pratchett?"

"Oh, really, Cranby! For a conspirator you are too blind!

My maid! I left her to spy on Jessica Whinburn for me, and she's returning here from Lady Emilia's later this week."

Sir Gordon Cranby yawned deliberately. "And what do you expect to learn from a lady's maid? That Miss Whinburn paints her eyebrows?"

Honoria shrugged her lovely shoulders. "I have no idea!" she said.

Chapter 9

Michael was shown in by the footman while Jessica sat alone in the parlor. The sunlight from the windows caught the golden highlights in his hair and shadowed the clean line of his jaw above his startlingly white cravat. He made her his elegant bow.

"It's a lovely day, Miss Whinburn," he said. "May I prevail upon you to take a turn in the Park?"

"I can't go," replied Jessica. She had stood up at his entrance and now she began to pace the room.

Michael walked over to the fireplace, but he did not take a chair. Instead he stood and watched her. "May I ask why not?" he asked casually.

"If only you had not forced me into that promise at Tresham! I shall never be able to do it."

"Do what?"

"Behave correctly!" She dropped into a chair and looked up at him. Her eyes seemed too bright. "You see I am choosing to be entirely honest with you, my lord, which I'm sure in itself is improper. But right now I don't care. The *beau monde* is a world that I would rather not be a part of."

Her distress seemed genuine. "What has happened?" he asked gently. "Someone has been actively cruel? Am I to assume that the dowagers have paid their morning calls?"

"How did you guess? Lady Vain and the Dowager Countess of Hawksley came here while Aunt Emilia was out."

"I see," said the earl gravely. "And you neglected to invite them to sit?"

She glanced back up at him. He didn't seem uncomfortable standing by the fireplace. The stance only accentuated his lithe grace. Then suddenly she burst out laughing. "Oh, heavens! Pray, take a seat, Lord Deyncourt!"

"Thank you," said the earl with a smile. He dropped to the chair opposite hers.

"You see, I cannot learn," she said simply.

"Yes, you can."

"I offered greetings to the ladies in the wrong order of precedence. I fumbled the tea things and dropped a spoon on the carpet."

"Which anyone can do."

"Yes, but I picked it up myself."

"Oh, I see. Thus depriving the maid of her duties."

Jessica stood up and began to pace back and forth once again. "Finally Lady Hawksley said I was charmingly unusual. She said it in French."

Michael casually resumed his stance at the mantel. "So she would."

"I don't speak French. Lady Vain translated. It was an insult!"

"I'm not surprised. Especially if you walked up and down the carpet like that."

Jessica stopped and turned to him. "Like what?"

"Like a soldier on parade! Ladies are supposed to mince. You must take the tiniest of steps, as if your ankles were hobbled together."

"But I shouldn't get anywhere walking like that."

"Alas, ladies aren't supposed to have anywhere to go." He came up to her and took her hand.

Jessica could feel her pulse beating beneath the cool touch of his fingers. She looked defiantly into his blue eyes. "I'll never be a lady. That was certainly your opinion at Tresham."

"Because I kissed you? Ladies get kissed all the time."

He raised her hand to kiss her fingers. His lips felt sensuously soft and warm against her skin.

"As part of a meaningless, exploitative game!" Jessica said. He must not! For she wanted it far too much.

Michael bent and touched his lips briefly to her temple. His breath warmed her cheek. "Don't you know that rakes have the simplest of rules? Flirtation is always harmless, but there are ladies for the night and ladies for the day. The great-niece of Lady Emilia Shay is by definition in the second category. I am trying very hard to prevent you mistakenly giving the wrong impression. Let us go for a sedate drive in the Park, shall we?"

"Don't," said Jessica. She felt stripped of her defenses. "This is all part of a scheme to make me a success in society and find me a husband, isn't it, my lord? But I don't need or want your help. I'll stay here for a month as I promised, but then I shall follow my own inclination."

"Is there no room in your plans for love, Miss Whinburn? The world would be a sorry place without the lovely dance of dalliance."

"But a more honest one."

"As Virgil said: *Quis fallere possit amantem?*"

Who can deceive a lover? "But flirtation is the very definition of deceit, my lord. I shall avoid scandal for the sake of my great-aunt, and thus I shall not drive in the Park with a rake."

There was no change in his expression as he made his exquisite bow and left the room.

But when Caroline came to call later that week, Jessica did not refuse her. They walked briskly into the Park. It was a bright blustery day. Everyone seemed to be out enjoying the sunshine. The walks were a display of fashion, and horses and carriages paraded up and down the broad rides. Soon the ladies reached the shallow waters of the Serpentine, where they lingered on the bridge and watched some children sailing toy boats off the far bank, while some older boys ran back and forth with a kite.

"I can almost reconcile myself to my fate on a day like this," said Jessica.

"Your fate?"

"Oh, my aunt and Lord Deyncourt conspire to find me an eligible match. I am to be taken to Almack's and paraded at routs and assemblies. Only the best places, of course! What on earth?" Jessica grabbed at her friend's arm and pointed.

Caroline looked for a moment, then she gasped. "Oh, it's a puppy! How horrid!"

A group of boys had just run off, laughing and joking, from the far bank of the lake. Floating rapidly toward the girls was a black and white puppy. He must have been tossed into the water and he was swimming valiantly. All his efforts to regain the bank were being frustrated, however, by the kite that had been tied to his tail. The breeze had caught the paper diamond, and was tossing it through the air above the water, dragging the struggling puppy in its wake.

"For heaven's sake!" snapped Jessica, rapidly taking off her bonnet and handing it to Caroline. "If the wind drops, that kite will hit the lake and become waterlogged."

"But then the puppy will drown!" exclaimed Miss Brandon.

"Not if I can help it! Here, hold these!" Jessica bent and unbuttoned her black shoes. Her shawl was next pressed into her friend's hand.

"Miss Whinburn! Whatever are you doing?"

Jessica grinned at her as she climbed up onto the parapet. "Don't worry, Caroline. I can swim like a boy."

"You must not! Oh, heavens! What of your reputation?"

But Jessica had already dropped into the water.

Within a few moments a curious crowd had gathered on the bridge. Caroline ran past them, carrying Jessica's shoes and shawl, and made for the edge of the lake nearest her swimming friend. She felt like laughing and crying at once. How could Miss Whinburn be so lost to all that was proper? Yet it would be splendid to rescue the puppy! She pulled up short as she ran straight into the firm chest of a gentleman. He caught her by the arms and steadied her. It was Lord Deyncourt.

"Miss Brandon? Has something happened?" He smiled kindly into her flushed face.

"Oh, Lord Deyncourt! It's Jessica!"

"It usually is," he replied with a wry smile. "What has she done now?"

"She's in the lake. Rescuing a puppy. London will be scandalized!"

Taking her arm, Michael allowed Caroline to lead him to the scene. He took in the situation at a glance. A crowd had begun to gossip and speculate, but Jessica seemed to be swimming very competently toward the little dog. Instantly, the earl kicked off his boots and shrugged out of his coat. Devil take it! Couldn't she see that this would be ruinous?

"Quickly, Miss Brandon! Set up a cry that she has accidentally fallen in." Without more ado, he dived elegantly into the water.

Just as Jessica had predicted, the wind took a sudden turn. The kite lurched wildly before hitting the surface and instantly beginning to sink. She reached out for the struggling puppy, and grabbed at it just as the black and white coat began to be dragged out of sight. At the same moment, she was caught from behind. "Pray, Miss Whinburn," said Michael. "Allow me to rescue you."

Jessica was treading water, clutching the puppy to her breast. "Whatever are you talking about?" she asked indignantly. "I am the rescuer!"

"I am talking about your reputation." He laughed, stroking the wet hair off her cheeks with both hands. "Look at the bridge!"

Jessica glanced up where he indicated. A gaggle of London's most fashionable gossips hung over the edge of the parapet. There was a great deal of gesticulating and pointing.

"Oh, Lord," she said ruefully. "I suppose this will set the cat among the pigeons!"

"Not if you will admit to having taken a fainting fit and fallen in. Please start drowning, so that I can complete my gallant rescue. Not for your own sake, but for that of your great-aunt, who loves you."

She allowed herself to drop below the surface for a moment, before spluttering up again. "Like this?" Jessica laughed. She had still held the puppy's head above water.

"That's an excellent start, though I've a good mind to hold you under until you beg for mercy."

"Pray don't, Lord Deyncourt! Though I held my breath under water once for several minutes in an attempt to break the stable boys' record at Whinburn House."

"And did you?"

"Not a chance!"

"Well, to nearly drown is your only hope now. It will turn you from a subject for scandal into an object of concern."

"Damn it all!" she replied. "I suppose this is much worse than dropping the tea spoon, isn't it?"

She went completely limp and closed her eyes. Instantly she began to sink like a stone. For a moment Michael's heart turned over as he thought she had really fainted. He caught her firmly around the shoulders, and began a strong kick toward the shore.

The water smelt faintly of duck weed. It broke over her floating skirts and eddied around her face, but Jessica hardly noticed it. Instead, she was conscious of the sensations that were being elicited by the feeling of the earl's flexible frame moving beneath hers. She did not want to be aware of him! Her mood was broken instantly when he unceremoniously dragged her from the lake and dumped her onto the grass. Caroline was ready with the shawl and surreptitiously slipped Jessica's shoes back onto her feet, then she caught up the puppy and handed it to Dover, who stood impassively awaiting his master with coat and boots.

"Good thinking, Miss Brandon," said Michael with a wink.

Jessica sat up and did her best to cough and splutter. The crowd was streaming off the bridge toward them.

"Dover, a cabriolet, if you please!"

The first of the onlookers had arrived, and at their head was Lord Steal. "Deyncourt? What happened?" He looked from the tall frame of his guardian, who was wringing water from his indecently wet shirt and breeches, to that of Jessica sitting as limply as she was able on the grass.

"Miss Whinburn took a fall from the bridge and nearly drowned. If you will kindly keep back the crowd to allow the lady some air and some privacy?"

"Oh, goodness!" cried Peter with a besotted look at Jessica. "You are too delicate for words, Miss Whinburn! Oh, hello, Caroline."

Caroline ignored him and matter-of factly added her own shawl to Jessica's shoulders, where the first one was beginning to soak through. Jessica gave her friend a wink, and was relieved to see Caroline smile back at her. Within a few moments the cab for hire had pulled up, and Michael was helping Jessica into the seat next to the driver.

"Now, sir," he said firmly. "This lady and I are likely to catch our deaths if we do not get to shelter quickly. You will allow me?" He took the reins from the hands of the astonished cabby, who was left standing on the grass as Michael climbed into the seat, whipped up the horse, and headed in the direction of Lady Emilia's elegant house.

"Will you allow that I am learning the rules, my lord?" Jessica asked as they swept around a corner at an extremely precipitate speed.

"What? It was hardly the done thing to go for a swim in the Serpentine!"

"Yes, but I allowed you to say that I had fainted and fallen in. Think how absurd that makes me appear!"

"It merely makes you interesting, Miss Whinburn; whereas to go for a deliberate swim makes you *persona non grata.*"

She laughed. "Then I am indebted to you. For your elegance and perfection make everything you do acceptable, don't they?"

"I am not perfect," said Michael with sudden ferocity. "And not everything I do is acceptable. I am only trying to help your aunt find you a suitable match; if you disgrace yourself, she will never be able to do so."

"You are all consideration, my lord," replied Jessica. "But I do not desire a match! What will you do with the puppy?"

"Probably ask Dover to wring its neck!"

"You will not!" She knew from his tone that he wasn't serious. "That would be a waste of both our gallant efforts, wouldn't it? Besides, it's a Border collie and would make an excellent sheep dog. Do you have sheep?"

"Of course."

"Then have your shepherd take it."

"I would have thought, Miss Whinburn, that after risking your reputation over the mutt, you would have demanded it as a pet."

"Should I wallow in sentimentality to match your demands of the behavior suitable to a lady? A Border collie would hardly make a lap dog. It's a country creature and wants a life of honest work. I couldn't bear to think of such an animal cooped up in town, where everything in life is ordered by absurd rules."

He grinned at her. "As you are?"

"You think I belong with the dog? Of course, when my month is up I shall pursue honest work. But I'm hopeless at herding sheep!"

He swallowed his laughter. He must stop her doing this! "Where will you live, Miss Whinburn?"

She glanced up at him. His hair, already drying in the breeze, whipped about above his soggy cravat. Duckweed had stained his shirt and jacket. He looked splendid. "I shall rent a room."

"Do you have any idea what a respectable room costs in London? How will you pay the deposit and live until your first wages are paid?"

"These are my problems, aren't they?" asked Jessica.

They entered Aunt Emilia's house under the astonished eyes of the butler, and Jessica swept away up the stairs to her room, leaving Michael to make explanations to her aunt. He offered Lady Emilia no gallantry at all before he took his leave. The old lady was extremely disappointed. How could she bring about her own little matchmaking scheme, if Jessica and the earl must quarrel all the time?

Jessica had known it for some time. If she was to win independence, she must have funds. The pin money which Lady Emilia gave her was nowhere near enough to rent her own establishment, not even a single room. If she had arrived alone in London in her donkey cart, God knows what she would have done. That Deyncourt was right, of course, made the problem all the more infuriating.

The answer when it came was so splendidly simple and so audacious that Jessica had no hesitation in pursuing it. There was to be a private party where the gaming would be very deep. The guests would be masked and in costume. The location was only one street away from Aunt Emilia's house, and the stables of the two houses fronted each other across a narrow alley. Jessica learned all this from the upstairs maid, who was courting the footman from the house in question. For the maid it was only idle gossip. For Jessica it seemed a heaven-sent opportunity. Cards were one of her only skills. She would win the money she needed.

The attics of Lady Emilia's town house proved to be a treasure trove. Jessica's great-aunt seemed never to have thrown anything away. Jessica found not only a costume and mask, but also a splendid, white-powdered wig. She would appear in the court dress of the previous century, with a large hooped skirt and boned bodice. When she dressed herself on the night of the gaming party, Jessica knew that no one could possibly recognize her. Her red hair was entirely hidden by the wig, her features by the mask. The dress was a little too revealing, but never mind. She was about to secure her future.

Thanks to the upstairs maid's influence with her sweetheart, Jessica's entrance to the house was not questioned. She took a seat at a table in the candlelit upstairs chamber without anyone giving her a second glance. The guests had no interest in each other, only in the cards and the dice. Jessica knew that her first game was critical. She must win right away, for all she had to begin with was the small stake of pin money she had saved. She need not have worried. It took nerve, concentration, and a certain amount of luck, but an hour later she had won two hundred pounds. If she could double it, she would leave.

As the cards were being shuffled again, Jessica quietly surveyed the room. Oh, dear Lord! That man leaning over the lady in the blue domino two tables away was surely Cranby? The lady bent her head as he whispered something in her ear. Her lovely mouth twisted into a grimace beneath her mask, but she shrugged, said something to her gaming companions, and stood up. As she hurried from the room with Cranby, the candlelight glittered on her blond hair. Jessica knew with certainty that the woman in the blue domino was Lady Honoria Melton.

In the next moment, Jessica realized why they had left so precipitately, for the door to the room opened again, and a gentleman and lady stepped inside. The lady was very lovely. She was dressed as Cleopatra. Her heavily ringed hand was laid possessively on her companion's sleeve, and she was blushing a little beneath her mask as he leaned down to whisper to her. The couple seemed amused, flirtatious, and intimate. The gentleman was Michael Dechardon Grey, Earl of Deyncourt.

"Why, what a splendid Cleopatra our former Lady Nest makes," said someone at Jessica's table. "But having married Caesar, she is still bedding Mark Anthony?"

Another player looked up and laughed. "She is still enamored, of course, in spite of her recent nuptials. And Deyncourt, damn his eyes, may bed where he will."

"But her new husband has a notorious temper," responded someone else. "Caesar's wife has shed her lovers with her previous name and her widowed state. I have it on the best authority: Mark Anthony has given her up."

"Then someone ought to tell that to the lady," replied the first speaker.

"And to Deyncourt," said the second, and there was general laughter.

Jessica's concentration was shattered. She lost one hundred pounds in the next five minutes.

Michael had seen her immediately. The wig and the mask should have made her impossible to recognize, but he knew the very turn of her shoulder and each of the drift of freckles that dappled her cheek. He left his old lover with a shared joke, and stalked across to Jessica's table. She glared haughtily up at him through the mask. Dear God, she might be foolhardy and obstinate, but she was brave! Michael pulled out a chair and entered the game. He began to steadily rob the table of their winnings.

Jessica sat opposite him and watched him do it in an impotent fury. He couldn't possibly know who she was, and they were very evenly matched. If he ever seemed to make a mistake, it was only in her favor. Thus she couldn't combat his strategy without putting herself out of the game and losing what she had won. One by one the other players bowed out and left.

"Well, madam," he said, giving her an intimate smile. "You play very high."

"Is there any point in gaming unless something is at stake, sir?" she replied.

He fanned the cards between his hands. "Indeed, the room is filled with the ecstasy of uncertainty: whether the erotic elation of winning a fortune or the unutterable despair of complete loss. The *beau monde* is prepared to risk all for that moment of pure and unsullied emotion. Which do you prefer?"

"To win, of course," said Jessica, blind with anger.

"Then you desire erotic elation? I will wager you my entire purse against an hour of your time."

He poured a small pile of gold coin onto the table. It was worth at least a year's wages to any clerk at Bromley and Finch.

"You wager me the naked power of your wealth against my virtue, sir?" asked Jessica.

The blue eyes looked straight into hers. "Do you possess virtue, madam? Perhaps I offer you a wager where you are a winner either way. You may gain a fortune in gold, or an hour of my time. For if I triumph, of course, you win me."

"But you won't win, sir. I shall." It was absurd. Only chance would determine the outcome of one more hand. But Jessica's anger drowned out any other voices. She pushed all her winnings out onto the table. "I stake all of it," she said, shaking.

"And so do I," replied Michael. "Now, let's play."

Jessica saw the cards dealt as if in a dream. Dear God! This was how her father finally had lost Whinburn—after wagering everything else he possessed! Piece by piece, over the years, everything had been risked. And she, out of some kind of dumb, blind, furious pride, was prepared to do the same? Deyncourt's elegant hands turned up the top card for trump. Jessica realized she had none of that suit. She traded in three cards in the draw and found three worse ones dealt in exchange. Finally she watched as he laid out his hand, with the aces and jacks, and knew she had lost.

"Come, madam," said Michael, taking her hand and seductively kissing the fingers. "Let us spend our hour together upstairs."

Chapter 10

Cranby hustled Honoria away from the gaming and into his carriage. Soon they were bowling back to her elegant town house.

"Good God!" he exclaimed and gave an unpleasant laugh. "That was a close one. Devil help us if Deyncourt finds you at a place like that!"

The Incomparable Melton pouted. "But I left several hundred guineas down, Cranby."

"Deyncourt will mend your purse after your wedding, my dear. But he will only marry you if he thinks you as pure as the driven snow. When the devil are you going to make him propose? It's damned tiresome that he seems to spend all his time these days with that red-haired chit."

Honoria laughed. "But I have discovered something which will banish her from town and leave her to scrub floors for a living. She is ruined, Cranby. Listen to this!"

Cranby leaned back in his seat and surveyed her through his quizzing glass as Honoria told the tale.

"How absolutely delicious," Sir Gordon said unpleasantly when she had finished. "Are you completely sure?"

"Cicely Pratchett saw them kissing in the corridor, and she spent the night in his room. What more do you want?"

"For you to keep this under your hat, my dear cousin."

"Cranby! You cannot mean it!"

He handed Honoria from the carriage and followed her up the stairs to her room. "Of course I mean it. I have spent the best part of the last six months getting Steal into my power. The young fool has also been gaming, my dear. He is heavily in debt to me and shall sink ever deeper. I intend to have him lose everything. Tresham has always rather appealed to me, but I shouldn't want to win it without some extra blunt. That problem evaporates when he marries Caroline Brandon. Her fortune also will fall into my hands. Now you tell me that Steal spent the night with Miss Jessica Whinburn at an inn called the Blue Boar. If this scandal gets out, Deyncourt will force Steal to marry Miss Whinburn instead of Miss Brandon; he will thus be penniless and my efforts in vain. I cannot allow that to happen."

Honoria pouted and flung her reticule across the room. "And what about me?"

"How can it affect you, dear Honoria? Surely our rufous Miss Whinburn is no rival for the Incomparable Melton? Besides, once Lord Steal is safely wed to Miss Brandon and all is mine, you may shout it from the rooftops for all I care!"

"Why should I care to help you?"

"Because if you don't, sweet Honoria," said Sir Gordon Cranby, pulling his cousin into his arms, "there are secrets of my own I might tell."

Michael took Jessica's elbow and hustled her from the room. A flight of stairs led to the bedrooms above, but instead he drew her down the corridor and into a small, disused study. He thrust her onto the couch that sat before the cold fireplace, stalked to the door, and turned the key in the lock. Then he came back and faced her.

"This is not a game, Jessica," he said coldly. "What the hell did you mean by coming here like this? And what the devil would you have done if you had lost such a wager to someone else?"

"You recognized me?" asked Jessica, stunned. And then to the complete astonishment of them both, she burst out laughing. "*Cantabit vacuus coram latrone viator,* Lord Deyncourt! In front of the highwayman the penniless sing! What did I have to lose? No one knew me, and I was in need of funds. If you hadn't interfered, as usual, I'd have been the richer by four hundred pounds. But quite obviously, I wouldn't have taken such a wager from anyone else; some other rake might have demanded I go through with it. Whereas with you I always have my aunt to protect me."

He sat down on a chaise longue opposite hers and leaned back, stretching his hands along the upholstered back in an extravagant gesture of exasperation. "Miss Whinburn, for God's sake! Are you determined on ruin? What if I had not recognized you, and had first taken you into a darkened room?"

"You would have forced me?" asked Jessica with sarcasm. "Since I'm dressed as Marie Antoinette, I thought it was my own head to lose. But this place is not ruin to Cleopatra? It was a source of great amusement at my table before you joined us to speculate whether she was still being faithful to Caesar."

His lids narrowed over the blue eyes. "*Aut Caesar, aut nullus.* To be honest I have no idea, and it's none of your business."

"And if Mark Anthony decides to risk all for her at a new Actium?"

"I shall know nothing about it. For God's sake, these aren't topics suitable for the ears of a young lady who is making her come out under the beneficence of Lady Emilia Shay. Cleopatra is married to her second husband. The rules which apply to you do not apply to her. Nor do they apply to me. Miss Whinburn, please will you let me take you home?"

"Oh, fiddlesticks," said Jessica. "The high and mighty Earl of Deyncourt speaks and mere mortals must obey. Like Io, couldn't I just be changed into a cow for once to escape the attentions of Jupiter?"

The mare arrived in Lady Emilia's stables the following morning: an elegant dappled gray, sensitive, gentle, perfect. Lord Deyncourt had picked out a mount for her. Jessica had not ridden such a horse since she had been forced to sell the stable at Whinburn. As soon as her aunt agreed it was the correct hour, Jessica, followed by a groom, took out the mare. She had barely reached the Park when her attention was caught by a curricle drawn by a small pony. The curricle was jammed with laughing young men, most of whom had obviously been drinking. It was far too heavy a load for the pony, which stood, flanks heaving, between the shafts.

"The wager's lost, Moore!" exclaimed one of the dandies. "This pony hasn't another step in him."

"By God, he has, sir!" cried the driver. "We'll make it to St. James's yet!" With that he began to flog the pony with his whip.

Horrified, Jessica impulsively spun her mare in front of the curricle. "Stop this instant! You will kill him!"

"What the devil do you mean, ma'am?" shouted the whipster. "You interfere in a private wager between gentlemen."

"No gentleman worthy of the name would treat an animal so," replied Jessica indignantly.

"Maybe she's right, Moore," said one of the passengers suddenly. "I concede the wager, and will stand the blunt for dinner tonight."

"Never say so, sir. It won't be a dinner earned unless this dratted beast makes it to the club."

Jessica instantly leapt down from her mare, and grasped the pony's bridle. "You shall not go a step further!"

"Get out of the way!" cried the driver and he raised his whip. At that instant his wrist was caught in the hooked end of a riding crop, and Moore was jerked from the curricle to sprawl on the pavement. Michael sat above them on his bay.

Moore struggled to his feet. "By the devil, sir! I'll call you out for this!"

"Shut up, Moore," hissed one of his friends immediately. "It's Deyncourt. No one could stand against him in a duel."

"No need for such desperate measures, gentlemen," said Michael, brushing an imaginary speck of dust from his sleeve. "I apologize freely, Mr. Moore, if I have accidentally dirtied your coat. Terribly careless of me—ham-fisted with my whip, I'm afraid. What do you say if I stand dinner for you and your companions tonight, as a gesture of my repentance? I rather like the pony, too. I'll give you a hundred guineas for him."

"He's got to get us to St. James's," persisted Moore doggedly. "It's a matter of honor."

"No honor, surely, sir," replied Michael with a cool smile, "if you displease a lady, and cause harm to a dumb beast? One hundred guineas and a dinner?"

The young man gave a drunken grin, and was hustled away by his cronies. Michael gave directions to the tiger to take care of the pony, and dismounted next to Jessica. "You are unhurt?" he asked.

"Why did you apologize to that brute? Surely you were not afraid to face him with a pistol?"

His face went rigid. "And if I was?" For a single unguarded moment, the blue eyes revealed only bleak dismay.

Jessica felt lost. "But he deserved a lesson," she insisted.

Suddenly he smiled and briefly touched her cheek, as if her fire could thaw the ice cold depths of his dread. Wisps of red hair had escaped from her hat and were straggling about her cheeks. Michael resisted the impulse to smooth them away, and dropped his hand. "Which you would no doubt have given him in your own inimitable style, Miss Whinburn? Our young bully has saved face for now before his friends, which prevented him from doing anything foolish. He may also boast in his club that he gulled the Earl of Deyncourt, connoisseur of horseflesh, into paying one hundred guineas for a five-pound pony. Meanwhile the beast is saved. When he is sober, Mr. Moore will receive a visit from me that will convince him to be more sensitive to his animals' welfare in future. There was no need for a duel. Are you satisfied?"

Jessica glanced down and bit her lip. He had been prepared to humble himself to save an animal? Or was he in truth afraid to fight? "Very well, you win, my lord."

Michael took her by the waist and tossed her onto her horse, before remounting his bay. "No, you do. How do you like the mare?"

He did not expect her open, genuine smile. "She's perfect. Thank you for choosing her, and for your assistance. Not for my sake, of course, since I assure you that I know very well how to handle the disasters of my life—but for the sake of the pony."

Michael knew he had shown her a glimpse of something that he always, always tried to keep hidden. He had seen the moment of confusion in her eyes. This was a brave courtesy that entirely disarmed him. "Then I trust you will know how to handle the company which is now approaching, Miss Whinburn?"

"My Lord Deyncourt!" It was Honoria. She was sitting in a little cream-colored cart, picked out in gold and drawn by matching cream ponies. Dressed entirely in blue, she made a dazzling contrast to the white leather cushions and the ponies' flaxen manes. Not a hair was out of place. She gave Jessica a coolly appraising glance. "Have you been galloping like a hoyden, Miss Whinburn? You look windblown."

"Oh, I am always windblown, even on a perfectly still

Say Yes to 4 Free Books!

COMPLETE AND RETURN THE ORDER CARD TO RECEIVE THIS $18.49 VALUE, ABSOLUTELY FREE!

(If the certificate is missing below, write to:
Zebra Home Subscription Service, Inc.,
120 Brighton Road, P.O. Box 5214, Clifton, New Jersey 07015-5214)

FREE BOOK CERTIFICATE

YES! Please rush me 4 Zebra Regency Romances without cost or obligation. I understand that each month thereafter I will be able to preview 4 brand-new Regency Romances FREE for 10 days. Then, if I should decide to keep them, I will pay the money-saving preferred subscriber's price of just $14.60 for all 4...that's a savings of almost $4 off the publisher's price with no additional charge for shipping and handling. I may return any shipment within 10 days and owe nothing, and I may cancel this subscription at any time. My 4 FREE books will be mine to keep in any case.

Name _____

Address _____ Apt. _____

City _____ State _____ Zip _____

Telephone ( ) _____

Signature _____
(If under 18, parent or guardian must sign.)

RF0996

Terms and prices subject to change. Orders subject to acceptance by Zebra Home Subscription Service, Inc.

day. It is just my careless habit. Surely you do not think that I would do anything out of the ordinary while in Lord Deyncourt's company?"

"And is Miss Whinburn to be introduced to your escort, Lady Honoria?" asked Michael innocently. "Sir Gordon Cranby is usually very jealous of your company, is he not? Yet today you favor another gentleman with a seat in your carriage."

A rotund figure sat stiffly beside Honoria. His beady eyes were fixed on Jessica's face, and he seemed to be steadily turning puce.

"Oh, this is Miss Jessica Whinburn, my lord," said Honoria to her companion. "She has recently traveled to town from Northumbria."

"I could swear I have seen you before, madam," snapped the newcomer. "How can that be possible, if you have just arrived in London?"

It was Judge Clarence.

Jessica noticed the earl unconsciously move his horse closer to hers. For God's sake, Deyncourt couldn't help himself, could he? "Oh, I believe I must have a very common face, Lord Clarence; several persons have remarked so since I arrived in London. Perhaps because I bear some resemblance to my great-aunt, Lady Emilia Shay."

"Lord Clarence has been telling me of a shocking misadventure with a highwayman," put in Honoria.

"Oh, how horrid!" exclaimed Jessica, as Michael coughed into his hand to hide his laughter.

"Indeed, Miss Whinburn. The roads will not be safe until every such brigand is caught and hanged."

"It was not a great hulking fellow with black hair, riding on a brown horse, was it, my lord?" added Jessica artlessly. "When I traveled down the Great North Road, there was nothing but talk of him at every inn. A most desperate and dangerous character, I heard."

"No indeed, ma'am. This man was dressed as a female. It was very shocking!"

"Alas," said Michael. "I had him in bonds at Tresham,

but his friends sprung him from confinement. However, Lord Clarence and I are satisfied that he died from his wounds. The most rigorous search turned up no sign of him."

"Lord Deyncourt put a bullet right through the fellow," added Judge Clarence with satisfaction.

"And as you know, my lady," said Michael, bowing to Honoria. "I could hardly have done other than give the rogue a fatal injury."

"But I hear that your coachman thought the assailant might truly be female, Lord Clarence," insisted Honoria.

Michael gave her an amused smile. "Good Lord! Do you think I wouldn't have noticed? I pulled off the creature's shirt myself. There was nothing in the least feminine or enticing about what was revealed."

"Well, thank goodness he is dead!"

"Indeed," Jessica said gaily. "I should not feel safe were you gentlemen to believe him still alive."

"Never fear, my dear," replied Lord Clarence. "He is in an unmarked grave."

"I trust you are entirely reassured, Miss Whinburn?" Michael asked politely. She looked down to swallow her reaction, but not before she had caught him giving her a slow wink.

Two days later Lord Clarence passed Jessica as she was walking in the Park, one of Lady Emilia's footmen trailing behind. He instantly signaled to his man, who drew up the horses.

"May I request the honor of your joining me in my carriage, Miss Whinburn?" he said gallantly. He was once again very red in the face.

"You are most kind, my lord, but I'd rather walk."

"Then perhaps I may join you?" And to Jessica's horror, with a great deal of panting and the aid of his groom, the hanging judge climbed from his seat. Jessica could do nothing else but take his proffered arm and allow him to escort her up the path. "There's something about you, ma'am. I can't seem to get your face from my mind."

"Indeed, my lord? Surely not!"

"Perhaps I have dreamed of you." He looked at her intently. "Do you think we are fated to meet?"

"I can hardly think so!"

He seemed to mumble almost to himself. "I could do worse. Indeed I could! Lady Emilia Shay's great-niece!"

"Do worse, Lord Clarence?"

"Ah, I was thinking to myself, my dear; mind was wandering. I'm on the hunt for a wife, don't you know. How long have you been in town?"

"A month," said Jessica. She had been in London for a month! And that was all that she'd promised Deyncourt, wasn't it? "I'm sorry, my lord," she said with no further warning. "I have the most unaccountable headache. I am going back to my aunt's!"

She came in from the Park and threw her gloves into a chair. She couldn't bear it! Would Lady Emilia think Lord Clarence a suitable match? And if not him, who? And what if she met someone she could really love? She couldn't continue this when it was impossible for her to marry. Far better to live in an attic and eat turnips! Running lightly upstairs she went into her room and rummaged through her few belongings. At last, she found it: the letter from Bromley and Finch, publishers of the classics. She frowned once again as she noticed how it was addressed. They couldn't conceive, obviously, of a female who was proficient in the ancient languages. Nevertheless, she sent a maid to order her horse saddled, changed into her habit, and jammed the missive into her pocket. Within half an hour she was riding her gray mare down the cobbled street. She hadn't gone very far when the groom who had accompanied her rode up alongside.

"Beggin' your pardon, ma'am?"

"What is it, Parker?"

"Where was you planning to go, ma'am?"

"I am going to Hunting Lane—in the City. Is it far?"

"Well, you can't go there, Miss Whinburn!"

Jessica pulled up her mare and looked at him. "Why ever not? Don't you know the way?"

"Well, I knows the way, right enough, ma'am. But a lady can't go there!"

"What do you mean?"

The groom looked awkwardly at the ground. "I could accompany you to the Park, ma'am, but it's not the done thing for a lady to travel about the City on horseback."

"You mean that I may ride for empty pleasure as long as it is the correct hour of the morning and the correct destination, but not as a means of transportation?"

"Well, I suppose you could put it that way, sure enough."

"Then how am I supposed to travel if I have business?"

He looked blankly at her face. "Business? Well, if you was to want to go shopping, we would gladly get out the carriage for you."

"I do not want to go shopping!" Jessica said desperately. "I intend to go to Hunting Lane, and if you will not accompany me, I shall go by myself!"

Parker turned quite white. "Lady Emilia would have me turned off, ma'am, if I was to allow it."

Jessica felt like cursing, but the poor fellow was shocked enough already. "Very well, then," she said calmly. "Let us return and put up the horses, and you may ask Coachman to ready the carriage."

"You still couldn't go to Hunting Lane alone, ma'am."

"I thought if I went in the carriage, I might meet the strictures of propriety?"

"Yes, well," returned the man stubbornly. "If you was to go shopping, see. But there's no shops on Hunting Lane; it's a business area, ain't it?"

Jessica could have wept with exasperation. If she went alone, no doubt Aunt Emilia would take it out on poor

Parker, who should stop her doing anything so out of the ordinary. "Then in order to get to my destination, what am I supposed to do?" she asked.

"Find a gentleman who will escort you, Miss Whinburn," said a smooth voice.

Chapter 11

It was Deyncourt. He smiled down at her from the seat of an extremely precarious-looking high-perch phaeton. A pair of matched bays fretted at the injustice of having been asked to halt, and the tiger who had been standing behind leapt down to take the horses' heads. A look of pure relief swept over Parker's features.

"Perhaps," continued the earl, "I might take you?"

"I should much rather not impose upon you, my lord."

"But if your journey is so important, you have little choice, do you? Mr. Parker is about to have apoplexy at the thought of losing his place. You could not be so cruel. Pray, allow me, Miss Whinburn!"

He jumped lightly from the phaeton and swung her down from the gray mare. In the next instant he had handed her up into the fine leather seat of his carriage.

"Take the horses back, Parker, and rest easy. You may inform Lady Emilia that Miss Whinburn is now under my care."

"Yes, my lord." The groom pulled gratefully at his forelock and rode away up the street, leading Jessica's mare by the bridle. Deyncourt's tiger stepped away from the team's heads and swung up onto his stand behind his master.

"Now, where was it that you were so eager to visit?" inquired Michael politely as the horses leapt ahead.

"Hunting Lane, my lord."

"Ah," said the earl lightly. "The premises of Bromley and Finch, publishers, no doubt."

Jessica whirled around. "However did you know?"

"I found out at Tresham."

"You went through my things?"

"Not deliberately. But it was impossible for me to avoid seeing their letter when you fell asleep with the missive in your hand. I assume you are now thinking of doing a few Greek translations? It will greatly disappoint Lady Emilia if she finds out you are not trying to land an offer instead."

"But there is a gentleman who seems to be developing an interest. I am giving his suit my most serious attention."

He gave her a keen glance. Suddenly, he didn't want to hear that she was truly considering marriage. Yet she was ineligible for him, forever. And what other future was there for her? "And that is?"

"Why, Lord Clarence, of course."

His gloved hands expertly guided the team around a sharp corner. "How could you hope to do better, Miss Whinburn?" he asked with a perfectly straight face. "I hear the hanging judge is very well heeled."

"Indeed, my lord. Well slippered too! And I might hope that he would not hang his own wife, might I not?"

"Oh, I wouldn't be too sure of that!" Michael laughed aloud, but then he turned to her and said quite seriously, "You do know that this journey to Bromley and Finch is a wild-goose chase, don't you?"

"I know no such thing," replied Jessica, instantly bridling. "But right now I would rather make my own living than marry for money, and sell myself body and soul for bed and board. That is the compact, isn't it, that's made in the wedding vows, an exchange of commodities?"

"But if you found the right man, dear Jessie, you might find that your body would enjoy the bargain."

She blushed scarlet, but he had pulled the team to a halt and leapt from the phaeton.

Within a few moments Jessica was face to face with Mr. Finch in person. He was an elderly gentleman in a monocle, which distorted one eye into a grotesque caricature of the other. "My dear young lady," he said in considerable distress, as soon as she introduced herself. "I'm afraid it is entirely out of the question!"

"My knowledge of the classical authors is as great as any male's, sir."

"No doubt, no doubt, ma'am! But it's simply impossible! Our clerks are all gentlemen, of course, but not of the *ton*, if you would indulge me with your understanding. For a young lady to join our staff would be unthinkable."

"Then perhaps you might sometimes have work that could be sent to me, sir?"

"Quite out of the question! No, no, I'm afraid we have all labored under a dreadful misapprehension."

It was no use. Angry enough to be close to tears, Jessica stormed out of the publisher's offices. Michael turned at her approach and raised an eyebrow.

"You were quite right, my lord," she said in unsteady tones. "My life consists of nothing but a string of petty humiliations. I may not ride when or where I like, I may not even shuffle a pack of cards, and I certainly may not make a living of my own. I had better give Lord Clarence my consideration, after all."

He made no reply except to hand her into the carriage. Something very strange was happening to him at the sight of her brave smile. For God's sake, she didn't deserve this! The horses plunged forward. After a few moments Jessica noticed that they seemed to be driving straight out of town.

"Where are we going, Lord Deyncourt?"

"We are going to take your mind off your troubles, Miss Whinburn. Trust me."

The horses stretched out into a steady fast trot as he

tooled them through the traffic. In an hour the stone streets and tall city buildings had given way to the dry dirt of a country lane and the thick green of leafy hedgerows. Villages, with their thatched roofs huddled around the central eye of a duck pond or a green common, passed every few miles. The rustics looked up at their approach and touched at their caps with gapped-toothed smiles. Before long the team swung in through a pair of imposing stone portals, each topped with a carved stone lion. The sun dappled through an alley of elms as they trotted up the gravel path, and then the trees opened up to reveal a mellow sandstone house basking in the heat. The façade boasted a series of stone arches over a matched row of mullioned windows. Behind them at each end of the roof rose a cluster of fantastic chimneys.

"Wherever is this?" she asked as he brought the team to a halt.

"Marchmont. It dates from the time of Good Queen Bess: witness the Tudor chimneys. It's one of my properties and a favorite—other than Castle Deyncourt, of course. But the Castle is halfway across England, and this, as you have just seen, is within easy reach of town. It's my secret retreat when I've had enough of gossip and intrigue."

"And is that often?"

He handed her down from the phaeton. "You have had the pleasure of enjoying the giddy pursuits of the *beau monde*. What do you think?"

They walked together into the cool hallway. Everything was in perfect order. Footmen silently appeared and took their hats and gloves, doors opened and closed behind them. Michael led her through a series of beautiful rooms, dappled with sunlight from the lead-paned windows. There was no clutter; yet every room held some object of real beauty, the accumulated treasure of a family who had traveled the world and brought back whatever distilled the most loveliness from each culture. The light from the tall windows was filtered and changed by the old glass and the greenness of the world outside. It was almost as if they were under water. Jessica could feel her sore feelings melting away to be replaced by a sense of peace.

"I believe my ancestor was inspired by Bess Hardwick; they were related. Of course, Marchmont is nowhere near as grand."

"*'Hardwick Hall, more glass than wall,'*" quoted Jessica softly. The dream house of that great Elizabethan was famous.

"It was revolutionary architecture for its time: a house built for beauty instead of fortification." He opened a door which led into a long gallery, lined with books. "Here is the library. It's nothing to the collection at Castle Deyncourt, but I like to keep enough books here to amuse me."

"Then you are hard to amuse, my lord. There are enough volumes here to fill a lifetime." Jessica wandered down past the shelves. "This is a rarity, isn't it?"

He pulled down the volume she indicated. It was a medieval treatise on herbs, written in a pidgin Latin. Soon he had her in hysterics as he deliberately mistranslated the language and worked absurd meanings out of the crabbed text. Jessica joined in the fun, as they attempted to outdo each effort with one both more ridiculous and yet close enough to the original meaning to sustain the conceit of a translation.

"Oh, God!" exclaimed Michael, throwing back his head and laughing aloud. "I yield, Miss Whinburn. Mercy! No more Latin puns, I beg you!"

"*Ab uno disce omnes,* my lord."

"I am outclassed! For heaven's sake, let us retreat to the safety of the gardens."

They stepped out of a solid oak door at the back of the house. A stone patio graced with more lions gave onto steps that led down to a formal garden, laid out with miniature box hedges and statuary. The sun beat down on them. Michael shrugged out of his jacket and flung it over his shoulder. The fine white fabric of his shirt shimmered in the light.

"This garden has looked like this for two hundred years;

it's a relic of more graceful times. Marchmont escaped my father's passion for things modern; it has not been naturalized. Aunt Sophy lived here until she died, so that may account for it.''

For some reason, Jessica had never thought of him as having a family. How very absurd! Everybody did. In fact he had told her at Tresham that he'd had a brother who died, and he'd mentioned this very Aunt Sophy. But he seemed so entirely self-contained and self-sufficient. Was he, like her, the last of his line?

"And apart from your brother, there were no other siblings?"

"My mother bore ten children, seven before me and two after. Only my brother and myself survived infancy."

"How terrible for her! I'm sorry," said Jessica.

"Don't be—it was the nurses who wept. You were an only child, I take it? There were no brothers or sisters to share the Whinburn inheritance?"

"To share in the debts, in my case," said Jessica. "No, Mama died when I was little. Thus all the obligation was mine alone."

He did not reply, but led her down a neat gravel path and through an arched opening in a box hedge. In front of them lay a cornucopia of roses. In a riot of color, English summer had reached its climax. The scent swept over them in a wave. Jessica was stunned.

"It's beautiful!" she exclaimed.

"Aunt Sophy's pride and joy. She had all this planted. I was occasionally allowed to be her solemn advisor when I was little."

"But you were never a child, were you, Lord Deyncourt?"

Michael gave her an astonished look. "Whatever do you mean?"

"I rather imagined that you had sprung already adult and fully armed from the brow of Zeus."

He laughed. "Like Athene, goddess of wisdom?"

"And also of warfare. What an odd combination of attributes! She could only have been invented by men. Women don't usually think war an act of sagacity.''

"But what other goddess can have wisdom? *Juno, which is queen of marriage*'? Hardly. Wisdom is never shared with love, so it cannot be an attribute of Aphrodite, either. Thus Athene gains wisdom by default. Yet men sacrifice in vain at her altar to get it.''

"You think ladies wiser than gentlemen?" asked Jessica, surprised.

They had reached the banks of an ornamental lake. A grove of birch trees hung over the dappled water and cast a welcome shade. Michael picked up a stone and skimmed it across the water, then he dropped onto the grass and stretched out under a tree, arms folded behind his head. He gazed up at her through slitted lids.

"Yes, for you will not allow me to charm you, will you, Miss Whinburn?"

She stood looking down at him. If he only guessed how fast her heart was beating, he would never have said it. The lithe tilt of his body where the shirt was stretched by the curve of his arm sent palpitations down her spine.

"And why should you wish to do so?" she asked.

"Because it is my profession, of course."

Jessica bent and picked up a flat rock; she wasn't sure what he meant, but it suddenly seemed dangerous to reply. She tried to send the pebble skimming after his, but the tight sleeves of her habit preventing her swinging her arm, and it plopped into the water. "Damnation," she said and laughed. "Even my clothes are fit for Bedlam!"

"Then take off your jacket! I wager you cannot throw more ducks and drakes than I!"

He leapt to his feet and began to collect pebbles. With a shrug Jessica shed her tailored jacket. In a few moments they were laughing together like children.

"That one was five!"

"Yes, but I have already done seven."

"I ought to have a handicap, my lord."

"You concede that I can throw further?" He looked at her in mock surprise.

"Yes, but not more skillfully! Watch this!" She had saved her best pebble for last. With just the right flick of the wrist, she watched in glee as it skipped exactly seven times over the surface.

He bowed. "A draw!" There was a light of warmth and humor in his eyes. "Now, we have lost all sense of propriety! And I have you just where I want you!" Jessica looked down at herself. Her blouse had pulled out of her waist, and without thinking she had rolled up her sleeves revealing her bare arms. No doubt her hair was as usual slipping from its pins. "You look like a wanton, Miss Whinburn. There is something so very enticing about the inner curve of a lady's elbow."

She flushed with anger and tugged down her sleeves. "Are you flirting with me, Lord Deyncourt?"

"Why not? That's what rakes do. And Marchmont cries out for it, don't you think? The very house enthralls the senses."

"Then I'm not sure that I ought to be here."

Her ferocity stunned him. "But you are quite safe because of your formidable great-aunt. So what harm is a little innocent flirtation? Since I know you intend never to marry, I can be sure you won't misunderstand."

"No, Lord Deyncourt," she said. "I shan't misunderstand."

Michael gently laid his fingers along her cheek, then slipped his hand behind her back, and pulled her to him. His lips touched the corner of her mouth. "Release me from my promise, Miss Whinburn?" he said softly against her lips. "Kiss me? Come, I won't bite." His voice was rich with amusement. "Or at least, not yet." He bent her against him, and kissed her. The most exquisite feelings flamed in the pit of her stomach. Jessica knew that if he demanded it, she would respond with a torrent of passion. The kiss deepened and flared into intensity. He must not! She wrenched away from him. He was slightly breathless, his eyes dilated, but instantly he regained that cool control.

"No wonder you think Aphrodite cannot have wisdom!" Jessica could hear her voice tremble.

"Oh, dear Lord, kisses are never wise. It was only a moment of madness, caused by the day and the roses. Never fear, other appetites may yet save us. Luncheon should be ready. Meanwhile, I beg you to forget that I so disgraced myself. I suppose if you like, you're entitled to slap my face."

"Good heavens," said Jessica. "A cuff in trade for a kiss? So warfare is an attribute of Aphrodite, after all!"

Jessica allowed him to escort her to the house. A maid appeared from nowhere and expertly repaired her hair. Why would he have such a person on his staff? The answer was obvious, of course. Marchmont was where he entertained mistresses, and they came without their personal maids. Cleopatra had no doubt spent many afternoons here being charmed by Mark Anthony. There was nothing about this day that was any different for him except that he had not yet bedded her. Oh, dear Lord, that despicable, easy charm! She remembered what he had said at Tresham before he knew who she was. If it were not for Lady Emilia, that would have been his answer: another mistress, for a while at least. But why had he brought her here? And why had she let him kiss her again?

Yet she quietly rejoined him in the dining room. The footmen served them in silence, then disappeared, while the earl distracted, then enthralled her, with stories about the history of the house. With an outward calm that was far from her emotions, Jessica filled her plate with fresh strawberries and raspberries, grown without question in Marchmont's kitchen garden. The food was delectable; the wine exquisite; the very house itself seemed seductive. It made it extremely difficult to think of spending the rest of one's life eating turnips in an attic.

"How many properties do you have?" asked Jessica at last.

"Besides Deyncourt and here? Well, there's a neat little manor at Kingston where I pursue the creation of a new line of Red Poll cattle, and a place in Norfolk that raises excellent turnips. Enough to keep me busy, I assure you."

"But you occupy yourself with more than just estates and Red Poll cows, don't you?" she said. "I have been led to understand that you have also embroiled yourself in heroics."

He glanced down and steadily peeled a piece of fruit with a silver knife. She could not see his face. "I did my bit against Napoleon, but there was a great deal more of dirt and squalor in it than anything glamorous."

"You were an officer in the cavalry?"

He looked up. His face showed no emotion. "I was one of Wellington's scouts, spending my days riding about after the French. When I came into my title, I turned gratefully enough to subtler ways to serve my country. Diplomacy is far more interesting."

"Yes, it comes naturally to you to manipulate people and their emotions," Jessica said a little desperately, "and that is what diplomats must actually do. I have been the object of your professional attentions today, haven't I?"

"If you say so," he replied with a smile. "Don't tell me you have been entirely immune, or I shall be forced to abandon intrigue and take up the sword again."

"Well, your roses and your fruit have done their work. I forgive Mr. Finch his narrow-mindedness. No doubt I should have made a dreadful botch of all his staid manuscripts. I shall return humbly to my aunt, happily resigned to my lot."

"Then I have succeeded in my goal, ma'am." He raised her hand to his lips. "Yet I kissed you and you dismiss it! I wish it was the charm of my company that had soothed your troubled soul, rather than my fruit and flowers."

But an hour later, as they returned to town, Jessica was forced to admit that in spite of all her defenses and her distrust of his motives, the eighth Earl of Deyncourt had succeeded only too well. She was damned if she would let him know it, but she had been thoroughly charmed. Yet he was as good as engaged to the Incomparable Melton. And her own future, since Bromley and Finch had refused to rescue her, now offered nothing but the hanging judge. Nevertheless, Jessica was far from resigned to her lot.

Chapter 12

Jessica entered the great portals of Mapleton House and looked around. Her aunt knew nothing of her disastrous venture to Bromley and Finch, and was taking her to her first real London ball. Lady Emilia still had hopes of a match. The entry was a blaze of light, and as her aunt ushered Jessica past the obsequious footmen, they faced a wave of heat and noise. Strains of music were almost drowned in a cacophony of laughter and chatter. Handing her cloak to the servant, Jessica realized that she would be glad of the lightweight silver gauze ball gown that Aunt Emilia—or, in truth, Deyncourt—had chosen for her. Her arms and shoulders were bare, and the neckline swept embarrassingly low, but Aunt Emilia had assured her that she must look just so if she was not to be dismissed as a country nobody. A single strand of pearls, borrowed from her great-aunt, encircled her throat, and more were woven into her hair. The heat from the dreadful crush of guests, added to that from the myriad candles, made her wonder how on earth the gentlemen in their formal jackets and high collars would survive the evening without passing out.

Lady Emilia swept her along toward the imposing group

of dowagers waiting at the side of the room. Jessica had a confused impression of enormous sweeps of greenery and fresh flowers garlanded about the marble columns, and of huge crystal chandeliers shimmering in the haze of heat that hung over the room. After making her curtsies to a seemingly endless string of matrons in a dazzling array of jewels, she was free at last to surrender herself to the flock of young men who were securing introductions. Her dance card began to fill with their names, and suddenly she was whisked away for the first country dance. Partner followed partner, until Jessica felt she would collapse under the strain of trying to remember so many strangers. Thus there was some relief mixed with her apprehension when she saw Caroline and Peter, wending their way toward her through the crush.

"Oh, Miss Whinburn! You look splendid!" cried Caroline. Her face was animated with pleasure. If only she didn't have quite so many frills and bows on her dress, thought Jessica, and if she wore her hair in a softer style as Honoria and Cicely had recommended, she might really look pretty. "I'm so glad to find you at last. This is always one of the grandest balls of the season. You shall have a dance with Lord Steal, because I declare I am fainting on my feet and must sit this one out."

Peter bowed low over Jessica's hand, and professed himself eager for the pleasure. As he led her onto the floor he nobly tried to avoid her eyes, but the measure of the dance brought them constantly face to face.

"Can't we make simple conversation?" asked Jessica at last. "I thought we were to be friends?"

"Oh, Lord, Miss Whinburn, don't you think I'm trying? A fellow was never in such a predicament! Do you still say you could never love me?"

Jessica groaned in exasperation. "Lord Steal, you are to be married in a month to one of the sweetest girls in London. How can you?"

"Oh, I like Miss Brandon, really I do, but she's not like you. She's actually quite steady and strong, not in the least

as delicate as a lady ought to be. She would never faint
away like you did at Tresham! It was like something out
of a poem when Deyncourt had to carry you into the house.
I've been desperately in love with you ever since. It was so
romantic!''

"Lord Steal, you have left me quite in the dark. You are
rambling, I swear it. For heaven's sake, when I arrived at
Tresham I had been shot and had twisted my ankle, but
I positively did not faint!''

Peter looked stubborn. "If I didn't have these dashed
debts, I'd still ask you to marry me—we could wait until
my majority and to heck with Deyncourt! Anyhow, I intend
to make it all come to rights. I've been having a run of
luck recently.''

"Oh, Lord Steal, you are being such a fool! I am not
what you imagine me. If you would only pay Miss Brandon
the attention she deserves, you would find her company
infinitely more appealing than mine. Before long, I shall
surely do something shocking enough to make the scales
fall from your eyes.''

"You could not!'' cried Peter.

The dance was over and she was led from the floor. She
almost stumbled into the gentleman that rose to his feet
as she and Lord Steal returned to Caroline.

"I should be honored by the pleasure of this dance,
Miss Whinburn,'' said Michael smoothly. "If you would
first refrain from stepping on my feet and leaving me a
cripple.''

Jessica looked up to meet his eyes. There was a cold,
dangerous look to their sapphire depths, as if ice had
settled at the bottom of a pool. What had happened? "I
am fatigued, my lord,'' she said quickly. "And would rather
go for a glass of lemonade.''

"Allow me to accompany you,'' he said firmly, and taking
her elbow, led her away from Peter and Caroline.

"On the other hand,'' she blurted, "I am not very thirsty,
perhaps . . .''

"Then you would rather dance?''

The band struck up the first bars of a waltz and he pulled her into his arms.

"I refuse to stumble around in public! I don't know the steps."

"Then let us stroll among the flowers—I expect they have been mute witness to many shattered hopes this evening." He led her from the room into an alcove, where French windows had been opened to give access to the gardens. Within moments, they were beneath the soft glow of the lanterns that had been hung from the trees. A few other couples were swirling together across the lawn. The lilting music wafted clearly through the open windows of the ballroom. His arm remained firmly around her waist as he propelled her down a little grassy path between the bushes. The air was heavy with the scent of blossom and the slightly damp, woodsy odor of the flowering shrubs. At last they reached a small stone bench, where the earl pulled her down beside him. They were entirely alone. Jessica felt her breath coming too rapidly. Through the thin silk of her dress, his strong thigh lay against hers. He turned her to face him, but in the dim light she could not read his expression.

"How lightly are your kisses given, Miss Whinburn?" He ran his thumb gently, deliciously, over her upper lip.

"This is a public ball!" she said shakily. "If a dropped teaspoon is enough to raise eyebrows, surely to be found here with you would be enough to ban me from society?"

"Perhaps," he said idly. "It is generally considered dangerous to play games with a rake."

Jessica pulled away. "Then are you determined to ruin me, after all?"

His hair was softly outlined by the lights of the distant lanterns. "A rake who steals a kiss has no further aim, my dear Jessica, than his own pleasure. Ought I to regret that I did not press my advantage at Marchmont when I had the chance?"

She completely lost her temper, as much with herself as with him. "Oh, fustian! You do nothing without hidden motives! What kind of game are you playing? Whatever it is, I do not appreciate being used as some kind of pawn."

Michael leant forward so that the light struck suddenly across his features. He looked completely astonished. "For God's sake! I have watched you succeed in attracting the attentions of my ward until you have him completely infatuated. I didn't want to believe it. Don't you realize or care about the depth of Miss Brandon's feelings? She has loved Lord Steal since she was ten years old. I shan't allow him to cry off because of you."

"Caroline loves him?"

"It was at her request that I asked him to consider her, but in your determination to intervene in what you perceive to be my plans, you have given Miss Brandon no thought at all, have you?"

"Are your wits completely to let?" said Jessica, stunned. "I have never given him a moment's encouragement! Is that why you have dogged my footsteps? Why you took me to Marchmont? Because in your insufferable vanity you thought to distract me from an imagined courtship with Peter?"

She had never seen him angry before. It was, as Lord Steal had said, like a killing frost. "Ah, *'Peter'*? How familiar! Forgive me, it seems I am indeed trespassing on his territory. Be careful, Miss Whinburn. I thought you would have the sense to pick a wealthy nabob for your efforts, not a penniless sprig of the aristocracy. Unless of course, you think that after his marriage to Miss Brandon, Lord Steal will have the blunt to set you up as his mistress? Are you completely the Jezebel?"

It was like a slap in the face. "How would you ever know?" hissed Jessica, fighting back angry tears. "Perhaps I have kissed Peter like this?"

She took his arms and fastened her mouth to his. Shame and anger and passion blazed from her lips and tongue. He shrugged from her grasp only to pull her against his body. Then his mouth burned down onto hers, overwhelming her senses as he returned the kiss with expressive mastery. Jessica felt the strength drain from her body. Her eyes closed and she knew that in the next instant she was about to surrender completely. His tongue searched her mouth, and eagerly she tasted him back, waves of desire running molten copper in her veins. His fingers trailed possessively over her jaw and neck, then down the sensitive skin of her shoulder as if to slide her dress from her breast, when suddenly he released her. He turned away and wrung both hands through his hair.

"Dear God!" he said, looking suddenly back at her. His eyes were dark with passion. "Jessica!"

She stood up and rubbed the moisture from her mouth with her hand. She was shaking. "Indeed, my lord! I am shameless! You offered me a career as a courtesan yourself. No doubt in your wisdom and experience you recognized that I was suitable for nothing else. Well, so be it! But it won't be poor Lord Steal who takes me to his bed in trade for trinkets, and it most certainly won't be you!"

She choked down the threatening tears and swept away up the path. Michael leaned back against the seat and gazed blankly at the canopy of leaves over his head. He had deliberately brought Jessica out here to confront her. She had seemed immune to his charm—so if diplomacy failed, he would indeed use the sword. For Caroline had just told him how she considered Miss Whinburn a very dear friend, then he had looked up to see Peter fawning over her! The devoted look on his ward's face had produced a sudden cold fury. After that day at Marchmont, he had truly begun to believe that Jessica Whinburn could not play such perfidious games. He had laid a trap for her at his beautiful house, and then he wasn't quite sure who had been caught.

And now she had kissed him, with passion, with anger, and with complete honesty, and left him to confront an appalling suspicion. All the pieces seemed to fall into place. Her reckless pursuit of independence. Her horror of marriage. Her anger and defiance at his casual flirtation. The

exquisite Earl of Deyncourt put his head in his hands. For
God's sake! For God's sake! What had he done now?

After washing her face in the powder room, Jessica
slipped back into the ballroom, only to be immediately
claimed for the next country dance. She looked away from
the sight of Deyncourt, taking his position further down
the line. No one should guess the pain that had flared up
in her heart. For the second waltz, her hand was clasped
by none other than Lord Clarence, who was perspiring
rather too freely in his high collar and garish coat. It was
too ridiculous.

"Would you object, my lord, if we were to sit and take
lemonade instead?" she suggested. "I confess, I am danced
off my feet."

"My pleasure!" replied her partner. "Awfully tuckered
out myself, never was much of a dancer. Probably step on
your toes, don't you know?"

They secured seats by a large palm and the judge brought
a lemonade for Jessica. As the couples sailed by, he began
to point out the people he knew. "There goes young Steal:
ancient family, huge old place in the country—caught
himself an heiress, though she's plain as a carriage wheel.
Can't imagine what he sees there but the blunt."

"No, indeed," corrected Jessica firmly. "We are
acquainted, and I assure you Miss Brandon is all kindness
and they are very devoted."

"Oh, didn't know you was acquainted. Shouldn't have
said anything if I'd known, assure you. Well, here comes
Deyncourt and the Incomparable. That's a love match at
any rate. She's dazzling!" Deyncourt and Honoria spun
by. As they passed, Deyncourt appeared to be listening
with doting interest to his partner. His lean fingers were
pressed against the blue silk at her waist. Her blond hair
made a shimmering contrast to the dark cloth of his coat.
"By God, she's a catch!" gushed Lord Clarence. "A beauty
and an heiress, and not a stain on her! All London's been

after Deyncourt, but my money is she's got him in the bag. The Melton can match her fortune and family to his, and she's a lovely, innocent creature—never a breath of scandal about her. Deyncourt's a man to demand perfection, and by God, he's found it there!''

It was a pain that threatened to entirely undo her. Jessica swallowed it down. ''Indeed, Lord Clarence, they are perfectly suited.''

''Yes, the Incomparable has the world of fashion at her feet.'' Then he turned to her. ''But for myself, of course, I don't mind something a bit out of the ordinary—russet hair, for instance.''

Jessica was finding her plump partner insufferable, but could think of no put-down sufficient to quell him. Until she thought of the evening slippers. ''But you are quite a leader of fashion yourself, aren't you, my lord?'' she asked innocently. ''How ever did you get quite such a perfect match between your shoes and stockings?'' Lord Clarence glanced down at his buff footwear. ''I declare, my lord, they are the exact same shade, as if both had been dipped in a puddle!''

The judge instantly turned puce. He spluttered and changed the subject. With infinite gratitude, Jessica relinquished his company for that of an elderly gentleman who claimed the next dance. Well, that had taken care of Lord Clarence! She had a far more pressing problem: she had just discovered that Caroline loved Peter. Now she must make Peter return that love.

As the evening drew to a close, the band struck up the final waltz. Having escaped her unwanted partner and scratched his name from her card, Jessica stood momentarily alone beside a marble pillar with its now wilting greenery and flowers. She fanned her hot cheeks, and attempted to tuck a few stray curls back into her rapidly disintegrating coiffure. Dancing was energetic work and although it made her blood race and her eyes shine, her hair was objecting to being confined for so long.

''Don't,'' said a voice at her elbow. ''It looks charming

as it is. We have unfinished business, Miss Whinburn. May I have the pleasure of this dance?''

Without waiting for a reply, Michael pulled her into his arms. She looked up into his face and met only a sardonic smile. In contrast to her, he looked completely unruffled, and the long fingers that held hers were cool and firm. But he did not swing her onto the floor. Instead, he forced her with him behind a tub of greenery.

"There is nothing further we have to say to each other, my lord!''

"Yes, there is, Jessica. Among other things, perhaps, an apology—''

"You won't get it!'' She wrenched away from him.

Immediately Michael released her, his eyes dark with pain, but without another word, he gave her his exquisite bow and took his leave. Even if she forgave him, what could possibly happen now to justify him being her savior? He had nothing, nothing he could offer her. The devil doesn't lightly give up a soul.

Chapter 13

The very next morning Jessica put her plan into action. She went with Caroline to inspect the latest fashions displayed at a stylish milliner's. They pored over ribbons and silk flowers, and hunted through straw-chip bonnets. Jessica knew and cared nothing about fashion herself, but she remembered very clearly the advice of Lady Honoria Melton.

"How do you like this?" Jessica said at last, holding up a very charming little hat with fine coquelicot ribbons, but no other adornment.

"Actually, I like it very well, but Mama always wishes me to wear the most modish bonnets."

"By which she means the most elaborate. Miss Brandon, you are almost a married lady, don't you think you should follow your own taste?"

"Do you think so?" replied Caroline with interest. "I confess that the gowns Mama picks out for me sometimes make me feel like a package wrapped up for Christmas."

"And look at this," said Jessica, pointing out some fashion plates. "This is exactly the style that would suit you." The lady in the print wore her hair in a simple cloud of curls around her face—the very style that Cecily Pratchett had recommended.

Caroline laughed. "Do you know, I have often longed to bob my hair, since it is not in the least pretty as it is, and it's such a nuisance to have it washed and dressed. Do you think I should?"

"Absolutely! I would cut my own hair, but I'm afraid that I should look like an orange chrysanthemum! Why don't you do it?"

"You mean, now?"

"Why not?" This was going splendidly.

Two hours later the two ladies emerged into the street from Caroline's home. Miss Brandon's maid had happily cut her mistress's hair, and all three females had giggled together as the stringy mouse-colored tresses fell to the floor. Caroline's hair sprang into natural curls when relieved of the burden of its own weight, and the color near the roots was deeper and richer. When it was done, she threw her arms around Jessica and laughed.

"You were so right! Now for the new bonnet! No one will recognize me!"

They hurried back to the shops together and Caroline tried on the straw-chip. She turned to Jessica with her face alight.

"It's perfect," said Jessica smiling. Indeed it was. The Incomparable had been right. Instead of looking like a frightened mouse, Caroline now seemed only sweetly vulnerable and feminine.

Jessica gave her friend a warm smile. "Now for your modiste! You need a new gown to compliment what we have done."

"Dear Miss Whinburn, you know, you are so like Lord Deyncourt! He'd help anyone, at whatever cost to himself, just as you rescued that puppy. I was ready to faint when you jumped into the water!"

Jessica swallowed her pain at the mention of his name. "Excellent, for that is the very thing that I want you to do, as soon as the opportunity presents itself."

Caroline gave her a puzzled look, but Jessica began to talk about dresses, and Miss Brandon was not to discover quite yet what she meant.

That evening Lord Deyncourt spent a great deal of time over his cravat. Dover assisted without murmur as his master cast aside one starched creation after another. Finally he was waved from the room. There was silence as Dover stood and waited patiently in the corridor, his brow contracted in worry—it hadn't been this bad for a long time. But when Michael strode into his club that night, his elegance seemed as simple and perfect as usual. There was no trace of his earlier torment. He looked about the room. To his considerable surprise, his eye fell upon the very man who might best be able to help him.

"Dagonet!" he said, holding out his hand.

Devil Dagonet looked up from his brandy and grinned. "For God's sake, my lord, you are exquisite! *Le style, c'est l'homme?* The cut of your coat is alone enough to intimidate lesser mortals."

Michael smiled grimly. "It serves a purpose," he said.

Charles de Dagonet gave his friend a sharp look. "But I am blinded, like Paul on the road to Damascus. Is this the result of becoming an earl?"

"It's an attempt to live down my past and my blasphemous friends, sir! What are you doing in town, Dagonet?"

"Pining for Kate, of course, but I unfortunately had to visit my cousin and she won't speak to him." The facile voice became suddenly serious. "How can I assist you, Michael? Your new responsibilities would seem to weigh on you like the globe upon the shoulders of Atlas. I won't join you in any desperate venture, you know! I am sworn to domesticity and have put our Peninsular adventures behind me."

"No, I don't need your sword arm, dear sir, all I want is gossip. Listen, you had your ear to the ground in the less salubrious parts of town last winter—Richard Acton told me something of it—can you tell me anything about Whinburn House in Northumberland?''

Devil Dagonet took a pensive sip from his glass. ''Not much. The place had a certain reputation, I believe.''

''For what?''

''For high gaming, for vice—a veritable den of debauchery it was whispered—but extremely private. I don't imagine it would have been known in London at all. I only heard of it myself because of some shady horse-trading connections.''

''And the owner, Sir Shelby Whinburn? What was his passion?''

''Le veau d'or, of course.''

''Dear God! Tell me,'' said Michael in a voice thick with dread, ''was there anything he wouldn't have sold for money?''

Dagonet looked up at his friend in alarm. ''Deyncourt, for God's sake! You would appear to have seen the writing blazoned on the wall. I'll gladly tell you everything I heard, but first let me order you a brandy, dear fellow.''

The following morning, accompanied by a maid, Jessica went to meet with Caroline for a walk in the Park. Somehow she had to make Miss Brandon appear as romantic to Peter as she herself had apparently seemed at Tresham. Lost in her reverie, she jumped visibly when she was accosted from behind. It was Lord Steal. His round face was ashen, and as he fell in beside her and her maid dropped behind, Jessica turned to him in alarm.

''Whatever is it, Lord Steal? You look all to pieces!''

''I am completely ruined, Miss Whinburn!'' he said dramatically. ''I have come to seek you out only to say goodbye!''

''Goodbye? Why, are you going away?''

''Further than anyone can reach!'' he exclaimed, wringing his hands. ''If only I wasn't such a fool! You know what I have felt for you, but now it can never be! And then there is Miss Brandon; she is truly the last person in the world to deserve this! I have lost everything. There is only one honorable way out."

"Lord Steal, you are quite wild! Pray, calm down and tell me what has happened." Jessica's heart went out to the young man, for though he flung out his words with a certain melodramatic bravado, he did indeed look quite desperate.

He groaned and wrung his hand through his hair. "I started playing pretty deep last autumn and fell in debt to Sir Gordon Cranby. I thought I could mend my affairs when I got back to town, and I'd been having the most tremendous run of luck recently. But then the luck turned. Last night—I was three sheets to the wind, of course, though that's no excuse—I wagered Tresham for all my debts on a single throw with Cranby—and lost!"

"How could you have done anything so hare-witted!" As if she did not understand!

"My entire estate and inheritance! Lost! I am ruined. I can never marry Miss Brandon under the circumstances and let Cranby get his hands on her fortune as well, for I promised him my future prospects as well as my present ones. There is only one action that I can take with honor. I could not end it all, though, without seeing you one last time. Say you will remember me with kindness?"

He grasped her hand, but at that moment they spied a solitary horseman coming down the ride toward them, and Peter cried bitterly, "Oh, dash it all! There's Cranby, the new master of Tresham! I can't face him."

Sir Gordon Cranby was almost upon them. Jessica had an instant idea. It just might work. It was worth anything to save the desperate young fellow at her side. Pulling Peter aside, she spoke to him rapidly and told him her plan. He looked at her with astonishment.

"You must," insisted Jessica. "What do you have to lose? Come, be a man. It's your last chance."

With a shaky laugh, Steal threw back his head, his face

flushed. "By damn, I'll do it! I might as well die in my shirtsleeves as in a coat!"

As Cranby drew alongside them Steal stepped into his path. "Another wager, sir!"

"You are mad, my lord," replied Cranby with a sneer. "You have nothing left to lose."

"You're wrong, sir! I wager my coat. It's very fine—the latest twig, don't you know—cut by Weston, cost me a pretty penny, too! I wager it against all my debts and Tresham!"

"You talk nonsense, my lord. Are you in your cups?" Cranby made as if to move on.

"Will you not hear the wager, Sir Gordon?" interrupted Jessica. "Do not say you are afraid of one more hazard with this young man?"

Cranby smiled unpleasantly. "This young man, madam, has already promised me his entire estate. What the devil would I want with his coat?"

"Then you fear to lose, Sir Gordon? Good heavens! I thought your reputation more audacious than that. Everyone will think you have lost your nerve."

"Especially when it's a sure thing," groaned Peter. "Oh, for God's sake! Ride on, Cranby. I'm not sure that I should offer the wager, after all. My best damned coat!"

While they talked, a crowd had begun, discreetly, to gather. The *beau monde*, always curious and ready for a new piece of gossip, would not miss this for the world. Seeing their faces, Cranby knew he was trapped.

"On what do you wager your exquisite garment, my lord?" he said silkily. "I am always in need of a new coat."

A fine bead of sweat lined Peter's upper lip. He looked quite ill as he threw out the words. "Why, that Miss Whinburn can shoot the top off that bush yonder."

A ripple of amusement went up from the spectators. "You've just won yourself a jacket, Cranby!" called out someone in the crowd.

"I accept with pleasure," grinned Cranby with relief. "Be our witness, sirs! Tresham for the coat off Lord Steal's back, that Miss Whinburn cannot shoot the head off that bush, or indeed any plant at all.''

"Done," cried Peter, and they shook hands on it. The crowd by this time was agog. What a splendid *on dit!* Jessica meanwhile was breathing rather fast. Could she in fact do it? It had been essential to come up with something unlikely enough that Cranby would accept the wager, but she was very out of practice. Sir Gordon of course was assuming that she could not shoot at all; it was not a common skill for young ladies, and even for a gentleman the distance made for a difficult shot. Some of the young bucks in the crowd were already pacing off the length to the bush. Had she been the complete interfering fool and overreached herself? Her thoughts were disturbed by the cool tones of the voice that had been haunting her.

"An interesting wager," said Michael casually. He sat above the crowd in his high-perch phaeton. The team of matched bays bent their heads fretfully to his steady feel on the ribbons. "Might I offer Miss Whinburn the use of my pistols? They are very fine, though perhaps a little heavy for such delicate hands."

"By all means, Lord Deyncourt," said Cranby. "Unless Steal has any objection?"

Peter shook his head and looked helplessly at Jessica. He was quite green. At that moment, Caroline appeared at Jessica's side. The only satisfaction that Jessica had at that moment was to see the color suddenly rush back to Peter's face as he noticed Caroline. He looked quite thunderstruck. The mousy girl he had thought himself engaged to had mysteriously turned into a rather appealing young woman. He came over to the ladies.

"Caroline! Whatever has happened to you? You look so different!"

"Oh, I have cut my hair and purchased a new gown, that is all." She brushed him aside. "What's happening, Miss Whinburn? There is such a crowd! What on earth has occurred?" Jessica was forced to tell her friend of the wager. "You cannot do it!" cried Caroline, her face ashen.

"It will be the talk of the town! Your reputation can only suffer. You shall not risk a scandal. I shall stick by Peter whatever happens. We can live well enough on my money."

Jessica could not bear to tell her friend that if she married Peter, he had promised Caroline's fortune to Cranby along with all the rest. Instead, she gave her a quick hug and drew her aside from the rest of the crowd, who were beginning to taunt Lord Steal in a good-natured way about the quality of jacket he was about to lose to Cranby. It was a particularly fine object, in a subtle cream-and-white stripe.

"Oh, fiddlesticks. Don't try to stop me! I shall win! Look, Caroline, will you do something for me? If the opportunity presents itself, can you faint near Peter?" Caroline looked completely astonished. "Oh, I know you think I have windmills in my head, but just do it! Promise me you will." The other girl stared for a moment, then laughed and nodded. "You won't regret it," said Jessica in a whisper. "Now go and comfort your betrothed. He thinks he is destitute, but then he's never had the occasion to witness my prowess with a weapon."

Caroline did as she was bid, and Jessica turned to Michael; he was still at the reins of his team, gently controlling their restive movements. She addressed him in a clear, cool voice. "Thank you for your gracious offer, my lord. I shall be happy to accept the loan of your pistols, since I gave you my grandfather's dueling piece."

He gazed at her for a moment, and the chatter of the crowd died away. "I perceive," said Michael calmly, "that we are creating both a public spectacle and an obstruction to traffic. Might I suggest that all parties concerned adjourn to Deyncourt House, where a suitable plant can no doubt be selected in the garden?"

His polite request might as well have been an order. Immediately the participants and the spectators began to leave in the direction of the earl's town house. He took Jessica up in the carriage beside him.

"May I trust you with my pistol, Miss Whinburn? You

did not actually fire at Judge Clarence, so I am not to know how much of this is bluff. My dueling pieces are both more delicately triggered and more accurate than your grandfather's weapon. I should not want one damaged."

"I learned as a child, my lord. I can shoot as well as anyone."

"Dare I doubt it?" he said unperturbed. "This whole little venture was your idea, wasn't it? I assume that my ward has finally disgraced himself completely?"

"He is threatening to kill himself!"

"I should hate to lose him so precipitately after all my efforts on his behalf. By the way, what has happened to Miss Brandon?"

"Nothing, my lord. I have merely persuaded her to cut her hair and change her style of dress."

"So I noticed. Then I pray you will win the wager." And he gave her that charming smile. "It would ruin all of your efforts if she was forced instead into mourning, wouldn't it?"

Chapter 14

They pulled up before Deyncourt House, an imposing and ancient mansion which sat back in its own grounds off Piccadilly. In front of the astonished eyes of the staff, the entire crowd was led into the garden. It was agreed that Jessica should have three shots at a particularly lovely rosebush that was just coming into bloom. There was a single red rose, fully opened, at the top, which was to be her target. Several youths paced back and forth to check the distance, and a line was drawn in the gravel path to be her mark. Michael poured powder into the barrel and rammed home the ball before he handed her his pistol. Out of the corner of her eyes, she caught sight of Peter's horrified face. She was finally about to do something that was not in the least feminine and delicate! Perhaps he would at last realize that he had thought himself in love with a mirage.

She took aim and fired. There was a deafening roar and the bullet tore through the bush to land with a thud in the bark of a tree behind. The red rose remained unscathed. Caroline gave a small scream and clutched at Peter's sleeve. With a look of pure shock on his face, he put his arm around her. Some of the dandies in the crowd cheered, Cranby gave a little guffaw, and Jessica saw the sweat running down Peter's pale face. The pistol was perfectly balanced, but every weapon was different. It was heavy in her hand: a man's dueling pistol, but the craftsmanship was such that she felt she held a work of art. Jessica reloaded, carefully cleaning the touchhole, and took aim once more. At the same instant, her attention was distracted as Caroline fainted into Peter's arms and he lifted her to carry her into the house. The shot went wild.

"I shall need to have Weston alter the coat," smiled Cranby, "if I am to wear it at Tresham. I am a little narrower across the shoulders than Lord Steal, I believe." There were several guffaws.

Jessica closed her eyes for a moment. The sun beat on her closed lids. She could hear the sudden trill of a bird and the distant clatter of the city above the laughter and talk of the crowd. This was the final shot. She reloaded again. She must concentrate! Michael stood casually to one side, and as he caught her eye, he gave her a slow wink. He did not believe she could do it! Challenged, she threw up her chin and taking quick aim fired for the last time. The rose exploded in a shower of petals that drifted slowly to earth like fragrant drops of blood.

"Be careful, you are about to drop my pistol," said Michael's voice in her ear as he gently removed the gun from her shaking fingers. Cranby stalked from the garden, as Peter's friends cheered and ran off to tell him of his restored fortunes.

"Come, Miss Whinburn," said Michael casually. "Perhaps you would care to come in for some refreshment?"

She went gratefully with him into the cool house. Suddenly she began to realize the enormity of what she had done. London would be scandalized. She would no doubt lose her voucher for Almack's at last, and Lady Emilia would be devastated. If it wasn't for that, the opinion of all these superficial, heartless people wouldn't matter at all. Well, she would just have to live it down. Only Deyncourt seemed unmoved by the entire incident. "I hope we shall never actually have cause to come to blows, Miss Whinburn," he commented lightly. "You would be a dangerous enemy."

She looked up at him quickly, but his expression remained unchanged.

"I trust I did not damage your weapon, my lord? It is magnificent."

"Thank you. No indeed, your touch on the trigger was as light as my own." He handed her a glass of wine, then began to pour another. "You have an extraordinary disregard for your reputation, Miss Whinburn. Whatever enabled you to persuade Steal to such an outrageous wager?"

"If you took the slightest real interest in him, you would know that he has been getting into trouble!"

Michael turned. "He has been losing at the gaming tables these last six months and Sir Gordon is the primary benefactor."

"You knew! Then why didn't you do anything about it?"

"Because I preferred to let him learn from his own mistakes."

"But he had gambled Tresham on a single throw with Cranby! Of course he lost and he was desperate. I do not share with Lord Steal the relationship that you seem to imagine, but he and Caroline are my friends and I would not stand by and do nothing when I saw a way out. Besides, Sir Gordon made me angry."

"Ira furor brevis est?" he said with considerable irony.

"Anger is a short madness? My scheme may have been mad, but it got Peter out of Cranby's hands."

"Steal is a thoughtless young puppy. As long as I have control of his affairs, Tresham is not his to lose. Cranby certainly wished to get him into his power before Peter married and came into his estates and Miss Brandon's fortune. But for God's sake, I should not have allowed it to stand! My ward's original debts were quite within my power to settle for him, if he had only kept his head and come to me."

"Perhaps if you were not such a bully he would have come to you!" Jessica flared. "He is afraid of you, my lord!"

"Really? I make most mortals quake in their tracks apparently, except you. Perhaps, however, in future you will refer my ward to me, before leaping so precipitately to his rescue?"

Jessica set her glass down so violently that the wine spilled. Why must she always quarrel with him? Deyncourt must think her all the more involved with Peter. It was too absurd, when she was hoping her strategy with Caroline had just done the trick to break his infatuation. But better that they quarrel than that he discover what she suspected was the true state of her emotions. She got up to go, but Michael suddenly caught her hand.

"There is only one thing you have forgotten, Miss Whinburn. You owe me for the rose."

"You offered it freely, my lord. We came here at your suggestion."

"Yes, but I did not expect you to hit it."

"It's rather an uneven debt, isn't it? I have absolutely nothing in the world. You have an entire garden at Marchmont and a glory of flowers here, but you cannot be generous enough to let me have just one, even for the sake of Caroline Brandon."

"It only caused her to faint," he said deliberately.

"So it did!"

He paced back across the room, desolate in the knowledge of what he suspected, and his complete helplessness in the face of it. Yet when he turned his face was once again the perfect mask. "Let me take you home," he said at last.

"And will that cancel the debt?"

"By no means. But I owe it to Lady Emilia to at least lend you that courtesy after allowing you to make yourself the center of the latest scandal."

"But I do not intend to go home, my lord, so I do not need your assistance." And she left him standing in the dark study.

Jessica marched up the street, maid in tow. Damn Deyncourt and all his arrogant pride! Peter had taken Caroline home after her dramatic faint, and she had to know if her ruse had worked. She was admitted to the Brandon home and shown into the parlor. As she waited while the footman inquired whether his mistress was sufficiently recovered to receive visitors, Peter entered the room. He looked extremely sheepish.

"Miss Whinburn, can I talk to you for a moment?" She nodded, and allowed him to guide her to a chair. "I have a confession to make. You will think me the worst kind of idiot."

"No, I shan't. Pray, go on."

"You see, I think I've misjudged you! I thought you so feminine! God knows how, after all the things you've done. I was willfully blind, I suppose. When I saw you firing that pistol in Deyncourt's garden, just as cool as a cucumber, I was taken aback, I can tell you! Do you know, you really are a virago? Deyncourt warned me that you were."

Jessica laughed. "How long it has taken you to see it!"

"You're not offended, are you?"

"Of course not, I have been trying to tell you so myself ever since we met."

He stood up and began to walk up and down the room. "When Caroline fainted in my arms, I suddenly realized how very dear she has become to me. She's not as dashing as you, of course, but she's as pretty and delicate as a dove. We have really become the very best of friends, and she needs a fellow who can protect and take care of her. I shall cherish her all my life. I swore her an oath that I'll never gamble again and I meant it. I shall be a model!"

"I'm very relieved to hear it, my lord."

"Are you really?"

Jessica leapt up and held out her hand. "I am in alt, Lord Steal. Nothing you could tell me would make me any happier. Now, let's be the best of friends and shake hands on it."

Her hand was grasped and pumped vigorously up and down. "And thank you for what you did, too," Peter added, coloring. "Winning Tresham back from Cranby like that! I only hope you won't pay for it. It wasn't the least ladylike, you know. Shooting flowers." He grinned.

"Fiddlesticks! Lord Deyncourt lent the entire scene his credence by inviting me into his garden. I have been led to believe ever since I arrived in town—by more people than I care to remember—that he is the very model of everything that is most admired and can do no wrong. How could I possibly suffer from acting under his auspices?"

"Well, I hope you're right, that's all. Now, you had better go up and see Caroline. She's resting, but she'll be all right."

Jessica shook him by the hand again, and went up the stairs. Miss Brandon had been reclining on the chaise longue, but when she saw her friend she jumped up and hugged her. She didn't look in the least delicate.

"However did you know to give me such good advice, Miss Whinburn?" she cried. "Was it so very wicked of me to pretend to faint?"

"Of course not! *Probitas laudatur et alget.*" Caroline looked puzzled. "Juvenal," explained Jessica. " '*Virtue may be praised, but it's often neglected*'—without a helping hand, that is."

Caroline laughed. "Yet I confess that I really was quite shocked. Where on earth did you learn to fire a gun like that? Never mind, you are my dearest friend. When I collapsed in Peter's arms, he became so solicitous; he has never been so before. We had the most wonderful talk." She blushed and looked down. "As he left, you know, he was actually so bold as to ask for a kiss."

"Then I hope you gave him one."

Caroline's cheeks flamed like a beacon. "Oh, Jessica, it was wonderful!"

Sir Gordon Cranby had stalked from Deyncourt House in a white rage. Shrugging off the little gaggle of cronies who had tried to offer their condolences, he was blind to all passersby. Within fifteen minutes he had stormed into the Incomparable Melton's boudoir. Honoria sat up at the sight of his face.

"For heaven's sake, Cranby! You look completely blue-deviled! Even you might at least knock!"

"Damnation, Honoria! Be quiet and listen!" Rapidly he told her of the wager over the rose and its dénouement in Deyncourt's garden. "The work and plans of six months, smashed in a moment! Deyncourt would never have found out. I had Steal right where I wanted him, in the very palm of my hand. I'd have had him on his knees if it hadn't been for that Whinburn chit! However was I to know that she could handle a pistol like that?"

"Well, it was a crazy risk to take! If you already had a promise of Tresham, why on earth did you wager at all?"

"How could I refuse such a bet? Half of London was witness to the transaction. I should have looked the complete fool!"

"Which you do now anyway! Half of London, you say?" The Incomparable Melton wrinkled her lovely brow. "What do you intend to do about it?"

Cranby laughed. It was a remarkably unpleasant sound. "Lord Steal may keep Tresham, debts and all." He picked up a lock of Honoria's bright hair and spun it thoughtfully in his fingers. "I think it's time that you told Deyncourt that little tidbit that you learned from Cicely Pratchett."

"About the Blue Boar? But how will that help you? He will only force Jessica Whinburn and Steal to marry."

"At which point I shall be ready to console the jilted Miss Brandon, dear cousin. I had hoped to gain her fortune and Tresham as well, but it doesn't pay to be greedy. The fifty thousand will have to be enough by itself. Of course, it's extremely tiresome to have to take on the milk-and-water miss with the blunt, but many a lesser man has managed an unwanted wife, no doubt I shall, too."

"Managed to totally ignore her, you mean! Really, Cranby, you are incorrigible."

"You are hardly in a position to carp! If Deyncourt knew that the fair Honoria had so carelessly depleted her own fortune at the tables and was hoping to bring it all to rights by battening onto his, he might not offer for you, after all."

Honoria blushed scarlet, but then she gave her cousin a lovely smile. "Then it would indeed seem to be time to tell him of the disgraceful behavior of his ward at the Blue Boar. It can only serve both our interests."

Cranby grinned back. "My thoughts entirely, my dear. Within three months we shall both be wed—you to Deyncourt and I to Caroline Brandon. Then we can have the pleasure of cuckolding them both at the same time. Lord Steal and poor Miss Jessica Whinburn will have to do their best to subsist at Tresham, the pariahs of society and poor as church mice."

Lady Honoria ordered her carriage and went straight to Deyncourt House. She took the precaution of bringing Cicely Pratchett with her. The earl was alone in his study, but he welcomed her in with perfect courtesy and ordered wine for them both.

"I have just heard, my lord, of the latest scandalous escapade involving our poor Miss Whinburn. Northumberland must be a perfect backwater, if she is an example of North Country manners."

"No doubt."

"I know you have done your noble best to cover for her, my lord, for the sake of Lady Emilia, so it gives me real pain to tell you that there is much worse." He raised an eyebrow. Honoria looked down at her reticule in lovely confusion. "I hardly know how to tell you this, except to come right out with it. Miss Whinburn's virtue has been compromised by Lord Steal, and it is bound to get out. Pratchett here witnessed it and by my orders has told no one, but these things never stay secret."

She peeked up at him under her eyelashes, and had the satisfaction of seeing the lines beside his mouth contract very slightly. "Go on."

"There is apparently an inn called the Blue Boar not too far from town, but not the sort of place where people of quality usually stop; nevertheless, Lord Steal took her there on their journey from Tresham to London. They spent the night together."

Michael's voice remained perfectly calm. "And you were witness to this, Miss Pratchett?"

"Yes, my lord," replied the maid boldly. "I could not be mistaken. Miss Whinburn did not sleep in her own bed; she spent the night in Lord Steal's bedroom. I saw him kiss her with my very own eyes. And she had a night rail of silk, more valuable than the rest of her clothes flung together. I reckon he gave it to her."

Lady Honoria was the very picture of maidenly modesty as delicate color suffused her perfect cheeks. "I hope you will not think worse of me, my lord, for being the harbinger of such dreadful news! I declare that not a word would have passed my lips, except that I was so shocked when I first heard of it that I told my cousin Cranby. He swore himself to secrecy, but after what has happened, I'm afraid he might try to drown his sorrows. And when he is in his cups—who knows?"

There was no further change at all in Michael's expression. He set down his wine and stood up. "Let me call for your carriage. The indelicate nature of this story has obviously quite overset you. Of course, you saw it only your duty to tell me and I am confident you will not breathe a word to anyone. Never fear, I shall take appropriate action. If Miss Whinburn is ruined, there will have to be a marriage, won't there?"

He bowed over her hand and kissed it. After she had gone he stared quietly at the fireplace for a few moments, then he rang for his manservant. Dover entered the room and stopped short.

"Is something wrong, my lord?"

"I am going to Lady Emilia's. I shall walk. Send a message to Lord Steal. He is to drop anything he is doing and meet me there immediately."

Jessica returned to her great-aunt's in a glow of satisfaction. Now, at last, perhaps she could give attention to her own problems. What would happen to her reputation now she had behaved so scandalously in public? Well, to the devil with it! It had been worth anything to see Caroline and Peter so happy.

Lady Emilia heard her out with her lips pursed together. "I have tried to impress upon you the necessity for a young girl to behave with the strictest decorum. To take an action that makes you the talk of the town! Whatever were you thinking of? I warned your father of the consequences, should he teach you such outlandish things." Then to Jessica's amazement the old lady's face suddenly broke into a merry smile. "Yet it was splendidly done. If you're going to do something, do it well!"

"Then I'm glad you approve, Aunt Emilia."

"Now I did not say I approved, but I do wish I'd been there to see their faces!" And the old lady went off into peals of laughter. "It will be all of a nine-days' wonder; then the *ton* will find something else to talk about. We'll defy the lot of them together! My dear Jessica, there's not much you could do that Deyncourt and I together couldn't brazen out for you!"

"I wish I could agree, Lady Emilia." Deyncourt stood in the doorway to the drawing room. His face was set like stone. "Lady Honoria has just been kind enough to inform me otherwise."

Lady Emilia looked at Michael in complete surprise.

"Whatever do you mean? Between us I should have thought we had enough consequence to offset anything Jessica could possibly do."

"Except one thing, my lady."

"Which is?"

"To share a bedroom at the Blue Boar with my ward."

Chapter 15

There was a perfect silence for a moment. "How on earth did Lady Honoria find out?" asked Jessica eventually.

"From Cicely Pratchett, Miss Whinburn."

Lady Emilia turned to Jessica. "Surely this is not true, child?"

The color flooded back to Jessica's face. "Oh, Lord!" she said at last. "I'm afraid that it is—but not in that way! I mean, it was all a silly mistake. Peter snored away the entire night in the chair with the key in his back pocket. He was unconscious till morning. Nothing happened!"

"For heaven's sake!" snapped Aunt Emilia. "I should think not indeed! But that is entirely beside the point. If this gets out, you are ruined. Will Lady Honoria feel obliged to tell her acquaintance, Deyncourt?"

"She as good as told me she was about to publish the tale in a penny broadsheet, Lady Emilia."

There was a commotion on the stairs and Peter burst unceremoniously into the room. "I received your message, Deyncourt! Has anything happened to Caroline? Oh, hello, Miss Whinburn." His face was red with the effort of running all the way from his lodgings and made a wonderful clash with a very fine puce coat.

"There is no need to have apoplexy!" announced Lady Emilia with authority. "Miss Brandon isn't involved. I think everyone had better sit down. I shall call for some wine, and we shall discuss this like civilized Englishmen and women. Tell him what Lady Honoria said, Deyncourt. Then I want an account from the beginning, young man."

Michael explained in a sentence, and then Jessica allowed Peter to tell the whole sorry tale. "It was dashed stupid of me," he said at the end. "Miss Whinburn was quite trapped, but it was all my silly blunder. I was completely foxed. You must believe that it wasn't her fault! And nothing improper happened, I swear it!"

"This is beyond the bounds of anything, sir!" cried Lady Emilia. "How could you have been so lost to all propriety? There is nothing else for it: You children will have to marry, and immediately!"

"But I can't marry Miss Whinburn," wailed Peter. "I'm in love with Caroline!"

"I am so glad to hear that you have had such a sudden change of heart, sir," said Michael. "It's a little late, isn't it?"

Peter leapt from his chair. "Oh, God! I shan't ruin the lives of three people just because of something so stupid! Miss Whinburn don't want to marry me. And what about Caroline? She loves me."

"You might have thought of that, Steal, before you kissed Miss Whinburn in front of Lady Honoria's maid." Except for the ice in his tone, Michael still seemed perfectly unmoved by the proceedings.

"Did I kiss you?" said Peter, looking blankly at Jessica. "Oh, I suppose I did! But it didn't signify anything! I thought she was a different person."

In spite of the gravity of all their faces, Jessica suddenly felt giggles bubbling up inside her. "That is hardly a flattering remark, Lord Steal," she said. "I don't want to marry you either, if it's any consolation. In fact, I refuse to do so."

"But you must," insisted Lady Emilia. "I want to hear no more on the matter. There is no living this down. If you shared a bedroom with a man, you shall marry him!"

"But Deyncourt did it first!" cried Peter. "Jessica spent several nights in his bedchamber at Tresham. Why doesn't that count?"

At which point, Michael began suddenly to laugh. The others looked at him in astonishment.

"I have never had the vapors in my life!" snapped Lady Emilia. "But this is enough to try the patience of a saint! Has my great-niece spent a night in everybody's bedroom?"

"I trust not, Lady Emilia," replied Michael quite seriously. "But Peter is right. I allowed Miss Whinburn to sleep in my bed. She wore my nightshirt. We shared a most improper intimacy of situation and manner. The fact that my motives were only to save her from the hangman does not excuse me. Miss Whinburn shall marry me."

At which point it was Jessica's turn to leap to her feet. "I shall do no such thing, my lord!"

"But you will, Miss Whinburn," he replied.

"It's capital!" cried Peter. "If you announce an engagement right away, it would only make Lady Honoria seem jealous if she was to spread tales!"

"Good heavens, Lord Steal," said Aunt Emilia innocently. "I believe you have hit upon something. For the Incomparable Melton to tell the story under the circumstances would reflect worse on her than on Jessica, for she would not be believed. She would merely appear piqued at being thrown over—as if she was making up scandal out of sour grapes. I have never had much use for Lady Honoria and I have not tried to hide the fact, but I'll allow this much: if an engagement is announced between Lord Deyncourt and my great-niece, she would have too much pride to breathe another word about the Blue Boar."

"And anything Cranby would say would be put down to spite over his loss of the bet!" added Peter with enthusiasm.

"Plus everybody knows that Deyncourt would not offer for Miss Whinburn if I had compromised her. He'd never take someone else's abandoned mistress to wife!"

"Indeed," said Michael, and he turned his bland gaze on Jessica. "So you see, Miss Whinburn, if you refuse my hand, you ruin Miss Brandon's happiness, for then the fable will out and you will have to marry my ward. Accept it, and all may be neatly settled. I think we shall have to give way with good grace, don't you?"

"But it is all nonsense!"

"It is a simple matter of honor. I am guilty of the worst indiscretion and meekly accept my punishment."

Jessica's face flamed. If Caroline's future were not involved, she would scrub floors before accepting such an offer. But she could not destroy Caroline's happiness after working so hard to accomplish it. This need only be a temporary solution. Jessica turned to Michael. "Very well, my lord. I accept."

The gentlemen got up to leave. For the plan to succeed, it was critical that the engagement be advertised right away. Jessica could not even guess at Deyncourt's thoughts as he bowed over her hand.

"You do believe us, don't you?" she asked. "Nothing improper took place at the Blue Boar."

"How can it be doubted, Jessica? As Lord Steal so cogently pointed out, no one in my position would dream of taking to wife a lady with a sullied reputation. Of course, it would have been the ultimate weapon in your determination to disrupt my plans—to force Miss Brandon to cry off."

"You may think what you like," replied Jessica acidly. "I can only wonder why, if you are determined to believe so, you do not take this opportunity to take the revenge that you promised."

"I am taking my revenge, madam. I can't think of a better punishment than marriage to me. Good day, Miss Whinburn."

* * *

"He has not!" cried the Incomparable Melton.

"I'm afraid so, dear cousin. The entire town is agog with it. Miss Jessica Whinburn is to become Countess of Deyncourt."

Lady Honoria picked up a very expensive cut-glass jar of French perfume and flung it across the room. "I shall be made the laughingstock of society!"

Sir Gordon grimaced as the powerful scent from the shattered bottle began to fill the chamber, and he snapped the delicate stem of his quizzing glass. "But more to the point, sweet Honoria, there will be no repining Miss Caroline Brandon to fall into my arms; she will have married Steal. If you act with sufficient panache, you need not even appear at a disadvantage. You have only to whistle and a dozen young bloods will offer for you."

"Yes, but they're not Deyncourt! He has done it just to spite me! Deyncourt knows perfectly well that now I should only look bad to tell the story of the Blue Boar. Worse, I should not be believed. How dare he do it!"

"Yet I am the one who is most damaged. The marriage of Steal and Caroline Brandon will now go ahead. I am nearly at the bottom of my resources. If one of us does not marry a fortune soon, what on earth will become of us?"

"What do you suggest?" asked Lady Honoria sullenly.

"I suggest that you bring Deyncourt up to snuff and make him marry you, my dear. If the orange-haired hussy were to disappear, for example, surely it would not be beyond your powers? You are the most beautiful woman in London. If necessary, cry rape."

The Incomparable Melton looked carefully at her cousin. "And why should Miss Whinburn disappear, sir?"

"Oh, I don't know," replied Cranby casually. "Perhaps she will decide to visit the Colonies? Or join a harem in the mysterious East? I understand she is an adventurous sort. There is no telling what she might get into her head."

"Cranby, you would not?"

"For the loss of fifty thousand pounds and one of the finest homes in the nation, there is quite a bit I might do. Miss Jessica Whinburn owes something to both of us. I know I can rely on your help, of course?"

Lady Honoria took a deep breath of the heavily scented air. "Of course, cousin. Have I ever let you down?"

Michael took Jessica out in his phaeton the very next day in order to promenade her in the Park. She had not wanted to go, but Aunt Emilia insisted, and Michael threatened to drag her bodily from the house if she did not immediately accompany him.

"If we are to carry this off, Miss Whinburn," he said as they bowled through the traffic behind the superb horses, "we had better begin to make a public demonstration of our affection."

"You are a consummate actor, of course, my lord. I shall do my best to match your artifice!" They smiled and nodded at their acquaintance as they passed them in their carriages. Several times they were forced to stop, and accept the congratulations and curious questions of society. "The entire *ton* thought you about to propose to Lady Honoria," Jessica commented as he let the horses go on. "I am glad that she will not be able to spread scandal and hurt Miss Brandon, but you don't seem in the least concerned about her broken heart."

He raised an eyebrow. "Do not tell me that you are full of sympathy for the Incomparable, Jessica. However, if it will put your mind at rest, be assured that she and I shared no tender feelings whatsoever. Her pride may be a little damaged, but that is all."

"But did you not intend to propose to her?"

"Of course. She would make anybody an admirable countess."

Jessica was silenced for a moment. "Did your parents not share any tender feelings?" she asked suddenly.

He looked amazed. "My parents? Good God! My mother claimed to be an invalid and spent her days reclining in the drawing room accepting the visits of a succession of young blades, who would read her poetry and sigh over her sapphire eyes. She was reputed a great beauty, and her primary interest in life was to perfect her toilette. My father, meanwhile, made no secret of his grand passion: a dancer—until she was replaced with an opera singer."

"It doesn't sound like a very happy home."

"Are you about to get misty-eyed over my deprived childhood?" He gave her an amused glance. "As it happens, I was very happy. I worshipped my mother from afar from the warm lap of my magnificent loving nanny, who spoiled me abominably. Then, when I was eight, I was sent off to school. It was a moderately brutal place, but I was able to hold my own and in the end I enjoyed it. On holidays, I was at Marchmont with Aunt Sophy. I fished, hunted, swam, ran, climbed trees, and did all the other things that boys are supposed to do. It was a wonderful place to grow up."

"What is Castle Deyncourt like?"

"It sits on a hill in a bend of the Avon River, in forest that dates back to William the Conqueror. From the battlements, you can see into Wales. It's older than Tresham or Marchmont; in fact, the heart of the house is the medieval keep. There is still a stunning collection of the mail that my ancestors wore, and I'm the proud possessor of a complete armory of pikes and maces. I am well positioned to form my own private army, should I wish!"

"Then it is a castle?"

"Essentially, though softened and changed with the years. The arrow-slit windows were enlarged in the sixteenth century. My father added modern chimneys and kitchens, and he had Capability Brown landscape the grounds, so the moat has become a lake with swans. The estate runs over some of the loveliest countryside in England. You will like it."

"Me?" asked Jessica.

"We are engaged to be wed, Jessie dear, remember? You are about to become mistress of Castle Deyncourt yourself."

Jessica looked down and was not surprised to find that her hands were clenched into fists. "Has it not occurred to you, my lord, that once Caroline and Peter are safely wed, I could cry off, and release us both from this absurd arrangement."

"Yes, but you will not. Unless we continue to block Lady Honoria's tongue, she could create misery for Miss Brandon, even after she becomes the new Lady Steal. We are stuck with each other."

They had pulled up in front of Deyncourt House, and Jessica was handed down and led inside. They went into the cool study where she had sipped wine after shooting the rose. She looked out into the lovely garden. The earl moved to stand behind her. "You must begin to call me Michael. I cannot have my wife mumbling 'my lord' in every other sentence."

She turned and faced him. She had no idea of his feelings. "Your word is my command, of course."

"Secondly, unlike my parents, I intend to have a large family. If we are to wed, will you accept me as a lover? I am aware that you hold me in considerable dislike. If it is sufficient that you will not be able to make love to me, then I'd like to know."

Her heart was in her throat. Deyncourt might wear a perfect mask of indifference, but he must in truth be both angry and disgusted that he had been trapped into marrying her. If he knew for a moment that she had fallen under his spell, it would be the ultimate mortification.

He smiled at her, but his eyes remained guarded, as if some dark secret lay in their blue depths. "Come here," he said at last. Jessica boldly stepped up to him. *He looks dangerous,* she thought, *as if a fire long banked was about to be given too much air.* "I already have reason to believe that we might be compatible, but it wouldn't hurt to be sure."

Casually he unbuttoned his jacket and waistcoat, and

then took both her hands and placed them against his fine shirt. Her blood began to hammer in her ears. She could feel the warmth and strength of his skin underneath. The clear, clean scent of his body ran into the center of her being. Under her fingers, his heartbeat throbbed steadily.

She looked defiantly up at him. It took every ounce of her self-control to speak calmly. "You are deliberately trying to humiliate me, my lord."

"Michael."

"Very well—Michael. I should like nothing better than a large family. It would mean that I should not have to accept your advances more often than once a year."

"Dear God, Jessie!" *He must know! How badly had she been hurt, how badly damaged?* He caught her head in both hands and kissed her, and her fingers ran boldly under his jacket to feel the smooth muscles of his back. When he pulled back, they were both breathless. Michael felt a desperate confusion of emotions. "Not once a year, dear Jessie! Whenever I like."

Suddenly she was furious. "I have agreed to this match entirely against my better judgment, my lord earl! If you are going to browbeat me, I shall cry off! And be damned to you, your ward, and everybody to do with you!"

"Miss Whinburn, you have already given me your answer. You cannot deny it."

"That I am not impervious to your practiced lechery? What kind of a basis for marriage is that? Of course, I find you attractive! But I'm damned if I will marry a bully who takes delight in my humiliation."

Light and shadow from the windows haunted his features. "Humiliation was not my intent, Jessica," he said softly, and strode away across the room. Then quite deliberately he faced his own demons, and knew he must give this up—whether from honor or cowardice, he couldn't say. When he turned once more to face her, his smile was as close as he could make it to the expression of the earl who took care of fluttering, unfledged chicks. What else could he do? "Forget it! Let us make peace! We shall squire each other around all the fashionable salons in apparent harmony, smile graciously at the flattery and congratulations of the *beau monde*, and marry in style as an earl and his countess should. Then, if you still cannot stand the sight of me, we'll annul the wedding, and I will set you up in a household of your own with an independent income. If such an arrangement was good enough for Henry VIII and Anne of Cleves, it is surely good enough for us."

"Anne of Cleves, the Flemish mare?"

"That's right: the only one not to die or be beheaded other than Katherine Parr, of course, who outlived him."

"Yes, Henry had met his match with Anne. Surely you don't concede that you have met your match with me?"

"Never. But I will marry you anyway, if you will accept the terms. Agreed?"

Jessica smoothed down her dress and refused to meet his eyes. He had offered her a way out! "Agreed. Though I believe it took an Act of Parliament to dissolve their union."

"As it would take one for ours, but the Lords will do it, just as a favor to me."

And with that, she had to be content. It was only afterward that she wondered to quite which set of terms he believed she had agreed.

Lady Emilia was unable to hide her glee. The dowagers made a grim procession of bobbing plumed hats and jewels as they came to offer their felicitations on the match. Lady Mapleton was among the first to arrive and she came to offer her house for a ball. Jessica would have tried to demur, but Aunt Emilia was adamant.

"It is the ultimate accolade, Jessica. It will also give the Incomparable Melton a chance to demonstrate to society her complete indifference. Deyncourt can lead her out in a dance or two, and she can use her beauty to attract every other man in the room. Lady Mapleton knows exactly what she is about for her niece, and I admire their grace in defeat. Nothing would be more churlish than for you to refuse such an invitation.''

Jessica sighed. "I believe I understand what Peter's mother meant when she said she had no desire to go to another dance or party in her life.''

"Stuff! You shall go and thoroughly enjoy yourself. After all, now that you are betrothed to Deyncourt it is unexceptionable if he dances with you several times. No man of my acquaintance is a more graceful dancer. Once you are married, he would look the fool to squire his own wife around more than once. So enjoy it while you may, my child.''

"I believe, Aunt, that I have had enough of society's absurd rules. Why on earth should a man marry a lady, if he is no longer to be seen enjoying her company once they are wed?'' And to Aunt Emilia's complete astonishment, Jessica burst into tears.

Mapleton House was once again a blaze of light. Since it was not at all done to be seen in the same gown twice, Jessica wore a new creation. Her objections about the waste of it were overridden by her great-aunt, who argued that appearances were everything if they were to succeed in their bluff. The new dress clung lightly to her figure as she moved. Over an underskirt of sheer white silk, ice green lace was worked into a pattern of tiny ivy leaves. Fine embroidered trails of ivy traced up over the short bodice and puff sleeves, so that her arms seemed to be coming out of a woodland bower. Around her neck lay a chain of gold with a simple oval gold locket. It was a gift from Deyncourt. Nothing else seemed to have so cemented their odd engagement in her mind as the gift of jewelry. She almost wished that he had delivered it in person, so that she could have told him in no uncertain terms that such presents were entirely unnecessary. Instead it had been brought by a messenger and she had been obliged to open the box in front of Lady Emilia, who insisted that of course she must wear it to the ball. Her only relief was that the locket was empty. At least he hadn't tried to embarrass her with a portrait of himself, or worse—a lock of hair. Suddenly she felt better about wearing the necklace. Aunt Emilia was vastly relieved.

Everybody she had met since she had come to London was there, and the ball progressed exactly as her aunt had predicted. Michael led Lady Honoria out into the first dance, and gave her a flatteringly correct amount of attention throughout the evening. The Incomparable Melton was able to laugh and look gracious, and never lacked for a partner. The ball might ostensibly have been inspired by Jessica's engagement to the earl, but the Incomparable Melton was still the belle of the evening. Michael also partnered Caroline while Jessica stepped around the room with Peter. Finally the four of them went in to dinner together. If any word of the events at the Blue Boar had already leaked out among the gossips, this performance would effectively crush it. Jessica only wished that she was having a better time. When Lord Clarence came over to offer his felicitations, she was beginning to develop a headache in earnest.

"Deyncourt knows what he's about, madam," cried the judge with forced gallantry. "Beat me to the punch. Something about you caught my eye the first time I saw you, and I don't hesitate to say it!"

"I also remember our first meeting, my lord," she replied with a smile. "But I did not believe we should suit."

Jessica would not allow herself to give up and go home. However, at last the carriage was called for, Deyncourt bowed over her hand and kissed it, and she could retreat with dignity.

Lady Emilia decided that discretion was indeed the better part of valor, and pretended to sleep in her corner of the chaise. It worried the old lady a good deal to see that her great-niece once again had big tears rolling down her cheeks, but she knew much better than to badger her about it. It was only natural that the poor child should feel overwhelmed. The Earl of Deyncourt was quite a catch for Miss Whinburn, even if she was a Shay on her mother's side. Aunt Emilia allowed herself one self-satisfied smile.

Jessica kissed her aunt goodnight and ran up the stairs to her room. The note was waiting on her pillow. "There is something I must say, Jessica. I beg you will come down to the stables right away. Deyncourt."

Chapter 16

Jessica took a good look at herself in the glass. Good heavens! He would think she was going into a decline! Splashing cold water into a basin, she vigorously washed her face. Whatever the earl had suddenly decided he couldn't wait to tell her, he would not have the satisfaction of seeing her looking so feeble! Without another thought, she went down through the empty house and took her cloak from its peg. The servants had long since gone to bed; she and her aunt had arrived back from Lady Mapleton's ball well after midnight. Only her aunt's maid and the butler had waited up for them.

Unlocking the big, heavy back door and sliding back the bolts, she slipped out of the house and walked quickly past the shrubbery into the cobbled yard. The carriage horses were contentedly munching in their stalls, and the ostlers had turned in for the night. The candle was blown out in Coachman's room over the stable as she turned the corner. Nobody seemed to waiting.

"Deyncourt?" she queried softly.

Her response was to be instantly suffocated in darkness. Something, a sack or a blanket, had been thrust over her head, and the ends wrapped somehow so that her arms were pinned to her sides. An extremely businesslike hand clenched her chin, so that she could not cry out. Without more ado, she found herself being rapidly hustled from the yard and bundled into a carriage. The horses sprang into action, and the seat swayed as they trotted away up the street. As soon as her initial shock subsided, Jessica was furious. Was this his idea of a joke? The hand relaxed its pressure on her chin a little and she was able to speak.

"I would very much appreciate," she said acidly, "having this blanket removed from my face. It stinks."

"Rough methods, my dear, are sometimes the most expedient," said smooth tones. "Never mind, we're almost there." Jessica had no trouble whatsoever in recognizing the voice. She kept silent. "What, Miss Whinburn, no maidenly protestations? No 'Oh, how dare you?' to enliven our journey?"

"I am not a great admirer of Gothic romance, sir," she replied. "I doubt seriously that having felt justified in abducting me for some unknown purpose you would be in the least moved by tearful entreaties."

"How right you are, my dear," the voice said.

"It is nonetheless extremely difficult to carry on a conversation with a horse blanket over one's head. Since I know you by your voice to be Sir Gordon Cranby, it really is not serving any purpose at all except to make it more likely that I shall be sick."

The suffocating blanket was removed, and Cranby looked her in the eye. Jessica glared back at him.

"You are not injured, I trust?" he inquired politely. There was no one else in the carriage.

"I have no broken bones, if that's what you mean."

"And you are not curious as to our destination?"

"Of course, I am raddled with curiosity. But I imagine that if you intended to tell me, you would have done so. Therefore I did not see the point in wasting my breath to ask."

"Never mind. We are here. Do not attempt any heroics. All the persons within earshot are my servants."

The carriage stopped, and Cranby handed her down. They were in a courtyard serving some small town houses. All the doors and windows were shuttered and dark. She had no doubt that Cranby would force her if she was to be awkward, so she walked quietly enough beside him into the dark hallway. A door opened and light flooded out, causing her to blink. She was thrust inside the room and pushed into a chair. It seemed to be a disused parlor. The furniture was originally of good quality, but old and shabby. Rows of leather-bound books were veiled in a thin layer of dust. No fire burned in the basket grate, but one brace of candles sat on the table at her elbow. The only other occupant of the room glittered like the sun, her golden hair glimmering in the candlelight. Sir Gordon Cranby sat down at the table opposite Jessica, and Lady Honoria Melton came and stood beside him.

"Was it any problem?" she asked.

"Miss Whinburn was all cooperation; your surmise as to a suitable bait was bang on the mark, cousin dear."

"And you will take her down there tonight?"

"I see no reason to not to set out right away, do you?"

Honoria laughed and sat down. "The sooner the better."

"I am not sure that I follow this conversation," said Jessica. "However, I would prefer it if you would not discuss me as if I were not here, like a child or an imbecile."

"Our apologies, madam," replied Cranby with a bow. "We have been shamefully negligent hosts. Let me give you a glass of wine." He stood and went to a side cupboard, where he poured three glasses. "A toast, I think! To adventure?"

"By all means," replied Jessica, gulping at her glass. "To adventure! I only hope you intend to let me choose my own?"

"Miss Whinburn," replied Honoria. Her wine lay

untouched at her elbow. "You didn't really think we would let you get away with this, did you?"

"Get away with what? It seems to me it was Sir Gordon who was trying to get away with something that did not belong to him."

"You refer to Tresham, of course." Cranby smiled, and stared at her through his quizzing glass. "Alas, I had so looked forward to being surrounded in the evenings with all those lugubrious portraits of the Steal ancestors. But my cousin refers to Deyncourt. She had quite set her heart on being a countess."

"Oh, be quiet, Cranby," snapped Honoria. She turned her velvet eyes on Jessica. In the soft light from the candles, she was quite lovely. "Miss Whinburn. It is as clear as a bell that you and Deyncourt have announced your betrothal for all the wrong reasons, so I have no compunction in asking you to do what I say."

"Which is?"

"Write a note to the earl, begging off from the engagement."

"And if I do not?"

"Then I will hurt you," said Cranby quietly.

"Goodness!" exclaimed Jessica lightly. "You are a nasty fellow, aren't you?" Cranby merely smiled. "Very well, then. I have no tolerance at all for pain. Since my acceptance of Lord Deyncourt is a matter of perfect indifference to me, I shall be perfectly happy to write whatever you suggest."

"Wise woman," replied Cranby.

"And when it is written, may I return to my great-aunt's house? I have not even had time to change my dress."

"Regrettably not, my dear. You will inform the earl that you are going away, but you will not tell him the truth."

"Which is?"

"That you will take ship from Bristol to whichever port in the Colonies is available."

She took another gulp of the wine. "And I am to make this journey in my little sprigs of lace ivy?"

"Only as far as Bath, Miss Whinburn. I shall see that you are suitably set up for your sea voyage. What on earth do you take me for, a barbarian?"

"Oh, my mistake, Sir Gordon!"

Jessica's brain felt like it was spinning, but the thoughts were totally clear. Her headache had entirely gone away. She had no doubt at all that Cranby would do exactly as he threatened. He would probably put her on a perfectly respectable boat, and might even provide her with some bare necessities for the voyage, but when—or rather if— she ever returned, Deyncourt would have married Honoria. Suddenly, she couldn't bear it. She finished the glass of wine. It wouldn't hurt to be a little fortified if she was to face a journey to Bath with Sir Gordon!

"What do you want me to say?" she asked.

There was a pen and paper on the table, and Honoria thrust it toward her. "My dear Lord Deyncourt," she began to dictate. "It is with great regret that I beg to inform you—"

"Oh, heavens!" cried Jessica. "He will know immediately that I didn't write it if I sound like a manners' book. Here, let me have the quill."

She pulled the paper to her and began to write. Her lovely copperplate handwriting flowed copiously across the paper. The capital letters in particular were done with great relish, their flourishes often running into the lines above and beneath.

"Here," she said when she had done. "Deyncourt will know that this was in my own words. I believe I have covered all the points you would have wished me to say?"

Honoria picked up the letter. "You do have a unique style, Miss Whinburn. Cranby, listen to this!" And she read it aloud:

"My dear Deyncourt: Vexatious as it may be to you, I have decided to go away. After the ball, my feelings have undergone a serious change. Absolutely nothing would induce me to marry you. Question your own behavior if you must. Very certainly you will do so when you get this.

An English gentleman's classic response! Squelch any thought of trying to find me. Vainly will you seek happiness unless you marry the Lady of your heart, the Incomparable. Signed, Jessica Whinburn.''

Cranby gave a titter. "Admirable, Miss Whinburn."

"Oh, wait," said Jessica. "I had better add a postscript, so that he will know that I am really distraught."

She whipped the letter back out of Honoria's hand and added: "PS. I know you will read this missive as carefully as if it were something from Phaedrus for Bromley and Finch.''

"Who on earth are Bromley and Finch?" asked Honoria suspiciously.

"Publishers," replied Cranby.

"I once had literary ambitions," announced Jessica. "Deyncourt is the only one who knows about it. It will confirm in his mind that I am serious, don't you think?"

"Undoubtedly," said Honoria with a smile of genuine amusement and relief. "You are a wiser woman than I thought, Miss Whinburn."

"Thank you, my lady. You know, I never understood for a moment why Lord Deyncourt did not marry you years ago. How could a carrot-top like me hope to rival the Incomparable Melton? Before I leave for Timbuktu, however, I do want to thank you for lending me Cicely Pratchett. She's a wonderful lady's maid. Not only did she teach me how to bully my own crowning glory into some semblance of a presentable style, but the makeover of Caroline Brandon—that helped Lord Steal fall in love with her—was partly Cicely's idea, and partly your own. You've been a truer friend to us all than you know.''

Michael received the letter by messenger the next morning. He had just shrugged into his coat after grimacing at himself in the mirror. The ball had gone perfectly. Lady Honoria had been able to save face; whatever stories she might already have begun to put about would now die a natural death. Peter and Caroline were saved—the only thing about the evening from which he could derive any satisfaction. As he had surmised all those months ago, Miss Caroline Brandon would be the making of his heedless ward. Beneath that unprepossessing exterior was a very sensible young woman who would know exactly how to bring Peter to heel. She also loved the boy with an abiding emotion and that love was going to be returned. Peter would start a family and probably settle down to be the very model of a country gentleman. The eighth Earl of Deyncourt was a successful matchmaker! And, of course, he had been aided, not hindered, by the impulsive Miss Whinburn. Valiant, beautiful Jessica! Oh, dear God, must he be glad that she despised him? For once this mess was over, he must let her go her own way—for what the devil could he offer her?

"You're a damned fool, Michael Dechardon Grey!" he said aloud as he tied his cravat. It was a great deal easier for Henry. He loathed Anne of Cleves—and he did not loathe himself.

And then the footman had brought in the missive from Jessica. Rapidly he read it through twice. Something very odd and distinctly painful seemed to happen to his heart. He folded the letter and thrust it into his pocket. Within fifteen minutes he was hammering on Lady Emilia's elegant front door.

"The ladies are not at home to visitors, my lord," said the astonished butler.

"Lady Emilia may still be abed, sir, but she will wish to see me, even in her dressing gown!"

"Perhaps you would care to wait in the parlor, my lord?"

"Damn it all, man! Where is her room?" And pushing the scandalized butler aside, Michael ran up the stairs. When he reached the landing, he called out for Lady Emilia. Instantly the door to her room opened and her head popped out.

"Deyncourt! For heaven's sake, sir! You will wake the entire neighborhood! Are you foxed?"

"My lady, I must see you immediately. Where is Jessica?"

"Asleep in her bed, sir, like all decent folk! Have you entirely lost your senses?"

"Where is her room?"

"This is beyond anything! You shall not enter her bedroom, if you were betrothed six times over!"

Michael went up to the old lady and thrust out the note. "Read this!"

Lady Emilia retreated back into her boudoir and fetched her pince-nez. She also took a moment to straighten her lace nightcap in front of the mirror. "Sit down, Deyncourt," she ordered. The earl ignored her, and paced up and down the corridor while Lady Emilia perused Jessica's note. "What an extraordinary letter! What on earth does she mean? She would not have gone off without telling me. Perhaps she is taking her revenge for your shabby treatment of her! When she comes down for breakfast, I will ask her myself."

"Lady Emilia, I beg you will make sure she is indeed still in her room."

"Oh, poppycock!" said the old lady, but she bustled down the corridor and knocked at one of the white-painted doors. There was no answer. Puzzled, Aunt Emilia knocked again. With an exasperated oath, Michael stepped past her, opened the door, and went into the room. It was empty.

"Good God!" said Lady Emilia, following him.

"Indeed, my lady." Michael quickly searched about the room. "The bed is not slept in. She has taken nothing with her, not even her nightgown." He stopped for a moment, the silk garment in his hands. A memory of her in his room at Tresham threatened for a moment to undo his composure. He tossed the gown on the bed and went to her wardrobe. "The dress she wore last night is not here. She must still be wearing it; neither do I see the locket I gave her. If she had decided to cry off, she would first have returned it to me. I very much fear, dear friend, that something untoward has happened."

Aunt Emilia dashed away the tears that had suddenly

sprung to her eyes. "Then let us waste no more time, sir! We must find her right away. Would she have informed Caroline Brandon of her plans, do you think?"

"I don't know," replied Michael. "Get dressed, ma'am, and have breakfast. I shall send for Miss Brandon and Peter immediately. Never fear, I shall find her!"

All the bland control was gone from his features. It suddenly gave Aunt Emilia great satisfaction, in spite of her anxiety for Jessica, to see the perfect earl look so positively haggard. Within an hour they had been joined by Lord Steal and his betrothed. Both the young people gave signs of having dressed too quickly and hastened out. Peter had so forgotten himself as to leave off his waistcoat entirely, and Miss Brandon was wearing stockings that didn't match. Nobody seemed to notice.

"It's very odd, my lord," said Caroline, when she had read the letter. "To say that her feelings have undergone a serious change! She never claimed to be marrying you for love."

"That thought has already occurred to me," replied Michael grimly. "But then I think she may have been forced to write the letter."

"But it's exactly her style," said Peter.

"Though why she would direct you to question your own behavior, I don't know," sniffed Aunt Emilia.

"Yes," added Peter. "Anyone would know better than that! 'An English gentleman's classic response,' my foot! Rather the other way I should have said. That's not your usual style at all!" He colored as the earl gave him a quelling look.

"I am aware, dear ward, that you consider me a perfect tyrant, but it is not unknown for even Attila the Hun to introspect upon occasion."

"Jessica also knows perfectly well," continued Aunt Emilia, "that the Incomparable is not and never has been the 'Lady of your heart,' in spite of your magnificent performance last night!" She snorted.

"What do you think has happened?" asked Caroline in a small voice.

"I'm afraid that she has been abducted," said Michael. "And I believe I know by whom."

"You don't think the Incomparable Melton's got anything to do with it, do you?" squealed Peter. "Dash it all!"

"Lady Honoria is fast asleep in her bed. I have made inquiries. The servants vouch that she returned very late from the ball at Mapleton House, but has not stirred since, and I believe them."

"What's this about Bromley and Finch?" asked Caroline.

"Oh, they publish all those dreadful Latin and Greek readers that gentlemen are tormented with in their schooldays!" Peter was almost able to grin. "I received many a beating for not knowing my Latin grammar, I can tell you! But what on earth does Miss Whinburn know about Phaedrus?"

"Good Lord!" announced Michael suddenly. *Things aren't always as they appear.* "Oh, clever Jessica! Look at this!" He laid the letter out on the table and the others gathered around. "You will notice, I'm sure, that there is a particular emphasis on the capital letters."

"Very florid," said Aunt Emilia. "I am surprised at it in my great-niece."

Michael began to laugh. "Call for my horse to be saddled and sent round immediately! I am going to Bath!"

"Bath?" queried Peter.

"Indeed, sir. The capital letters in this note read: V I A—by way of—A Q V A E S V L I S. Aquae Sulis: the Roman name for Bath."

"But who on earth does she know in Bath?"

"Nobody, if my guess is correct. But Sir Gordon Cranby hails from there, doesn't he?"

"Cranby? The devil!"

"Exactly, sir."

"Can Lady Honoria give you the direction, do you suppose?" asked Caroline uncertainly.

"Undoubtedly she knows it, but short of torture, I would never get it out of her!"

"And what about that invincible charm?" said Aunt Emilia. "Pretend to believe this missive, go to the Incomparable, and declare your passion. Could you not get her to tell you her cousin's address?"

"My dear friends," said Michael, pulling on his greatcoat. "That is probably exactly what she hopes I will do. If I go near Lady Honoria, I would not put it past her to claim ravishment at my hands. I am not interested in compromising another lady's honor. Jessica is quite enough. For God's sake, a man's address is not so hard to obtain!"

"You will find her, won't you?" cried Caroline. "Peter and I owe all our happiness to her! You may not have known it, but Peter thought himself in love with Jessica for a while before he fell in love with me. She soon put a stop to that!"

"Oh, God, Caroline! Don't throw it in my face!" groaned Peter. "Jessica never gave me the least encouragement. I was just being my usual dumb self!"

Michael gave the pair of them an extremely penetrating look. He wriggled his fingers into a pair of fine gloves. "Wish me Godspeed!" he said quietly. "There is no time to be lost; they are already seven or eight hours ahead of me. But if Jessica is still in the country, I shall bring her back, never fear."

"And if she is not?" asked Aunt Emilia, her blue eyes very bright.

"Then I shall go to the ends of the earth to find her!"

Chapter 17

Jessica woke up with a dreadful thirst and a splitting headache. She was lying on a cot in a small bedroom. There was a tiny window and she gazed at it in a distracted way. Outside, the branches of trees were faintly silhouetted against a gray sky. This must be Bath. Sitting up and looking about her at the shadowed room, she thought about it. Cranby had bundled her into a coach, and they had rattled away through London. The blinds were drawn on the windows and two footmen rode behind; there had been no point at all in trying to escape from the moving carriage. She had ridden beside Sir Gordon for some time in silence, listening to the faint nighttime noises of the city and waiting until they should reach the turnpike. What if she were to scream at the tollbooth and cry out that she was being abducted? Good Lord! It was like something out of a Gothic novel! How would a real-life turnpike man respond? In books they were always sinister imbeciles, nothing like the stolid Englishmen of her experience. It surely wasn't really that easy to kidnap a lady and carry her halfway across England undetected?

Then, unaccountably, she seemed to have fallen asleep.

She remembered nothing of the journey. How on earth could she have passed the rest of the night and the best part of the next day in a deep sleep? With a wince, she remembered the glass of wine. Cranby must have drugged her. In which case, she had better not eat or drink anything else from his hands. It was bad enough to be about to be sent to the Antipodes, but she had no desire at all to be carried on board ship unconscious. How long had it been since they left London? Assuming that Cranby had made no stops, but merely changed horses every few hours, it must be at least early afternoon. Would he have had time to contact the captain of a vessel?

It was cool in the room, and she realized that she was still wearing nothing but the ball gown with the ice green ivy leaves. There were goose bumps on her bare arms. Wrapping a blanket from the bed around her shoulders, she stood up and tested her legs. They were distinctly unsteady. How soon would Honoria deliver the note to Deyncourt? Would he decipher her code? Or would he believe the surface message and go to Honoria in relief? Surely if the earl had followed her, he would have been here by now? A vision of the Incomparable Melton with Deyncourt leading her out into the set at the ball came clearly to mind. Lady Honoria was as beautiful as an angel; she would make him a much better countess. Jessica sat back on the bed, and was horrified to find hot tears welling up in her eyes. What on earth had happened to her, that she should be turning into such a watering pot? With that thought she fell back against the pillows and into another deep sleep.

Not even the bay thoroughbred could gallop nonstop from London to Bath. Michael rode the horse like a demon, but he was forced to pace himself and keep to the gait that his mount could maintain. It had been mid-morning by the time he was able to leave London, and the streets were jammed with carriages and horsemen. He must ride at a crawl through the crowds or risk killing someone. Even when he left the city behind, and was able to open the horse into his ground-eating stride, he must still negotiate the main street of a town or village every few miles. Gaggles of geese and flocks of sheep, farmers with their slow wagons and gangs of farm boys on foot, everything conspired to slow him down. By traveling at night, Cranby would have met no such obstacles. If he had arranged his post horses ahead of time, he would have met almost no delay. Wherever possible, Michael left the road and set off across country, leaping his mount over hedge and ditch, as if on some wild steeplechase. The farm laborers looked up in amazement as he passed, and a couple of times he was given a cheer as the bay soared over a stone wall, or in and out of a lane. Miles were cut off from his journey, but the effort took its toll on the horse and at Reading he left the exhausted animal at a posting inn. After that, he must ride hired hacks, and even if they were the very best that money and influence could muster, they seemed to dawdle in comparison to the thoroughbred. With a deadly determination, he rode on. The day passed in a blur. At every tollbooth he made inquiries, but of course there were innumerable gentlemen's equipages passing by day and night. No one had noticed anything odd; no, there was no young lady in distress that anyone had noticed. Suppose he had misread her message? What if he got to Bath and she wasn't there?

Jessica woke again with a start. The gray light still filtered into the room and a constant steady noise was drumming in her ears. It was raining. She slipped off the bed and went to the door. It was locked. She rattled at the handle, but there was no response. Turning to the window, she worked valiantly for some time at raising the sash. Eventually it gave a little to her efforts. It was anyway far too small to crawl through, but she was able to thrust out her arm. There must have been a hole in the gutter, since a spout of rainwater splashed down in front of the glass. She cupped her hand under the water running from the roof and drank a little. It tasted perfectly good, so she drank her fill. Cranby should not drug her again! She peered out. The window looked onto a garden thick with unkempt trees and shrubs. Every piece of property that Cranby possessed seemed to be in a ramshackle state. What would he have done at Tresham, had his scheme succeeded? Old Lord Steal may have gamed away much of his ready capital, but the estate had not visibly suffered. Would Cranby have allowed that beautiful house to fall to rack and ruin? On the far side of the overgrown shrubbery, a rambling rose ran wild over a tall brick wall. It was the typical garden of a small country house. So she had not been brought into the city. Just on the other side of that wall was surely a road, with people passing by about their normal daily business. They might as well have been on the other side of the moon. She closed the window and went back to the bed. There was a noise behind her, and Jessica turned to see Cranby in the doorway.

"I trust you slept well, Miss Whinburn?"

"Excellently, thank you, Sir Gordon."

"Would you like some breakfast?"

"I couldn't eat or drink a thing, sir. I believe that I must have taken something that disagreed with me, for the thought of food or drink quite turns my stomach."

"You have a remarkably vulgar turn of phrase for a lady, my dear," he replied. "Won't you come downstairs?"

Jessica followed him down through the still house and into the dining room. A meal was spread out on the sideboard, and her mouth watered at the sight of cold beef and fresh bread and fruit. A flagon of red wine sat beside the food. Would that contain the drug?

"You will surely take a glass of wine, madam?"

"Thank you, sir."

He handed her a glass and she pretended to take a sip. Thank goodness she had been able to drink some rainwater! Cranby turned to the table and Jessica quickly poured some of her drink into a vase. Was he relieved that she had taken the wine? Whatever he had planned, it would surely be easier if she was unconscious. Jessica sat down in a chair beside the empty fireplace. The sound of rain beat heavily in the room.

"Pray, make yourself comfortable, Miss Whinburn. There is a library next door and a withdrawing room, but do not attempt to leave the house. I have menservants at the door, with instructions concerning you."

"Are they to knock me on the head, sir, if I attempt to pass them?"

"They are instructed to do whatever is necessary. I trust you will behave in an appropriate manner, so that such behavior will not be called for."

"I understand. Very well, Sir Gordon. By all means go about your nefarious business. I feel unaccountably sleepy during my last few hours in England."

He left her alone in the room, and Jessica immediately began to explore the limits of her prison. As Cranby had said, there were three rooms linked with connecting doors and she was free to sit in whichever one she chose. The windows, however, were securely fastened and the doors locked. The one door that opened when she tried it gave onto a small anteroom, whose occupants looked up suspiciously when they saw her. They were two burly footmen and they were playing cards. There was no point whatsoever in testing their loyalty to their master. She was only too sure that these unpleasant fellows had been handpicked for their jobs as jailers.

"Good afternoon, gentlemen," she said gaily. "How about a game?"

"You're to stay in the drawing room, ma'am, if it's all the same," stated one of the men.

"Oh, surely not? I shall expire from boredom! Cards are my passion. I'll wager you'll not beat me!"

The footman guffawed. "Bob and I aren't playing a ladies' parlor game, ma'am."

She came and stood at the table. A considerable number

of coins lay scattered about its surface, and an ale jug sat at each man's elbow. "No, you're playing High-Low-Jack. And not for penny stakes, either, thank goodness. I'll play for first winner of seven games takes all. Your pot against this!" She took the gold chain and locket from her neck and laid it on the table. The man called Bob gulped visibly.

"No tricks, now," said the first. "You shan't cozen us into letting you out of this room."

"Get away, Harvey!" Bob's eyes were as round as saucers. "That's real gold, that is!" Harvey still looked wary.

"How should I leave the house more easily if I am sitting under your eye at this table, than if I am reclining with the vapors in the drawing room?" asked Jessica. "But if you prefer not to play, it's your loss." She picked up the necklace and began to move back toward the door.

"First to win seven games total, right?" said Harvey. Jessica smiled. "Very well, you're on, miss! Deal her in, Bob!"

Bob dealt the first round of cards and turned the card for trump. It was the queen of spades.

"I'll stand," said Harvey, and play began.

Jessica looked at her cards and smiled to herself. She had both the three and knave of spades. Without difficulty, she took points for Low and Jack, while High and Game points went to Harvey. It was Harvey's deal.

"I beg," said Jessica. Diamonds had turned trump and she had none. Harvey refused gift and ran the cards, until spades turned trump again. This time, Bob took three points. The pack was passed to Jessica. She gave it her very best shuffle, with every fan and waterfall that she knew. The man called Bob laughed.

"You're no stranger to high stakes, are you?"

Jessica laughed back. "Neither are you, sir!" She turned the card for trump. "Do you stand or beg?"

"I beg."

"But I'll take it," said Jessica. "Gift to you, Bob!"

She had a superb hand and cleaned up all four points. Bob dealt again. One more point and Jessica would win this round. Quite deliberately, she discarded three good cards after the run, and Harvey and Bob split the points. She did it again in the next round, and Bob took first game.

It was early evening by the time they had reached the tenth game. Copious amounts of ale had poured down the throats of the two men, and Jessica had managed to get through one glass. She didn't care at all who won the game, but it was essential to her plan that the footmen have a good time and relax, and accept her as one of them, if only for a moment. She remembered once reading somewhere that laughter makes a poor jailer. If that was the case, she was half free already. Both footmen were as merry as rattles.

"Your deal, missy!" cried Harvey. He had loosened his collar and was in a grand humor. He had already taken five of the ten games. Two more wins and the necklace would be his. "How about another glass of brew?"

This was her moment! "My turn, gentlemen! I have already drunk some of your poison. Let me treat you to some of mine! Hold on!"

She got up from the table a little unsteadily; she was not used to strong liquor and the ale had been as raw as mud. Concentrating her mind, she went back through to the dining room and took up the flagon of red wine. Supposing she had guessed wrong? Then the only result of this entire caper would be that either Harvey or Bob would get Deyncourt's necklace, while she passed out under the table from an overdose of coarse ale! She came back with three wineglasses and filled them while Bob dealt the cards. Harvey took a sip and laughed.

"So this is what the gentlemen tipple! Drink up, Bob!"

Jessica smiled and winked at Bob as she raised her glass. He took a deep draft. She hoped that neither man would notice that she set her own down untouched. She had also better stop Harvey winning for a while; her entire aim now was to make the game go on as long as possible, while the men drank Cranby's wine. She managed to win the next

round, and then began to slip points to Bob. Before long
they were almost even. Five games to Harvey, and four
each to Bob and herself. Then Harvey took the next. One
more and he would win, and the game would be over.
Jessica watched anxiously to see if either of the men would
get sleepy. Perhaps she had miscalculated and there was
nothing in the flagon but wine! Neither of these fellows
would ever pass out from alcohol alone. It was her deal.
She turned up the knave of hearts. Hearts were trumps
and one point to her.

"Stand or beg, sir?" she asked Bob.

"Beg, miss, begging your pardon," cried Bob. "Can't
seem to stand!" And with a giggle he slumped to the floor.

"Damn me!" said Harvey looking at his friend. "Never
thought that Bob couldn't hold his liquor." He looked at
Jessica and his eyes crossed. "Pretty good stuff you gentle-
folk drink," he said, and he followed Bob to the floor.
Stentorian snores shook the room. Jessica leaned over each
man and shook him gently by the shoulder. There was no
response but another nasal explosion. Instantly she went
to the door. It was locked. Without compunction she went
back to the two men and began to search their pockets.
Pray that they weren't lying on the key, as Peter had done
at the Blue Boar. She giggled aloud. Oh, Lord! She had
taken nothing for a day but two glasses of extremely potent
ale. It would be beyond anything if Cranby returned and
found three unconscious bodies around the card table.
The key was in Harvey's pocket. Moments later, she had
the door open and stepped out into the garden. It was
almost dark, the long summer twilight shortened by the
black clouds. Instantly, the rush of rainwater sobered her
up as she was soaked to the skin.

The hired horse cast a shoe exactly halfway between
Marlborough and Chippenham. With a curse, Michael was
forced to dismount and lead the animal to the next village.
He had just passed the extraordinary antiquities of West

Kennet, where a row of barrows hugged the ridge top. The rain swept across the Marlborough Downs in torrents, hiding the windswept landscape of chalk hills and hidden valleys. Mud ran in rivulets around his boots, and water poured off the brim of his hat and soaked the shoulders of his greatcoat. This mishap would cost him at least another half hour. The earl had already ridden for nine straight hours, with little more sustenance than his brandy flask and a sandwich that Dover had miraculously produced and thrust into his pocket as he left, and which he had eaten as he rode. God bless John Montagu, fourth Earl of Sandwich, for his invention! For a moment he wished that his estimable manservant was with him, but Dover, capable as he was, could never have kept up on this bruising ride. Michael grimaced to himself. He had once done something very similar in the Peninsula in order to carry an urgent message for Wellington, before his brother had died and he had come into his title, but at least then it hadn't been raining. He cursed again as a violent little squall sent a spray of water straight into his face.

The village of Cherhill boasted a smithy, but the smith had retired to his cottage for the day. There was not another horse to be had.

"For God's sake, man. I'll pay in gold!"

"Very sorry, sir," said the man he had accosted on the main street by the crossroads. "John Smith shuts up shop at six o'clock sharp and starts in on his cider. He'll not be capable now till morning."

"Can he be roused?"

"Not if it was judgment day, sir!"

"Very well, I believe you. Where is the smithy?"

"Just over yonder, sir."

Michael looked where the man pointed, at a ramshackle stone and thatch building. "I'll pay a guinea to the man who will blow the bellows!"

"You can't go in John's smithy without his say-so, sir."

"Try me," said the earl.

The man gave him a shrewd glance. This tall fellow

would obviously have his own way, in which case he might as well profit by it as another. "Then I'll blow for you myself. But if John were to catch me, he'd have my hide."

"A big man, is he?"

"Bigger than you and me both, and mean in his cups!" The fellow took a bite at the coin that Michael had dropped into his palm, before thrusting it deep into his inside pocket.

"But he'll be like a lamb by morning. I have met your John Smiths before. Never fear, I shall make sure that he forgives you."

Michael threw open the door of the smithy and led his horse inside. There were still coals in the fire, and the man set to with a will blowing up a fierce blaze. Word has a way of traveling in villages; before long a little gaggle of rustics gathered to watch the extraordinary sight of a gentleman shoeing his own horse. The sly nudges and winks turned to a reluctant respect as the tall stranger peeled off his expensive coat and rolled up the sleeves of a shirt that was surely silk, to reveal a pair of strong brown arms and workmanlike hands. Their silent respect turned into a murmur of approval when those fine hands set about the humble task with dispatch. Within fifteen minutes Michael had trimmed up the hoof and reset the shoe.

He laid a golden coin on the anvil. "For Mr. Smith, for the use of his equipment, and to ensure that he doesn't run out of cider. I trust he will share his good luck with his friends." There was an enthusiastic cheer and a wave as Michael remounted and splashed away up the street at a canter. It was at least another twenty miles to Bath. He made a final change of horse at the Bull in Chippenham and rode on. It was already getting dark.

Jessica slogged through the damp garden. She had a sudden rush of reluctant sympathy for Judge Clarence as her evening slippers sank into the soft mud. She had no idea what Cranby had done with her cloak, so she was exposed to the entire force of the storm as water rushed over her bare head and arms. Her hair was instantly plastered to her head, and her wet skirts wrapped insistently around her legs. She pulled them out of the way and hurried over to the wall. There was no gate anywhere that she could find, except the main gate at the front of the house, and she was afraid that it would be guarded. She looked up at the rambling rose. A bedraggled spray of white petals nodded in the rain like soggy paper, but the thorns would shred her skin. She worked her way beneath the dripping trees. At last an old apple tree stood close enough to the wall that with agility she could climb high enough to leap to the flat brick top. With a grin she remembered climbing trees as a child. Her father had encouraged her. She sent him a silent prayer of thanks. Without more ado, she shinned up the tree and swung to the wall. A great strip of her lace ivy caught on a branch and tore away. She shrugged and looked down into the road. Both sides of the way were walled with solid brick. Sir Gordon would undoubtedly be returning from Bristol at any moment. If he found her out here, recapture would be as easy as penning a pig. Now, which way to go? She decided at random to go to the right, and dropped into the lane. As she did so, a horse came thundering down at a canter, and a chaise turned into the end of the road to the left. She screamed as the rider caught her by the wrist and swung her onto the horse behind him.

Chapter 18

"Now, don't faint, Jessica!" said Michael over his shoulder. "I've come a hell of a long way to rescue you, and I'm damned if you don't seem to have already rescued yourself."

"I don't know what I'm going to have to do to convince the gentlemen of my acquaintance that I don't faint!" *He had understood the message! He had come after her!* "So you had no problem deciphering my note?"

"Ne fronti crede, my dear! It should be our motto!"

"Don't trust appearances? But I'm not rescued yet either!" Jessica pointed to the carriage that was rapidly bearing down on them. Two armed menservants rode on the box with the coachman and someone was leaning from the window. "It's Cranby!"

A shot rang out from the chaise. Michael whirled his horse around. "I think it's time for discretion, my dear. There are several of them and only two of us." Firing one returning shot, he clapped his heels to his horse and they bounded away. She looked over her shoulder. The carriage horses were also being whipped to a gallop. Their horse reached the end of the walled lane, and the countryside opened up. "Can you hang on, Jessie?"

"Try me!"

He laughed and in the next moment had jumped his horse over a stile and away down a footpath. There was no way that the carriage could follow. Jessica clung to his back as they thundered away through the night.

Michael pulled the horse down to a trot, and then to a halt.

"We've lost them. Now get down."

Jessica slipped from the horse's back. The rain continued to beat down on their heads and she was wet to the skin. Michael pulled off his greatcoat and wrapped it around her shoulders. It was little comfort. The coat was also wet through, but at least it was warm from his body.

"Where on earth are we?" she asked, and found the words would barely come out for a shivering chatter that seemed to have seized her jaw. It had become entirely dark. All she could see around them were huge oak trees, part of some thick wood. His face was entirely lost in the gloom.

"We are on the edge of my own domain. It is not how I imagined bringing you here, but this is Castle Deyncourt."

"You mean we c-c-can get to your house?"

"We can get to shelter. Come along." He slipped an arm around her waist, and leading the horse with the other hand, guided her down a small path beneath the overhanging trees. Before long they arrived at the dark outline of some low-roofed building. Michael tied the horse, and pulling the key from its hiding place, opened the door and led her inside. Just to step out of the rain was a huge relief. He struck a tinder and lit a lamp. They were standing in a cramped stone-flagged entry. A single door led off to one side.

"I thought Deyncourt was a real c-castle, my lord," she managed to whisper when she could get her teeth to stop banging together for a moment. "Where on earth is this?"

"This is just a retreat that I use sometimes. It's a remnant of the original forest assart. The house is several more miles; neither you nor the horse can make it.''

Hanging the sodden greatcoat from a hook in the hall, he led her through the low door and into a little room; the pump handle and stone sink in the corner, and the wall ovens next to the basket grate, proclaimed it to be the kitchen of a cottage. He knelt in the fireplace and within moments had a blaze roaring up the chimney. With a smile he turned to her where she stood in the ruins of her ball gown making a large puddle on the floor. ''Now take off those wet things before you die of an inflammation of the lungs.'' She had never seen him look this way before. His expression was entirely stripped of artifice, the hair stuck to the curve of his head, water shining on his cheekbones. His blue eyes seemed as clear as a summer sky in comparison. She hesitated, and he ran his hand over his face. ''I have ridden more than ten hours today! Don't argue! Just do it, please!'' He threw open the door to a linen press that sat in a corner of the room. There were neat stacks of towels and some folded garments. ''I shall go and see to the horse. Dry yourself!''

He ducked back out through the low doorway and Jessica forced her sodden feet to walk across the stone floor. She pulled out a white towel. As she went back to the fire, the remains of her evening slippers disintegrated entirely and she pulled them off. Her feet and legs were thick with mud. No wonder Judge Clarence had been so annoyed! It was extremely tempting to simply lie down on the floor and give up, but she could not allow herself to be so feeble. Summoning all her reserves of strength, she dried her face and rubbed vigorously at her hair and arms, then shrugged out of the shreds of silk and lace, and dried herself to the knees. Somehow she could not bring herself to cover the towel with mud, so with another dry towel wrapped around her body, she padded barefoot across the kitchen and worked energetically at the pump. Water gushed into the sink, which was carved from a single block of stone. She pulled a large brass kettle from its shelf and filled it. There was a hook that swung out over the fire for the express purpose of receiving it. Now in a few minutes she would have hot water. In the meantime, she had better put something on. This situation was irregular enough, without having Deyncourt find her dressed in a towel!

The earl led the horse into a shed that adjoined the cottage and stripped off the tack. The poor beast hung its head for pure weariness. There was a cozy stall well bedded with dry straw, and plenty of good feed in the loft. The staff at Castle Deyncourt knew better than to leave any part of the estate not in constant readiness for its master. Taking a wisp of straw, Michael gave the animal a thorough rubbing down and filled the manger with fragrant hay. With a final pat to the horse's rump, he plunged back out into the downpour. Would Jessica have managed, or would she be in a helpless state of the vapors? He grinned to himself; the latter was extremely difficult to imagine!

He pushed open the door to the kitchen and stopped short. The fire burned happily in the grate, casting its warm glow over the entire room. Over the flames the kettle bubbled and sputtered. Jessica sat on a three-legged stool by the fire, bent from the waist as she dried her hair in the heat. Her bare feet were soaking in a basin of hot water, and she looked around at the sound of the door.

"I took the liberty of helping myself to one of your shirts, my lord," she said merrily. "It's a bit big, but I discovered that a cravat makes a fine belt, and since there was nothing for a skirt, I made do with some of your breeches. Do you think I might start a new fashion?"

She straightened up and pushed the cloud of hair from her face; she looked beautiful. Ignoring the odd look on his face, she dried each foot in turn and thrust it into one of his stockings, which she tied up using her own lace-trimmed garter. "You would appear to have a very competent housekeeper, my lord, even for your cottage. There is a complete selection of clean clothing in that press."

"I am aware of the fact," he said dryly.

"I also found some potatoes in the bottom of the cupboard and put them under the coals to bake. All we need is a pair of turnips and we can have a real feast. In the meantime, how about a dish of tea?''

The full teapot sat on the iron plate near the fire. Hanging to dry in the chimney angle were her shift and stockings, already washed out. The ball gown was past saving, so she had used it to clean the mud from the floor, and she had left it in a sorry bundle in the corner of the room.

''If I could have found some bran, I would have made a bran mash for our noble steed, but then that would have made it necessary for one of us to go back out in the rain again. Good Lord, Michael! You're hurt!''

Michael shrugged and looked down to where a red stain was spreading across his thigh. ''Cranby's man was unfortunately a decent enough shot to wing me. It's of no consequence.''

''For heaven's sake! You mean to tell me that we rode all the way here and walked through the wood—and I let you see to the horse—and all the while you were bleeding like a stuck pig?''

He laughed. ''If you want to put it like that! The rain has cleaned it and it's only a flesh wound.''

''Nevertheless, it ought to be seen to.''

He grinned and sat by the fire opposite her. He was as pale as a ghost, the planes of his face stark with fatigue. Pulling off his cravat, he quickly bound the injury. It seemed ridiculous, but he hadn't even been aware of being hit. Then he remembered a fellow officer in the Peninsula. The poor chap had ended up losing his left arm, yet not even known he was hurt until the battle was over.

''What do you suggest, Jessie dear? That I remove my breeches and let you minister to me?''

She replied perfectly steadily. ''Stuff! What do you intend to do? Sit there all night in your wet clothes and bleed to death for the sake of my modesty? I shall tend to our potatoes and keep my back turned. For heaven's sake, get dry and bind that up properly, or it'll be your turn to die.'' Carrying the copper basin, Jessica stepped carefully across the floor to avoid the wet patches. She poured away the dirty water, and fetched two cups from the dresser. Michael took several gulps of hot tea. Color slowly came back to his face. Jessica poured a liberal splash of hot water into the basin and set it on the rough pine table. "Now, my lord. Get washed and dry."

The shirt had turned transparent on his body and rivulets of water ran from his boots. The blue of his eyes had turned into a deep indigo. A complete physical exhaustion lay like a shadow over his wet skin. "As you suggest, madam. I do feel absurdly like Odysseus washed up on the beach."

"Well, you'll wait all night for Athene to appear to you in the guise of a shepherd."

"Shall I?" he said casually. "I rather thought the vision of the goddess was at hand."

She ignored him. The way he was looking at her was making her temperature rise in a distinctly uncomfortable way. "And Odysseus didn't drink tea. Here, let me get you a towel."

"To stuff in my ears as protection from the sirens?"

"That was wax. And besides, Odysseus listened . . ." Jessica turned from the linen press, cloth in hand, and the rest of the reply died on her lips. Deyncourt was peeling off his soaked shirt. The muscles of his back were outlined in firelight and shadow. He was magnificent, like a hunting wild cat or a fine horse in racing condition. He held out a hand and she tossed him the towel.

"My thanks, madam." Michael gave her a formal bow before proceeding to rub the cloth over his head until the hair stood up in a wild halo. With both hands he splashed warm water over his face, then dried his body. She stood rooted to the spot, fighting the most shocking impulse to touch that smooth skin and pass her fingers through the dark down on his chest. He bent over to work off his boots. Jessica went hurriedly to the fire and turned the potatoes. Her heart had begun that heavy irregular beat that made her feel she was about to suffocate. Her eyes were glued on the ash surrounding the humble tubers as she heard each boot thump to the floor, followed by the slither of his wet buckskins and undergarments. She had thought it bad enough to be trapped with him at Tresham, when she had been inadequately clothed. This was far worse!

"You may look up now, dear Jessie!"

She turned. How on earth had he done it? His damp hair was once again swept back from his forehead as neatly as if his valet had just finished with it. He had dressed in a fresh white shirt and linen pantaloons. He looked immaculate. The unguarded look she had caught a glimpse of earlier had disappeared, as if he had put on his emotional protection along with the dry clothes. Pray that he would not have noticed the effect his nakedness had on her!

"The potatoes are ready, my lord."

"Michael."

"Michael. Shall we eat? I have had nothing since the ball, which was at least seven lifetimes ago. This unassuming root looks like ambrosia to me."

"Cranby did not feed you?"

"He fed me some kind of narcotic and I did not enjoy the effect."

He came and sat down at the fireside. "Then how did you come to be climbing over his garden wall?"

As she dug into her roast potato, Jessica told him rapidly what she remembered of her abduction and of her card game with the footmen. The corners of his mouth began to twitch.

"I'm glad you can laugh, when I was almost shipped out to the Antipodes!"

"I had better laugh, sweet Jessica, than get too angry. Cranby has had a lucky escape so far."

"I'm so glad that you care."

"For God's sake, you're my affianced wife! Did you think I would let him ship you away?"

"What will you do about it?"

"I think I might just leave him to the Incomparable Melton. She will have his eyes."

"It was her plan to have you."

"So it was," he said, as if that was something which had happened in another lifetime.

"And will the Incomparable Melton meekly accept her fate?" Jessica asked. "She was extremely angry with me."

He leaned back in his chair and gave her a lazy smile. "I don't see why not. Doubtless, she will marry someone else and Cranby will cuckold him. After all, she and her cousin have been planning it a long time."

Jessica knew that her jaw had dropped open, but she couldn't help it. "What? How could you have wanted to marry her, knowing that?"

"Why not? We didn't pretend affection. Besides, Honoria has no doubt been careful to keep her virtue intact—technically, at least. How could she marry an earl otherwise? So I wasn't in the least worried that she would return to Cranby after spending a honeymoon with me."

Jessica leapt to her feet and made for the cupboard. "That statement shows an insufferable arrogance!" As she passed, he caught at her hand and pulled her to him.

"Just a statement of fact, my dear. I do not believe in false modesty. Didn't it occur to you that you may have leapt from the frying pan into the fire? You have escaped the clutches of the charming Sir Gordon, only to fall into mine."

"Fustian! Cranby never once threatened my person!"

"But I do, don't I?" Without more ado, he swung her onto his lap.

"Your wound, Michael!"

"It doesn't hurt, forget it. Now, madam, it is time for us to get some things straight."

Lady Emilia's personal dresser thought she might faint. Her mistress had not left London since that disastrous trip to Northumberland all those years ago. Now, she intended to pick up and leave for the West Country with no notice whatsoever.

"What would you wish me to pack, my lady?" she gasped at last.

"Pack anything you like, but do it now!"

Lady Emilia swept out into the hallway and opened the door to her withdrawing room, where Peter paced restlessly. "Are you children quite ready?"

Lord Steal looked up at the old lady. "It's only a two-day journey, Lady Emilia. Caroline and I would go in the clothes we stand up in!"

"It's the first time I ever heard you be indifferent to your wardrobe, young man. Nevertheless, it is expected of those in our station in life to keep up appearances even if the sky falls."

Caroline came in at that moment and joined them. "I have packed clothes for Jessica. She has nothing with her but her ball gown. I think she might be glad of a few muslins."

"Assuming Deyncourt has found her," said Peter glumly.

"Oh, stuff and nonsense!" cried Aunt Emilia. "The man has never failed in any adventure yet. No, I am more concerned about what he may do when he does."

"What ever do you mean, Lady Emilia?"

"Haven't you eyes for anyone's situation other than your own?" snapped the old lady. "Jessica is in love with Deyncourt and has been for these months! But she believes he despises her. The earl has discovered, I believe, reciprocal feelings, but he is such a stiff-necked idiot that he will never admit it. I'm very much afraid that he will make a complete botch of the whole situation."

"Lady Emilia!" Peter's eyes were as round as cartwheels.

"Oh, you have been accustomed to thinking Deyncourt everything that's perfect, but he has had his emotions on a rein for so long, he wouldn't recognize them if they came and bit him on the rear."

It was Caroline's turn to be shocked. "Oh, dear," she said. "Whatever can we do about it?"

"Get down to Castle Deyncourt right away, which is

where he will take her, before they murder each other. Now, are we all packed? Coachman has had the chaise and four ready this past hour.''

"There is nothing to get straight, Michael. We are trapped into this mockery of a marriage. You have made your feelings perfectly clear, and I shall do nothing to disturb your independence.''

His hand lay on her thigh, threatening to burn right through to the flesh.

"So you won't kick up a fuss if I leave you at Castle Deyncourt to tend to our flock of children, while I take opera singers and dancers to Marchmont?''

"If that's what you want.''

"Well, devil take it, it's not what I want!''

"It would seem to be the life you had planned with Lady Honoria.''

His fingers had begun to work up her back in little circles. "How true! It's not such an unusual life for an earl, is it? My father was an excellent example. Except that Aunt Sophy would never have allowed him to entertain his lightskirts at Marchmont.''

"Then I am to suppose that you haven't had much respect for her memory! For that's the use to which her home has been put ever since, isn't it? I am probably the only female you ever took to Marchmont who didn't spend her visit in your bedroom. But perhaps it's the normal way to go on. Apart from you, I haven't had too many dealings with earls.''

"Then you had better get used to them.'' The long fingers had reached the neckline of her shirt, and he deftly began to pull apart the strings. She felt that she would begin to melt from the inside out.

"What are you doing?'' she asked.

"This discussion will get us nowhere. We're going to bed, dear Jessica.''

With a violent movement, she pulled away from him and leapt to her feet.

"Over my dead body!"

"I would much prefer it alive," he said with a grin. He stood up and crossed to the side of the room. There was a set of sliding doors, which he pushed back. In a kind of wood-lined cupboard was a bed, ready made up with white linen sheets and wool blankets. "This is the only bed in the house. I intend to get into it and go to sleep, and I would suggest that you do likewise. However, I don't intend to do so fully clothed."

"Michael, you can't!"

"Can't what?" He had begun to strip off his pantaloons.

"You can't just take off your clothes! Where am I to sleep?"

"In this bed with me, my dear; unless you prefer the floor?"

"Michael, stop it!"

He grinned up at her as the pantaloons fell to the floor. The tails of his shirt effectively covered him. He slipped between the covers and pulled the shirt off over his head. "You are already compromised, dear Jessie; you might as well be hanged for a sheep as a lamb. Besides, I have already obtained a special license. We can be married in the morning."

"Damn you! I shall never marry you!"

"Very well, but you might as well share the bed. It will get cold out there when the fire dies down." He lay back and gave her that devastating smile.

"You are no gentleman at all!"

He sat back up and looked at her. "Yes I am. I will cry truce! Come to bed and go to sleep. I am in desperate need of innocent slumber. It's not every day that I ride *ventre à terre* across England. I shan't touch you. I give you my word."

"Can I trust it?"

"You did at Tresham."

"And once again I have no choice at all, do I?"

She was to have no reply. He simply turned his back and pulled the covers up over his head. Jessica paced the room for a moment. How dare he be so impossible! At last, she was forced to concede. There was nowhere else in the cottage to sleep. The simple pine furniture of the kitchen was extremely hard and uninviting. The rain still beat heavily at the roof. The floor was of stone. So, dressed as she was, she slipped gingerly between the covers and lay as far from his graceful back as she was able. Michael did not move.

Jessica awoke to moonlight streaming in at the cottage window. It had stopped raining. She sat up. She was in an extremely compromising position with the eighth Earl of Deyncourt, who intended to marry her in the morning. She looked down at him for a moment. His hair was tumbled over his forehead. The carved lips were slightly apart, as if he were about to whisper. The planes of his face looked softer, a little blurred by shadows. No wonder he had London at his feet. Her heart gave an uncomfortable lurch. She slipped quickly from the bed and built up the fire.

Michael turned over. Jessica crossed back to the bed. He still slept. The moonlight outlined the clear, strong line of his nostril and the turn of his jaw. She suddenly realized how defenseless even he was in slumber. To go to sleep with the same person night after night in the same bed was somehow the ultimate expression of trust, wasn't it? She put her face in her hands. She loved him! And thus, she could never marry him; it would be the ultimate betrayal. Was there nothing that would turn him aside? The earl's own words echoed in her mind: *Besides, Honoria has no doubt been careful to keep her virtue intact. How could she marry an earl otherwise?* It was the only way out, wasn't it?

Before she should lose her nerve, Jessica stepped out of the pantaloons and peeled off her stockings, then quickly pulled the shirt over her head. The cool night air raised goose bumps on her thighs and arms. Naked she slipped back into the bed. Shaking with her awareness of him, she pushed back the covers. Moonlight and firelight flickered over him as he stirred. Jessica let her palm drift across his shoulder, feeling the warm strength of his flesh. As desire flamed through her blood, she blinked back hot tears. To go through with this would break her heart! Yet quite deliberately she ran her hand down the smooth muscling of his chest, over the springing hair and firm skin, to the delectable tautness of his belly. With the tears pricking painfully at her lids, she followed her fingers with her lips and tongue. There was a sudden quickening of his breath and she moved against him, burning with her own shame and longing. As his lashes parted Jessica pressed her open mouth to his, and felt the kiss returned with naked, hungry passion. The earl's oath would be broken. Lord Deyncourt was going to have to learn the truth.

Chapter 19

Sunlight woke him. He reached for Jessica, instantly aroused, a memory of her sweet body entwined with his sending fire through his blood. They had made love again and again, without constraint. Michael sat up and looked about the room. She was gone. There was something on the table. He slipped naked from the bed and went to it. A spray of dog roses spilled from a cup, and next to the flowers was a note: "I have paid my debt, Michael. These roses for the one I shot in your garden. I cannot marry you. Now you know why. Jessica."

Lady Emilia's ancient carriage cracked a wheel hub near Thatcham, and the three rescuers spent fretful hours at the only inn before they could secure a repair. Peter stalked up and down the little parlor, while Caroline and Aunt Emilia calmly played cards.

"For heaven's sake, sir!" snapped the old lady at last. "It is like being in a cage with a parrot that hops back and forth on its perch."

"Not a parrot, Lady Emilia," said Caroline with a shy

smile. "Parrots are both as bright as day. Peter is more like a pheasant, I think, for the female pheasant is just as dull and brown as I am, and only the male struts in glorious plumage."

Peter grinned at his fiancée. "I intend to be much more faithful than any old pheasant, Caro!"

"Well, I wish you had shown such sense earlier, young man," said Lady Emilia. "Your absurd mooning over Jessica is part of the cause of this entire tangle."

Peter blushed scarlet, but Caroline laughed. "I would have thought the less of him if he hadn't fallen in love with Jessica first. How could anyone not? None of us has ever met anyone like her!"

Lady Emilia sighed and laid down her hand. "But will Deyncourt see it in time, my dears? That's all that really counts."

Michael rode up through the Deyncourt estates on a horse borrowed from a tenant. Jessica had taken the hired nag. There was no way to trace her, yet he would find her if he had to tear England from its chalk bed, stone by stone. How could Sir Shelby Whinburn have been such a damned bastard? Had Lady Emilia known? Perhaps she had guessed, but if so, how could she have displayed her great-niece on the Marriage Mart? For if Jessica had wed, she would have been found out and her marriage destroyed on her wedding night.

Lady Emilia's cavalcade turned off the turnpike. It was not more than ten more miles to Castle Deyncourt. Peter rode up on the box with the coachman, and when the carriage lurched to a halt, the old lady called to him. "What is it now, Steal? We shall never arrive at this rate."

"It's a lad, my lady! In some kind of trouble."

Lady Emilia opened the window and leaned out. A boy sat at the edge of the road with his head in his hand

Beside him, a nondescript nag cropped at the grass. "Can we be of assistance, young man?" The boy looked up. The face was white against the flame of red hair. "Good Lord! Where on earth are your shoes, child? Caroline, quickly, it's Jessica!"

Caroline and Peter helped Jessica into the carriage as Lady Emilia offered her handkerchief. "Whatever is the meaning of this?"

Jessica gave her great-aunt a wan smile. "The horse went lame. Deyncourt rode him too hard yesterday."

"And where, may I ask, were you going?"

"To London. I have sold a book of stories. It's not much, but it's a beginning, and I can survive modestly on the proceeds. I can't stay with you any longer and I can't marry Lord Deyncourt."

"Why ever not? The man loves you!"

Caroline took Peter by the elbow and steered him away. They climbed together onto the box, out of earshot. Jessica laughed a little unsteadily. "Do you think so? It doesn't signify, for I shall never marry him."

"I won't hear another word until you are warm, changed, and fed."

"I don't care. I couldn't eat anything," replied Jessica.

"Nonsense! Coachman! Back to the inn!"

An hour later, Jessica sat alone with Lady Emilia in a shadowed parlor at the inn. She was dressed now in one of her own muslins that Caroline had brought, but she had taken nothing but a cup of coffee. Lady Emilia glowered at her.

"Why? What is this about, Jessica? You will tell me!"

"I cannot."

"There is nothing in this world that cannot be faced. You are no coward, child. Why won't you marry Deyncourt? Now, tell me the whole."

The freckles were stark on Jessica's cheeks like a mockery of tears. "Very well, I will. Then you will see that the marriage is impossible."

Some time later, Lady Emilia gazed grimly from the

window. She turned stiffly and confronted her great-niece. "I see," she said. "Of course you can't marry him and I won't let you be made his mistress. It would destroy you both. Will there be a child?"

"It's not the right time. I learned such things years ago, you see."

"Dear God! If your father were not in his grave, I would put him there myself. Nevertheless, you must tell Deyncourt. Let him repudiate you if he will, but to run away now is the act of a craven deserter. You will face him over this, Jessica. You made him break his sworn word last night—when he has nothing in the world but his honor to stand between him and despair. Do you think in his disgust, he'll forget you? You leave him to think you are yet another damned burden for which he must be responsible. He won't rest until he finds you, for he will feel obliged to provide for you and possibly a child. If you are going to leave him, you must free him from that encumbrance first."

The coach lumbered toward Castle Deyncourt. Jessica wasn't in the least surprised to see everything in such good order. There were no untended cottages or neglected fields. The tenants that they passed looked cheerful and dignified as they went about their work. "There aren't any children," she said suddenly. She had seen almost no children working in the fields or gardens.

"They are in school," Lady Emilia replied shortly. "Deyncourt believes that these people must have the full rights of Englishmen—the vote, a fair chance at representation in Parliament—in which case, they must read and write. He has built dame schools in each village, and he pays for the costs and insists the children go."

"And he has made Peter do the same at Tresham. Lady Mary told me."

"Indeed, it creates some grumbling and he has to constantly enforce it. He tries to make it up to them in reduced rents and I believe he is beginning to win a few hearts on the issue, but change is a hard thing for the English countryman to swallow."

"You mean they don't want their children to read and write?"

Lady Emilia sniffed. "Why should they? It takes a pair of hands from the field work."

And thus they resent him! Jessica thought.

The carriage crossed a stream by an arched stone bridge, and suddenly she saw it. At the top of the rise cresting the skyline, white limestone towers gleamed serenely in the sun. From the battlements flew the ancient banners of Dcyncourt; the earl was in residence. The entire façade with its soaring archways and intricately carved corbels was reflected in an ornamental lake, graced with swans. Around it lay the deer park, the trees in full leaf. Castle Deyncourt beckoned like the magic castles of Camelot, and Jessica felt tears welling up in her eyes.

Aunt Emilia's carriage pulled up in front of the great doorway with its Norman arch. Jessica climbed down alone and stood in her simple green muslin in front of the steps.

"I shall not return until I'm sent for," said Lady Emilia, leaning from the coach window. "This is between you and Deyncourt, Jessica. I shall not interfere." She rapped on the panel and her carriage lumbered away.

Jessica looked up at the banks of gleaming windows soaring away above her head. So magnificent! A seat of power and prestige since the Middle Ages—and Michael's home. Her courage drained away. Oh, dear God! She could not! She could not face him! Someone opened the door.

Michael stood on the threshold. "Welcome to my castle, Miss Whinburn," he said gravely. "Come inside. Be careful, do not knock down the armor—the favorite garment of my fourteenth-century ancestor." He indicated the figure of a steel-clad knight that stood in the hallway. "I tried it on as a lad, but I've outgrown it now."

A footman had appeared at his elbow. The earl had a

quick word with him, and the man scurried away. Taking Jessica by the hand, Michael led her into a sunny parlor.

"First things first, I think," he said. He sounded as remote as a priest. "Have you had breakfast?"

Jessica shook her head. Within moments Michael sat her down before a feast of fresh food. Jessica stared at it.

"Oh, dear Lord," said Michael. "I can't eat either. Come into the study."

"And leave all this? What will your servants think?"

"The staff know better than to question anything I might do."

She followed him through a stone-flagged hall into a neat study, lined with books. "As they're used to your bringing odd females into the house at any time without notice?" Not a single eyebrow had been raised at her appearance by any of the servants.

"Of course. They won't concern themselves about it. Most of them have known me since I was a baby."

"And you were a baby?" asked Jessica.

"When we have our first, maybe it will make it easier to imagine. The poor mite will indubitably have the misfortune to look just like me."

Jessica studied him. He was dressed in a superbly tailored dark blue coat above buff pantaloons, and his cravat fell in crisp folds beneath his freshly shaved chin. His hair caught the shine of the sun streaming in at the window; subtle shadows outlined the planes of his face. They were looks that he knew how to use like a sword.

"But your appearance is . . ."

"Something I have learned to accept and wield to my advantage as an adult, Jessica. But it cost me many a fistfight as a lad. It's not easy for a boy to be too out of the ordinary."

"It won't matter," she said quietly. "There won't be any child. You are under no obligation at all."

"But a wedding would please the old stone knights in the chapel."

She looked down. "We are not getting married, so your ancestor's effigies will have to wait for another time."

The blue eyes widened slightly. "Really? Why?"

It took all of her courage. "After last night? Surely that was enough?"

"That you were not a virgin, and offered me a seduction skilled enough to make my word worthless and my body like putty in your hands? No, it's not enough, Jessie. If your father gambled your maidenhead to a friend and lost it, it wasn't your fault."

She looked back at him, wide-eyed. "How did you know?"

"I suspected it after the Mapleton's ball, when you lost your temper and kissed me." His voice seemed stripped of emotion. "And then I found a friend who had heard about Whinburn—it seemed the only logical conclusion."

"You offered me marriage, knowing that?"

"So I did. Is that what happened? A wager?"

"I don't ever remember anything at Whinburn but gambling and drinking. There were women, too, of course, and parties that went on for days. When I was little I was kept out of the way in the nursery, but it couldn't last for ever. I suppose it was inevitable. Father was drunk and he owed a lot of money to a man from Scotland who had visited quite often before. The man won me from my father that night at hazard. His name was Ben Cameron."

"How old were you?" asked Michael quietly.

"Just sixteen."

"So you thought that marriage was out of the question? What of our debt to Caroline and Peter?"

"Go back and marry Honoria. She won't hurt them if you wed her; and she can give you the kind of marriage that people like you expect."

"I don't want the kind of marriage that people like me expect."

"Then what kind of marriage do you want?"

"I want to marry you, wild Jessica!"

She put her head in her hands. "So instead of repulsing me because of my past as I'd hoped, you nobly offer yourself in our marriage of convenience. Then you will put me

aside like Anne of Cleves, or perhaps you will keep me
to mother your children while you take your women to
Marchmont. This is a gesture of pity, isn't it? You think it
wasn't my fault—that I was raped. But I wasn't! I was willing
enough and he brought me nothing but pleasure."

"Then I'm very glad, Jessica."

"How can you be? He was beautiful and I loved him. I
happily became Ben's mistress, but he was killed three
months later. I wept very bitterly for him, I'm afraid. My
father suffered the most dreadful remorse; it never happened again. You offer me your name out of compassion
or some misplaced obligation, even when I caused you to
defile your own honor. Well, that's generous of you, but
I'm not going through with it. I can't face the rest of my
life in your power, sinking into a relationship based on
artifice and recrimination, all tempered by your damnable
efficiency and control. You said that *ne fronti crede* should
be our motto. Well, I think I want to be able to trust to
appearances. I don't want to keep up a pretense week after
week, year after year, and I think you deserve better."

"Better?" he said. "You think I deserve better?" He
seemed completely detached and calm, but his eyes were
like still pools of clear water reflecting a summer sky. "What
pretense?"

Jessica folded her hands in her lap. She took a deep
breath. "It will no doubt sicken you to hear it, because
you must have heard it a thousand times from women far
more beautiful and desirable than I am, but I'm in love
with you." She could not look at his face. "After last night,
I know that I always will be. I don't expect you to do
anything about it, except to find a way to release me from
this wedding. You must see that it's the one fact that makes
the whole thing impossible."

He did not reply for a moment, and she forced herself
to glance up at him. He looked stunned. "Why?" he asked
at last.

"Because I should not be able to keep up my side of
the bargain, like your mother did. I couldn't take solace

in flirtations while you entertained your mistresses at Aunt Sophy's beautiful house. It makes me vulnerable to you. It makes it matter to me that you think I deliberately encouraged Peter's infatuation. It makes the sight of your indifference a torment. You are able to hurt me, and in spite of all the fights we have had, you have too much honor to do it with impunity when you know that I care. Both our lives would be miserable, Michael. I should rather live alone, and leave you your freedom."

"I don't want my freedom."

Jessica's brows came together in a frown. "Why not? So that you can plague me and revenge yourself forever over my every transgression, real or imagined?"

"Because I shall never be happy until I have you."

She leapt to her feet. "I don't want to be had, my lord! Damn you! Can't you have the grace to leave me any dignity?"

Suddenly his expression was as stripped as it had been the night before, when the rain and exhaustion had carved away all of his control. "Jessie, don't!"

"Don't what?"

He wrung his hands through his hair, instantly disordering the careful arrangement that his valet had labored over. "Don't do this! I love you! I have loved you for months. How could I have guessed you returned it? If I thought for a moment that you encouraged Peter as a well-deserved revenge for my treatment of you, I don't anymore. I suppose I was angry that you were so indifferent to me. I know he didn't touch you at the Blue Boar, but if he had, what difference would it make? I would still love you. I shall always love you. Isn't that enough grounds for marriage?" He threw back his head and laughed. "I have never botched anything as thoroughly in my life as this courtship! Forgive me, my love, please?"

Jessica stood stock-still. Eventually, she sat back in her chair. "But you cannot. You cannot be in love with me."

"Then you don't think that I proved it last night?"

"Does the body reveal love?" she said.

He looked genuinely surprised. "Of course it does, dear Jessica. When Ben Cameron taught you all that beautiful expertise, be assured that he loved you, too. If he hadn't been killed, you'd have known it. I love you with my skin and bones and flesh, but my soul and mind and spirit want you, as well."

Jessica could not look at him. "It won't wash, my lord. You cannot marry someone like me. You're a paragon in society—a man fit to entertain heads of state! You're being gallant, but it's not an even match."

He glanced down at his hands for a moment and his face seemed laid bare to the bone. "No, it's not," he said. "You are right." She stood up to go, blinded by tears, but his next statement stopped her. "You had your lover at Whinburn, Jessica. For me there was Lady Beaumont."

"Lady Beaumont? Who is she? I know you've had lovers! It doesn't make any difference."

"Yes, it does." He shuddered, then he laughed with the old self-contempt. "I was twenty-two. Her husband found me in bed with her. It was a wager I'd made with some friends—that I could seduce her when they'd only been married two weeks. She was young and naive and very vulnerable—he was years older—but I didn't love her. It was an idle gesture of arrogance and pride. I was a great drinker and gambler—a younger son, what responsibilities did I have? Dear God, if I had come to Whinburn then, instead of Ben Cameron, it might have been me. I shall never forget how Lord Beaumont looked when he found us. Yet he would simply have called the footman and had me thrown into the street."

"But he did not?"

"I was foxed. I made him challenge me to a duel. We met the next week, with pistols. I had so little respect for his feelings that I caroused away the night with my friends, and came to the field almost too drunk to stand."

"So you were humbled? It has happened to other young rakes."

The remarkable blue eyes met hers in open derision, but it was directed only at himself. "No, indeed, dear Jessica. My brother hushed it up, of course—I was banished from the country and ended up in the Peninsula. You see, I had so little discretion that I killed him."

Chapter 20

There was silence.

"And Lady Beaumont?" whispered Jessica at last.

He was torn open, defenseless in the face of his pain. "She was married off to an Irish peer. Seven months later she was confined; the baby was stillborn, and she killed herself. It might have been my child."

"And it might not, Michael," Jessica said gently.

"I will never know, of course," he said with some bitterness. "I have learned to accept that. And nobody knows of it now."

"Except me?"

"Lady Emilia knows—my Aunt Sophy told her. And a friend of mine in the Peninsula. We shared our stories one night after one of our comrades was killed—Dagonet had been accused of murder, but unlike me he was innocent. Lord Beaumont died because of my arrogance and stupidity. And I have relived daily how Lady Beaumont must have suffered—I deliberately risked leaving her with child. What is your poor innocent transgression compared with that?"

Jessica put her head in her hands. "But thank God,

Michael. Thank God for poor Lord and Lady Beaumont. It's the one thing that makes us even."

He looked at her, his expression uncertain. "You do not despise me?"

She dropped her hands and reached for his. "How could I, my dear earl? I love you. You have lived this down long ago, haven't you?"

"I have tried, God knows. Day in, day out." *Six years in the Peninsula courting the favors of Death. Yet the devil always protects his own.*

"You didn't mean to kill him."

"I was too damned foxed to have intentions, but he still died."

"For heaven's sake, it was an affair of honor! Lord Beaumont could have found another way out if he'd wanted— you said he was much older. He should have known better. I suspect he had more stupid arrogance than you. And Lady Beaumont welcomed you to her bed, didn't she? You didn't force her."

Michael wrung his hand over his face. "Hardly," he said wryly.

"But you have taken all the responsibility on yourself. Lady Beaumont was not helpless just because she was young and female. She knew the risks. When she lost the baby, she may have been temporarily deranged—that was hardly your fault. My dear earl, it was a tragedy. But if it can't be forgiven, then neither can my sins. I was a wanton! I willingly threw away any chance for a respectable future, and though I loved Ben, I didn't care that he didn't offer marriage. I knew nothing of his circumstances and never asked him. Haven't we both learned our lessons?"

There was nothing left of his elegance. He was stripped to the soul. But a great burden had been laid down, and what remained still shone with brilliance.

"Jessica, I don't deserve happiness. I don't deserve you." His voice became vibrant with sincerity. "Yet, dear God, I love you, as you are and with everything you have done.

If you still love me, as I am and with everything I have done, will you marry me?"

She began to cry, openly and without shame. "My lord, I am overwhelmed that you have so honored me with your proposal. I should be pleased to accept. Now, let's go and wed before we have another argument!"

He pulled her into his embrace and kissed away the tears. It was some time before Jessica was able to extricate herself.

The coach pulled up before the door of Castle Deyncourt. Peter and Caroline helped Lady Emilia alight.

"Dear Lord! I am as stiff as an old board. Why does no one come out to greet us? If I ever receive another such disgracefully cryptic message from my great-niece, I shall disown her. Where on earth is the butler?"

No one had come out to welcome them. The castle stood smiling secretly in the sun. Lady Emilia swept up to the front door and pushed it open. The young couple followed her into the hallway, where the suit of armor stood blankly at attention.

"No footmen? What is going on here? Is there not a servant in the house?"

"Hark, Lady Emilia," said Caroline. "I hear something!"

The sliding sound of metal crashing against metal could be faintly distinguished through the thick walls.

"By God, it sounds like a sword fight!" Peter's young face looked remarkably grim; he grasped Caroline by the hand. "Who but Sir Gordon Cranby?"

The three of them hurried in the direction of the sound. No one intercepted them. At last Peter opened a heavy oak door.

"Good God!" cried Aunt Emilia.

The two combatants put up their rapiers at the sound of her voice, and stood panting and laughing together.

'What on earth is this? Is this any way to go on? Lord Deyncourt! Whatever do you think you are about?"

Michael put his arm around his opponent. His face was open and free from shadows. He laughed aloud. "Lady Emilia! May I not practice fencing in my own home?"

"But with Jessica! I am shocked to the core, young lady. Where are your shoes, child? Has the world gone mad?"

Jessica looked down at her bare legs and feet beneath her rucked up skirts. "No one fences in shoes with heels, Aunt Emilia."

"And where are the servants?" asked Lady Emilia. "Are they so shocked at all these goings-on that everyone has given notice?"

"They have the day off," said Michael. "Jessica and I have some catching up to do." He pulled Jessica to his side and kissed her on the mouth, then released her and gave Lady Emilia an immaculate bow. "I have been busy telling her that a countess may do as she pleases. Lady Deyncourt will set fashion and arbitrate manners, and she will publish Greek tales for her pin money."

"Countess?" asked Aunt Emilia. "I need salts."

Jessica ran to put her arms around her great-aunt. "We are to be wed this afternoon. The priest is arranged, so if you came to stop it you're too late."

"Now, why should I try to stop it, young lady?" Aunt Emilia's rouged cheeks were crinkled into a huge smile. "I have been working at nothing else for these last months."

"You see?" Michael laughed. "We didn't stand a chance, love. All the world conspired against us."

"Except me," said Peter ruefully. "I'm dashed sorry I was such an idiot. Caroline has forgiven me, so can you?"

"Omnis amans amens, Lord Steal," said Jessica.

Caroline gave her a puzzled look, but Peter laughed. "It means 'every lover is demented,' Caro."

"Shall we shake hands, Steal?" said the earl with a wink.

"Gladly, my lord. For a minute there I thought you were fighting a duel with Cranby."

"Alas," said Michael with a shake of the head. "Sir Gordon has taken ship from Bristol for Australia."

"Well done!" exclaimed Lady Emilia.

"And we have a piece of news that might interest you, Deyncourt," said Peter with a grin. "The announcement of the engagement of Lady Honoria Melton."

"So who is to be the lucky fellow?"

Lady Emilia sank onto a chair. "Dear God, Deyncourt! Do not tell me you also had a hand in this?"

Michael laughed openly. "Alas, I sent a note to disabuse the Incomparable of her hopes before I left London, dear friend. And regrettably I also informed the prospective bridegroom—very tactfully, of course—that I had done so. The outcome was natural enough, don't you think?"

"I don't understand," said Jessica. "Who is she engaged to?"

Peter could hardly keep a straight face. "Why, Hanging Judge Clarence, of course."

Michael and Jessica were married that afternoon in the mellow medieval chapel of the castle. A sleeping crusader had a sudden blush brought to his stone cheek by the sun streaming in through the rose glass of the west window. It was not surprising that Michael was once again impeccable, but Jessica stood at his side in one of her London gowns that Caroline had packed, and with diamonds around her neck. The jewels had appeared from the family safe; it had never occurred to Jessica before that the Countess of Deyncourt would possess such things, but Michael had put into her hands a treasure chest of precious and beautiful jewelry. While Peter nervously clutched the ring, Caroline stood behind the bride holding a great armful of roses from the gardens, and Lady Emilia Shay, to her own considerable annoyance, wept copiously into a large handkerchief. Lady Emilia's coachman and servants stood awkwardly at the back of the chapel and grinned.

* * *

"Well," announced Lady Emilia once Michael and Jessica had signed the necessary papers. "I believe we had better go straight on to Bath. We are hardly going to hang around here and act the gooseberry!" Jessica kissed her wrinkled cheek.

"Peter and I," said Caroline as Jessica embraced her, "also can't wait to get to Bath and try the waters."

"But you will join us for luncheon first?" Michael teasingly kissed Caroline briefly on the lips, and she blushed scarlet as he winked at Peter. "For the Blue Boar," he said.

They followed the earl from the chapel into the great dining room, where a selection of cold food was already laid out. The wedding feast was beautiful, elegant, and festive, with chilled champagne from the castle's deep cellars.

"You do everything to perfection, don't you?" Jessica whispered. "How can I ever live up to it? Here I sit in diamonds when I would have married you in the breeches I fled your cottage in!"

Michael put his hand on her shoulder and spoke softly against her cheek. "Yes, but you would have shocked the priest, my love. And besides, your gown will be a great deal more fun to take off."

Jessica's lips brushed his ear. "Won't a maid remove it for me when it's time for me to retire tonight?"

His thumb strayed to her bare neck and up to the hairline, where he wound a thread of red hair around his finger. "No, she won't, because the maids won't be back until tomorrow."

Suddenly ravenous, Jessica savored her wedding lunch, and drank a little too much champagne.

At last Lord and Lady Deyncourt stood together under the Norman arch, and waved as the carriage pulled away down the driveway to begin the journey to Bath. Michael pulled Jessica against his heart.

"And now, my dear wife, we are alone. It's time to go to bed."

"Michael! It's afternoon!"

His grin made her heart contract. "So?"

Taking her hand, he led her up a set of winding stairs into a vaulted chamber tucked somewhere beneath the roof. There was little other furniture besides the four-poster. Sunlight streamed into the room.

"What about my maidenly modesty?" she asked shakily.

"It's fortunate you have none, my wild rose. Come here. It's my turn to seduce you."

Jessica stepped into his encircling arms and his lips met hers. There was all the subtlety and skill that she had come to expect in his kiss, but this time there was something else: passion without restraint, without doubts, and without shame. Any last vestiges of fear and guilt melted like frost flowers on a windowpane under the clean, burning heat of the sun. Her muslin slipped with a whisper to the floor, to be followed by his shirt and cravat. She helped him out of his silk knee-breeches and delighted in the warmth of his body under her hands. As he kissed the sensitive flesh of her neck, he slid her shift slowly from her shoulders, leaving her clad in nothing but diamonds. They sank together onto the bed, where sunlight poured over their naked skin. Her fingers traveled with wonder over his smooth flank. He would always, always, entrance her. Willingly, she held out her arms to him and he lost himself in her embrace.

Author's Note

The most famous highwayman who dressed as a woman in order to ply his dastardly trade was one Thomas Sympson, known as Old Mob. In this charming disguise he is said to have enticed a lord into leaving his guard of six for a tryst in the woods. Immediately he set about "taking up the petticoats," but then his lordship is reputed to have cried out: "What a plague's the meaning of your wearing breeches, madam?" Needless to say, the lord lost his purse and the highwayman kept his virtue! Old Mob was hanged in 1691, but public executions continued until 1868. The death penalty applied to many crimes and could be carried out within days of the trial, thus Deyncourt's concern for Jessica. During the Regency the death sentence was sometimes commuted to transportation—but probably not by my fictional Lord Clarence!

Readers of my other *Reward* books have already met Charles de Dagonet and Richard Acton who are mentioned in these pages: in *Scandal's Reward, Virtue's Reward,* and *Rogue's Reward.* They were both members of Wellington's intelligence forces in the Peninsula—as, of course, was Michael, Lord Deyncourt. For fans of the Actons, never fear, they are destined to reappear in my next book, *Folly's Reward,* in March 1997. I do hope you'll write and tell me your favorites. I may be reached at P.O. Box 197, Ridgway, CO 81432. Please enclose your SASE if you would like a reply.

ZEBRA'S REGENCY ROMANCES
DAZZLE AND DELIGHT

A BEGUILING INTRIGUE   (4441, $3.99)
by Olivia Sumner

Pretty as a picture Justine Riggs cared nothing for propriety. She dressed as a boy, sat on her horse like a jockey, and pondered the stars like a scientist. But when she tried to best the handsome Quenton Fletcher, Marquess of Devon, by proving that she was the better equestrian, he would try to prove Justine's antics were pure folly. The game he had in mind was seduction — never imagining that he might lose his heart in the process!

AN INCONVENIENT ENGAGEMENT   (4442, $3.99)
by Joy Reed

Rebecca Wentworth was furious when she saw her betrothed waltzing with another. So she decides to make him jealous by flirting with the handsomest man at the ball, John Collinwood, Earl of Stanford. The "wicked" nobleman knew exactly what the enticing miss was up to — and he was only too happy to play along. But as Rebecca gazed into his magnificent eyes, her errant fiancé was soon utterly forgotten!

SCANDAL'S LADY   (4472, $3.99)
by Mary Kingsley

Cassandra was shocked to learn that the new Earl of Lynton was her childhood friend, Nicholas St. John. After years at sea and mixed feelings Nicholas had come home to take the family title. And although Cassandra knew her place as a governess, she could not help the thrill that went through her each time he was near. Nicholas was pleased to find that his old friend Cassandra was his new next door neighbor, but after being near her, he wondered if mere friendship would be enough . . .

HIS LORDSHIP'S REWARD   (4473, $3.99)
by Carola Dunn

As the daughter of a seasoned soldier, Fanny Ingram was accustomed to the vagaries of military life and cared not a whit about matters of rank and social standing. So she certainly never foresaw her *tendre* for handsome Viscount Roworth of Kent with whom she was forced to share lodgings, while he carried out his clandestine activities on behalf of the British Army. And though good sense told Roworth to keep his distance, he couldn't stop from taking Fanny in his arms for a kiss that made all hearts equal!

Available wherever paperbacks are sold, or order direct from the Publisher. Send cover price plus 50¢ per copy for mailing and handling to Penguin USA, P.O. Box 999, c/o Dept. 17109, Bergenfield, NJ 07621. Residents of New York and Tennessee must include sales tax. DO NOT SEND CASH.

ELEGANT LOVE STILL FLOURISHES —
Wrap yourself in a Zebra Regency Romance.

A MATCHMAKER'S MATCH   (3783, $3.50/$4.50)
by Nina Porter
To save herself from a loveless marriage, Lady Psyche Veringham pretends to be a bluestocking. Resigned to spinsterhood at twenty-three, Psyche sets her keen mind to snaring a husband for her young charge, Amanda. She sets her cap for long-time bachelor, Justin St. James. This man of the world has had his fill of frothy-headed debutantes and turns the tables on Psyche. Can a bluestocking and a man about town find true love?

FIRES IN THE SNOW   (3809, $3.99/$4.99)
by Janis Laden
Because of an unhappy occurrence, Diana Ruskin knew that a secure marriage was not in her future. She was content to assist her physician father and follow in his footsteps . . . until now. After meeting Adam, Duke of Marchmaine, Diana's precise world is shattered. She would simply have to avoid the temptation of his gentle touch and stunning physique — and by doing so break her own heart!

FIRST SEASON   (3810, $3.50/$4.50)
by Anne Baldwin
When country heiress Laetitia Biddle arrives in London for the Season, she harbors dreams of triumph and applause. Instead, she becomes the laughingstock of drawing rooms and ballrooms, alike. This headstrong miss blames the rakish Lord Wakeford for her miserable debut, and she vows to rise above her many faux pas. Vowing to become an Original, Letty proves that she's more than a match for this eligible, seasoned Lord.

AN UNCOMMON INTRIGUE   (3701, $3.99/$4.99)
by Georgina Devon
Miss Mary Elizabeth Sinclair was rather startled when the British Home Office employed her as a spy. Posing as "Tasha," an exotic fortune-teller, she expected to encounter unforeseen dangers. However, nothing could have prepared her for Lord Eric Stewart, her dashing and infuriating partner. Giving her heart to this haughty rogue would be the most reckless hazard of all.

A MADDENING MINX   (3702, $3.50/$4.50)
by Mary Kingsley
After a curricle accident, Miss Sarah Chadwick is literally thrust into the arms of Philip Thornton. While other women shy away from Thornton's eyepatch and aloof exterior, Sarah finds herself drawn to discover why this man is physically and emotionally scarred.

ZEBRA REGENCIES
ARE
THE TALK OF THE TON!

A REFORMED RAKE (4499, $3.99)
by Jeanne Savery

After governess Harriet Cole helped her young charge flee to France — and the designs of a despicable suitor, more trouble soon arrived in the person of a London rake. Sir Frederick Carrington insisted on providing safe escort back to England. Harriet deemed Carrington more dangerous than any band of brigands, but secretly relished matching wits with him. But after being taken in his arms for a tender kiss, she found herself wondering — *could* a lady find love with an irresistible rogue?

A SCANDALOUS PROPOSAL (4504, $4.99)
by Teresa DesJardien

After only two weeks into the London season, Lady Pamela Premington has already received her first offer of marriage. If only it hadn't come from the *ton's* most notorious rake, Lord Marchmont. Pamela had already set her sights on the distinguished Lieutenant Penford, who had the heroism and honor that made him the ideal match. Now she had to keep from falling under the spell of the seductive Lord so she could pursue the man more worthy of her love. Or was he?

A LADY'S CHAMPION (4535, $3.99)
by Janice Bennett

Miss Daphne, art mistress of the Selwood Academy for Young Ladies, greeted the notion of ghosts haunting the academy with skepticism. However, to avoid rumors frightening off students, she found herself turning to Mr. Adrian Carstairs, sent by her uncle to be her "protector" against the "ghosts." Although, Daphne would accept no interference in her life, she *would* accept aid in exposing any spectral spirits. What she never expected was for Adrian to expose the secret wishes of her hidden heart . . .

CHARITY'S GAMBIT (4537, $3.99)
by Marcy Stewart

Charity Abercrombie reluctantly embarks on a London season in hopes of making a suitable match. However she cannot forget the mysterious Dominic Castille — and the kiss they shared — when he fell from a tree as she strolled through the woods. Charity does not know that the dark and dashing captain harbors a dangerous secret that will ensnare them both in its web — leaving Charity to risk certain ruin and losing the man she so passionately loves . . .

Available wherever paperbacks are sold, or order direct from the Publisher. Send cover price plus 50¢ per copy for mailing and handling to Penguin USA, P.O. Box 999, c/o Dept. 17109, Bergenfield, NJ 07621. Residents of New York and Tennessee must include sales tax. DO NOT SEND CASH.

Taylor-made Romance from Zebra Books

WHISPERED KISSES   (0-8217-5454-8, $5.99/$6.99)
Beautiful Texas heiress Laura Leigh Webster never imagined
that her biggest worry on her African safari would be the handsome Jace Elliot, her tour guide. Laura's guardian, Lord Chadwick Hamilton, warns her of Jace's dangerous past; she simply
cannot resist the lure of his strong arms and the passion of his
Whispered Kisses.

KISS OF THE NIGHT WIND   (0-8217-5279-0, $5.99/$6.99)
Carrie Sue Strover thought she was leaving trouble behind her
when she deserted her brother's outlaw gang to live her life as
schoolmarm Carolyn Starns. On her journey, her stagecoach
was attacked and she was rescued by handsome T.J. Rogue. T.J.
plots to have Carrie lead him to her brother's cohorts who murdered his family. T.J., however, soon succumbs to the beautiful
runaway's charms and loving caresses.

FORTUNE'S FLAMES   (0-8217-5450-5, $5.99/$6.99)
Impatient to begin her journey back home to New Orleans,
beautiful Maren James was furious when Captain Hawk delayed
the voyage by searching for stowaways. Impatience gave way
to uncontrollable desire once the handsome captain searched
her cabin. He was looking for illegal passengers; what he found
was wild passion with a woman he knew was unlike all those
he had known before!

PASSIONS WILD AND FREE   (0-8217-5275-8, $5.99/$6.99)
After seeing her family and home destroyed by the cruel and
hateful Epson gang, Randee Hollis swore revenge. She knew
she found the perfect man to help her—gunslinger Marsh
Logan. Not only strong and brave, Marsh had the ebony hair
and light blue eyes to make Randee forget her hate and seek
the love and passion that only he could give her.

FROM AWARD-WINNING AUTHOR
JO BEVERLEY

DANGEROUS JOY   (0-8217-5129-8, $5.99)

Felicity is a beautiful, rebellious heiress with a terrible secret. Miles is her reluctant guardian—a man of seductive power and dangerous sensuality. What begins as a charade borne of desperation soon becomes an illicit liaison of passionate abandon and forbidden love. One man stands between them: a cruel landowner sworn to possess the wealth he craves and the woman he desires. His dark treachery will drive the lovers to dare the unknowable and risk the unthinkable, determined to hold on to their joy.

FORBIDDEN   (0-8217-4488-7, $4.99)

While fleeing from her brothers, who are attempting to sell her into a loveless marriage, Serena Riverton accepts a carriage ride from a stranger—who is the handsomest man she has ever seen. Lord Middlethorpe, himself, is actually contemplating marriage to a dull daughter of the aristocracy, when he encounters the breathtaking Serena. She arouses him as no woman ever has. And after a night of thrilling intimacy—a forbidden liaison—Serena must choose between a lady's place and a woman's passion!

TEMPTING FORTUNE   (0-8217-4858-0, $4.99)

In a night shimmering with destiny, Portia St. Claire discovers that her brother's debts have made him a prisoner of dangerous men. The price of his life is her virtue—about to be auctioned off in London's most notorious brothel. However, handsome Bryght Malloreen has other ideas for Portia, opening her heart to a sensuality that tempts her to madness.

Available wherever paperbacks are sold, or order direct from the Publisher. Send cover price plus 50¢ per copy for mailing and handling to Penguin USA, P.O. Box 999, c/o Dept. 17109, Bergenfield, NJ 07621. Residents of New York and Tennessee must include sales tax. DO NOT SEND CASH.